Storybook Ending

Also by Poppy Alexander

The Littlest Library
25 Days 'Til Christmas
The 12 Days of Christmas

Storybook Ending

A Novel

POPPY ALEXANDER

AVON

An Imprint of HarperCollins*Publishers*

STORYBOOK ENDING. Copyright © 2024 by Sarah Waights. All rights reserved. Printed in the United States of America. No part of this book may be used or reproduced in any manner whatsoever without written permission except in the case of brief quotations embodied in critical articles and reviews. For information, address HarperCollins Publishers, 195 Broadway, New York, NY 10007.

HarperCollins books may be purchased for educational, business, or sales promotional use. For information, please email the Special Markets Department at SPsales@harpercollins.com.

FIRST EDITION

Interior text design by Diahann Sturge-Campbell

Book illustration © Hey Rabbit/Stock.Adobe.com

Library of Congress Cataloging-in-Publication Data has been applied for.

ISBN 978-0-06-334062-6

24 25 26 27 28 LBC 5 4 3 2 1

For my little mate, Saffy

 *Chapter One*

*O*nce *upon a time, there was a marmalade cat.*
His best friend in the whole world was a little girl called Ruth. She thought Tango—because that was his name—was the cleverest, handsomest, most magical cat in the whole world. And she wasn't the only one, because Tango thought so too.

One day—

The telephone rang.

Imogen jumped, dropping the writing pad in a flurry of paper.

"Imo," said Nigel without preamble. "We've just bought a house!"

"Oh my God!" she replied, clutching her pad to her chest, her heart inexplicably starting to race. "Already?"

"Yep. I told you we didn't need a property solicitor slowing things up."

Nigel had insisted on doing his own legal work, she remembered, even though he was a matrimonial lawyer, not the property sort.

"I'm coming home to celebrate," he announced. "Put some champagne on ice, would you?"

"That's fantastic!" she said, taking the pencil out from

behind her ear and twizzling it nervously into her auburn curls. "Only, can we celebrate tonight, do you think? It's just that Sally's coming for lunch . . . I'm showing her my sketches."

"Bloody Sally again? You only saw her the other day. Isn't this much more important than some boring old designs?" he snapped. "Sorry, babe, I don't mean your designs are boring, of course."

She knew he did.

"Anyway," he continued, "I'm leaving the office now. Call Sally and tell her you can't make it."

He hung up without waiting for a reply.

Guiltily, Imogen looked around the flat as she wrenched free the pencil, which was now hopelessly entwined in her hair. The flat had become shamefully untidy since Nigel had left that morning. Her drawings were spread out all over the carpet. Colored pencils were scattered on and around the coffee table, and Tango was lounging fatly in his favorite outlawed place, on the seat of Nigel's armchair. Unforgivably, the overstuffed velvet cushion now had a generous sprinkling of orange fur.

The doorbell made her jump. Guiltily, she went to shoo Tango off the chair before realizing it couldn't possibly be Nigel so soon.

"Sally?" she asked, with her finger on the intercom button.

"Chardonnay . . . chardonnay . . ." a voice croaked weakly.

"The door switch thingy is broken," she said, grinning. "Try to survive until I get down there."

Downstairs, throwing open the wide, stained-glass-paneled

door, she stepped aside sighing as Sally crawled into the communal hall, dragging her briefcase in one hand and wrapping her other arm around Imogen's legs.

"Honestly," Imogen complained mildly, "you're such a drama queen."

"It was horrible," Sally gasped. "I thought I'd never get away."

"Really? Because you're actually quite early."

"I am?" Sally asked—miraculously recovered as she stood up and brushed off the trousers of her immaculately cut suit. "Blimey, it felt like forever. I had the CEO of Grantley's Mushrooms Inc. determined to waste his money telling his advertising agency how to do their job according to the advice of his wife, who he can't possibly have married for her brains, by the way."

"Tell me more."

"Well, she's got massive tits, for one thing. Mind you, I don't reckon they're real—"

"Not the wife, you twit, the campaign."

"Oh, right. Well, how about a prime-time TV campaign—he wants it on during *Love Island*, dunno why—based on a series of cartoons, starring—no less . . ." Sally paused for effect. "Martin the Mushroom," she declared in an I-rest-my-case sort of way.

"Could have been worse," said Imogen as they reached the flat door.

"Really? How?"

"What about Toby the Toadstool," she suggested, "or Mike the Morel, or even Fergus the Fungus . . . Actually, that one's quite good, although it's a bit familiar, I think it might have been done before . . ." She continued to ramble as she went to collect wine and glasses from the kitchen.

By the time she returned, Sally had slipped off her shoes and was padding around the sitting room, examining Imogen's drawings and paintings from every angle.

Bursting with the news, Imogen told her friend about Storybook Cottage.

"Wow, that's it, then," said Sally. "It's the country life for you from now on. How are you looking forward to sticking on your Crocs so you can wade through the manure to feed the chickens every day? It'll be a far cry from playing eeny, meeny, miney, mo with the Wimbledon wine bars every lunchtime."

"I don't," said Imogen. "I may not have an actual job, but I work very hard on my pictures and designs when I'm at home. I don't often take time for lunch anyway."

As she spoke, she was wrestling awkwardly with a bottle of champagne and a tea towel. "Nigel just phoned to say he is coming home to celebrate. I thought we'd get a head start."

"Good thinking," said Sally, "but I'll make myself scarce when he gets here, don't worry. Don't want to get in the way of any celebratory couple stuff, do I?" Sally gave a theatrical shudder.

"You wouldn't be in the way," Imogen replied, flushing slightly.

"No?" Sally threw her an incredulous look. "I can't see our Nigel up for a ménage à trois somehow." She pretended to consider. "Well, maybe I can, but not with me, I don't flatter myself . . . Anyway, surely the whole deal about the rambling country house is to keep you barefoot and pregnant. You might as well crack on."

"I don't think that's 'the whole deal,' no," protested Imogen. "There's no hurry with the baby thing, is there?" She was definitely not going to admit to saying the same to Nigel a little too often recently.

"Not getting second thoughts, I hope, my love?"

"No-o . . ." said Imogen. "Well, not about the move to the country. You know I adore the idea. It's going to be such a good social media story, it could really launch my stuff. I've set up a new Insta account. I've called it @Storybook_Ending because it felt weird using my name, and—well—I want to feature this children's book I'm working on. I've got followers already . . ."

"Ha! @Storybook_Ending, eh?" said Sally knowingly. "Is this what it is? This move to the country? Your 'happy ever after'?"

"Maybe," said Imogen, alert to the possibility she was being mocked. Was it wrong to want a happy ending? "You will come to visit me, won't you?" she added. It sounded like a plea.

"Try and stop me," said Sally, giving her a searching look and then turning her attention to the pictures.

"I love the ones with the cat. It's Tango, isn't it? He'll be insisting on having his own agent."

By the time they had eaten lunch and nearly finished the champagne, Sally had enthused over Imogen's sketches for her children's book and was looking regretfully at her watch. "Sadly, I can't leave the office unattended too much longer, or it'll be carnage."

It suddenly struck Imogen it had been nearly two hours since Nigel had called to say he was coming home.

"Funny that Nigel isn't here yet," she said.

"He probably decided to stop off and get you a huge celebratory present. Either that or he got delayed showing off to all his colleagues about his great big expensive house . . . and his beautiful, clever, surrendered wife," she added, naughtily.

The doorbell rang.

"Speak of the devil?" queried Sally.

"That'll be him. He's probably lost his key again," said Imogen, relieved.

"I'll let him in on my way out." Sally gave Imogen a brief hug and headed for the door.

COMING OUT OF the kitchen, having dumped the lunch plates in the dishwasher, Imogen was surprised to see Sally in the doorway again. "What have you forgotten?"

Sally didn't speak. She walked unsteadily into the room, holding out her arms. Imogen was shocked to see her friend's face was waxy and white, as if she were about to faint. Then she caught sight of a policeman and policewoman coming through the door, and her heart thudded violently in her chest.

"Imo," said Sally, reaching out and grasping Imogen's hands, "I'm s-so sorry."

NIGEL'S PARENTS WERE quick to take over the organization of the funeral. "Nigel's wife? She's an artist . . ." she could always imagine them telling their friends. "Pretty girl, but—well, *you* know—you've got to let them make their own mistakes, haven't you?"

They made a gesture at keeping Imogen in the picture, but the consultation was peremptory; she was informed of the guest list, the catering arrangements for the post-funeral reception, and the announcement in the *Times*. All that was left was to contact their few mutual friends and acknowledge the messages of sympathy.

The service was held at the crematorium next to the gasworks. Perfectly manicured grass dotted with memorial plaques and plastic flowers surrounded the one-story building. Nigel had not been remotely religious, Imogen knew—except where propriety demanded it—so the context seemed fittingly godless. He would have wanted a bit more drama, she thought, or at least a little more gravitas than the suburban dispatching of souls as the priest chanted singsong through the shortest of services necessary to preserve decorum.

She should have reckoned on his family to provide the entertainment.

"My darling boy!"

A wail broke through Imogen's reverie as the coffin began to jerk toward the curtained furnace. She turned to see Nigel's mother swaying, handkerchief clutched to her cheek.

Imogen watched with interest, to see if she was going to throw herself after the coffin, but instead—having made her point—the older woman sank dramatically back onto the pew to be fanned and patted consolingly by her acolytes.

What a pity, thought Imogen.

Her mother-in-law had made no secret, during her depressingly frequent visits to the flat, that Imogen had failed badly in her responsibilities as the perfect wife. Her sins, she was informed, were many and varied, ranging from failing to iron his underpants to giving him frozen pizza for supper.

Nigel had never once defended her either, she remembered.

AFTER THE FUNERAL they all piled back to Nigel and Imogen's flat, where Imogen planted herself inconspicuously—she hoped—against the drawing room wall. She had borrowed a chic little black dress from Sally. "An LBD, darling, you can't go wrong!" But as Sally was a good six inches taller and Imogen hadn't been eating much, the effect was more like a child dressing up in its mother's clothes. She desperately wished Sally was there. She could have done with an ally, but Sally had been the first to admit she and Nigel had not been close, and the two women agreed it would have been a little hypocritical of her to attend.

Clutching a glass of warm white wine to her chest, she watched the throng of guests milling around the room and spilling out onto the roof terrace. She had enjoyed making the garden. It had been a wasteland of broken chairs and rusting barbecues when she first knew it. Despite Nigel joking about her killing plants on sight, the little terrace had flourished, and she had cherished every leaf. It was the one part of his flat she had been allowed to put her stamp on since she and Tango had moved in with him two years before.

Noise levels rose steadily after the first half hour. With most guests onto their second or third glass of wine, tongues had loosened, and raucous anecdotes were following one from the other, punctuated with explosions of laughter.

The ebb and flow of sound lulled Imogen into a near trance. She felt like one of the nodding dogs in the backs of cars, smiling politely as Nigel's relatives, friends, and work colleagues paraded before her, each with an expression of regret and a memory to relate. She was pretending to listen to a dusty old aunt plowing through endless tales of Nigel's childhood misdemeanors—he was really quite evil, apparently—when she spotted Richard Spencer, his boss at the law firm. He was pointing straight at her for the benefit of an elderly man that Imogen didn't recognize. As she idly wondered who he was, Richard spoke emphatically into the ear of the older man, who screwed up his face in the way of someone who is deaf and denies it.

". . . not the one I remember," she heard the elderly man say, too loudly. "Pretty little thing, mind you, but I assumed his wife was that blonde . . . we saw having lunch in . . ." She struggled to hear the next bit and then the other noise in the room momentarily dropped a little: ". . . seemed a bit embarrassed about her, now you mention it . . ." was the last Imogen heard as Richard hurried him away with a—was it a guilty look in her direction?

The next minute a clawlike hand gripped her upper arm. Resisting the temptation to yank herself free, Imogen regarded Nigel's mother with pity. She was a bitter and complaining woman who took the loss of her only son as the final insult after her beleaguered husband had escaped her by dying three years before.

"He was worth ten of his father, you know," was her opening declaration. "You'll go and find someone else soon enough, I'll be bound. But me? I've nothing to live for now." She snuffled, choked into temporary silence by the drama of the picture she had drawn for herself. "I hope you never know the agony a parent feels when a child dies before them," she continued, her eyes boring into Imogen's.

Probably right, thought Imogen as she patted the woman's arm helplessly. No chance at all if I fail to have any children—and it's not looking good at the moment.

LATER, WHEN THE drink was drunk, the food gone, and the guests beginning to think about Tube journeys home, supper, and the relief of removing too-tight shoes, Imogen turned to see Richard Spencer at her elbow.

"Imogen! What a terrible thing this all is," he boomed. "Nigel will be sorely missed at Brandon and Spencer, I don't need to tell you. He was destined for a great future with us, you know. A partnership, I'm sure of it."

"Thank you, Richard. I know he would have appreciated hearing you say that."

"If there is anything we can do, my dear. Anything at all? If you need financial assistance . . . ?" He raised his eyebrows.

"I'll be fine," she said, hoping it was true. "Oh, except I think the paperwork for the house purchase is still in the office. I don't suppose it could be sent, could it?"

"That's certainly something we can take on for you. Tell

your estate agent to ask for me personally and think no more of it. Anything else?"

"Just one more thing—who was that older gentleman I saw you talking to earlier?"

"Do you mean old Winterton? He's a long-ago-retired partner. He met Nigel a few times through work functions, that's all."

"Only that I couldn't help overhearing him . . . something about a blonde? He thought he had met me before?"

Richard flushed, reluctant to meet Imogen's eye. "Oh, you don't want to listen to anything he bangs on about, although he's pretty good for a chap in his eighties, I suppose. He gets things mixed up, and he's as deaf as a post, which doesn't exactly help."

A sickening, heavy lump settled in the pit of Imogen's stomach.

Richard was lying.

She didn't blame him. He had always been avuncular and had flirted harmlessly with her at dinner parties, but she was realistic enough to know that men stuck together in his world. Betraying a male confidence or—dare she even think it—an indiscretion, would be anathema to him. Swallowing hard, she gave him a wan smile and pecked him on the cheek. "Thanks for coming, Richard. I know Nigel would have appreciated such a good turnout from the company."

"Not at all, my dear girl," he said, bolting with obvious relief.

SHE SAT BLANKLY through the inquest at the civic offices, an ugly gray sixties building with a warren of small, airless rooms, brown carpeted and mean. Several witnesses gave their reports of a reckless motorcycle rider weaving in and out of rush hour traffic and then plowing at full speed into the side of a van turning right. He had always loved his motorbike, reveling in avoiding traffic queues on his two wheels. As a note of pure farce, Imogen learned, the van's contents had been scattered all over the road from the force of the collision. Traffic had had to be held up for nearly an hour while police cleared away the boxes of novelty condoms.

"Wow," SALLY SAID when Imogen met up with her later at Julio's, over flat whites and avocado on toast. "Fancy being killed by a condom. With all this talk about safe sex, I think you ought to launch a campaign to let everyone know they can be lethal in the wrong hands."

"Seriously?" Imogen blurted in a rare moment of exasperation with her friend. She knew Sally and Nigel were enemies, but was there anything Sally wouldn't joke about?

"Imo—I'm so sorry." Sally was instantly contrite. "I don't know what makes me say things like that."

"Are you okay?" Imogen asked, stifling her indignation on noticing Sally looked strained. Her face was gaunt, and she was fiddling with her hair constantly.

"Yeah, yeah. I'm fine," Sally replied, waving her hand. "Come on, I don't want to dump my problems on you, of all people. Not now."

She knew better than to push. Sally would tell her when she was ready.

THE NEXT DAY there was an embarrassed letter from the estate agency dealing with the house sale: . . . *so sorry for your loss . . . our deepest condolences . . . awaiting your further instructions . . .* The look of relief on the face of the smooth-scrubbed agent was obvious when she went into the office and confirmed the sale of their Wimbledon flat and the house purchase should carry on.

She was uncertain about the move, but she also yearned to escape from the flat and from the city that sweated and reeked in the grimy summer heat. In any case, Nigel dying was so seismic, Imogen thought she had nothing else to lose in changing every other aspect of her life while she was at it. There was simply no conceivable way things could be any worse than they already were. Not that she was idealizing the past. Their marriage had been far from perfect— wasn't everyone's?—but the move to the country together had been a shared dream. Maybe—in Nigel's memory— she should try and live the dream for him. For them both.

The reading of the will was the final hurdle and did nothing to dispel her feeling that her whole life had been transformed into a bad soap opera. Arriving at the solicitor's offices, she was relieved to see only her sister-in-law, Anne, was present. Nigel's mother had excused herself, claiming exhaustion brought on by the heat and the strain. Imogen sat, hands folded in lap, as the elderly solicitor applied himself to explaining the contents of the will.

"It is fortunate that my late client saw the wisdom of preparing a will, you know, especially given that his . . . er . . . demise was so tragically unexpected."

The solicitor continued with a sigh, "Of course there are

the formalities of probate to be observed. However, the terms of the will are broadly as follows. Nigel Hewitt—that is, the deceased," he clarified unnecessarily, "leaves the sum of his estate to his wife, Imogen Hewitt, with the standard provision for offspring, of which I understand there are none?" He regarded Imogen over the top of his wire-rimmed glasses.

"No," she confirmed, clearing her throat. "No children."

"I see," he continued briskly. "Anyway, the value of the estate is straightforward. There are a couple of small investment policies, and a 'death in service' benefit payable from his firm equivalent to a year's salary. In addition to these, there is simply the matter of the properties. It would appear that the sale of a flat in Wimbledon had been agreed and contracts exchanged. In addition, the purchase of a property known as Storybook Cottage in Middlemass, Devon, had also been agreed, with funds from the flat sale and the provision of a substantial mortgage loan.

"This is an interesting situation," he droned, in a tone that suggested it was the most boring thing he had ever heard. "The contracts, being exchanged but not completed before the death, are arguably no longer enforceable. In addition, the purchase can no longer depend on the mortgage loan that was granted to your husband alone and is not transferable."

Imogen, feeling her eyelids droop, struggled to stay awake. She suddenly realized he was looking at her, waiting to deliver his big moment, and wanted her full attention.

"However," he said, brightening considerably, and planting both hands firmly on the desk in front of him, "it appears a life assurance policy set up to cover the mortgage debt is valid given that it was set to begin on exchange of contracts rather than on completion, as one might, perhaps, have thought.

"Therefore, my dear," he continued, positively avuncular now, "as your husband's death occurred a full hour after the official exchange of contracts, the life assurance company is obliged to pay out. This means that, providing the sale of the Wimbledon property proceeds as planned, with the consequent release of equity, Storybook Cottage is yours absolutely, without debt or encumbrance."

 *Chapter Two*

Imogen drifted awake to birdsong and opened her eyes to see faded chintz curtains, the fabric worn practically transparent. As they billowed at the open window, she glimpsed a hazy blue sky, framed with honeysuckle tendrils, and the tops of the fruit trees in the orchard. The bed, the only piece of furniture in the room, stood on bare floorboards. The removal men, exhausted after the long trip from Wimbledon, were not pleased when she asked them to take it right up to the little attic room, rejecting the larger bedrooms on the floor below.

She jumped as a soft weight landed on her chest with a thud. Tango yawned widely in her face and then stalked, tail held high, to his favorite spot at her feet, leaving four perfect paw prints in mud on the white pillowcase.

"How on earth do you manage to keep all that muck on your paws as you come up the stairs? What do you do? Walk on your knuckles?" she scolded as he purred like a chainsaw and dribbled, ignoring her until she shoved him ignominiously onto the floor with her feet.

He had spent the first few hours in his new home cowering in the bathroom cupboard. After a night of cautiously patrolling his new domain, he had mostly regained his usual savoir faire, and he made it clear he was in the mood for a hearty breakfast.

She rolled out of bed. Feeling lightheaded, she pulled on yesterday's clothes and gingerly descended the steep attic stairs. Tango insisted on staying just half a step in front of her, continually in danger of an inadvertent kick, as she tried to hurry him on. Ignoring the bathroom for the time being—there had been no hot water the previous night, and she had mentally added this to her Urgent Tasks list—she padded barefoot across the wide, sunlit hall and through to the kitchen at the back of the house.

Despite the promise of another hot, cloudless day outside, the flagstones in the north-facing kitchen were cold underfoot. Giving the cast-iron range in the chimney recess a doubtful look, Imogen went first to the deep stone sink with her kettle and then across to the modern gas cooker she had thankfully spotted tucked into the corner. With the kettle heating, she dug a big earthenware mug out of the first box she saw in the selection piled against the huge wooden dresser.

Then she delved into the "essentials box" Sally had packed for her. It came up trumps. Not only had it provided the vital instant coffee, Sally—who pretended to despise Tango—had also thought to pack two tins of cat food and—miracle of miracles—a tin opener. Tango, who looked as if he had expected no less, hovered mewing as Imogen dusted off one of her best saucers and loaded it with cat food on the floor.

She poured boiling water directly onto the coffee

granules—sadly, the magic box hadn't managed to produce a bottle of milk—then opened the back door into the kitchen garden. Cradling her mug in both hands, her bare feet winced across the gravel path that dissected the overgrown parterre garden. She pushed through the ivy-trailing archway in the stone wall and, thankfully for her now bruised feet, reached the dew-soaked lawn beyond. The grass was overgrown, and the bottoms of her jeans were soon wet through.

The last time she had seen this garden, she was being ushered by the local estate agent, who had largely ignored her, keeping up a constant patter with Nigel as he asked tedious questions about deeds and dry rot guarantees. Imogen had wandered off in a reverie, drinking in the springtime freshness and ravishing prettiness of the gardens that were then more abundant than abandoned. She had daydreamed about their children playing football on the lawn. In her imagination, there was even a family dog—a red setter—barking frantically and trying to steal the ball.

Three months on, the neglect was more obvious, with rose branches straggling to the ground and the contents of the flower beds spilling across the width of the paths. The weeds were winning the battle too, with bindweed smothering plants and shrubs in a blanket of heart-shaped leaves.

She headed for an arch cut into the yew hedge. This, Imogen thought, was the house's best secret. Directly on the other side of the yew hedge was a fast-flowing stream with a tiny wooden bridge leading into an orchard with some fifteen or twenty mature fruit trees in a meadow. Beyond them was a low stone wall marking the edge of the property and a gently rising hill dotted with grazing sheep. Probably half a mile farther was a Georgian mansion. Imogen had been intrigued by it, asking the agent to tell her more, but he confessed he was new to the area and had simply dismissed it with a wave of the hand as "the old manor house." No longer a family home but a conference center or something similar, he thought.

There was an apple tree in the orchard with its trunk split low down into three sturdy branches. She hauled herself up into this rough seat, sloshing her coffee a little in the process.

In the weeks since Nigel had died, she had got used to a constant gnawing anxiety, reliving the moment when she heard the news about his death twenty times a day, each time with a flip-flop of the stomach and a lurch of shock. Eating little and sleeping less, Imo—reliant on the carefully rationed diazepam her London doctor had persuaded her to accept—had become quite fragile.

Of course, the plan of action when Nigel was with her had been perfectly sensible.

He: rising commercial lawyer, soon to be offered partnership in prestigious London law firm.

She: perfect wife maintaining children, dog, and roses around door of picture-postcard house.

He would work from his study at home on Mondays and Fridays, commuting to London and staying in a pied-à-terre for the rest of the week. The mortgage would be large, and his career was at a crucial point, so cutting back on work would be out of the question, but then, Imogen remembered, he had dismissed the idea of her sharing the financial responsibility.

"I thought I might take the chance to develop some of my illustration ideas—try my hand at some children's books, perhaps," she had suggested.

"I hardly think the income from your drawings is going to transport me to a life of leisure," he told her crushingly, "and anyway, I want you to settle down properly in our new life. It might not be a particularly feminist thing, but we're a team, Imo—and I need you providing the backup—food, house, ironing, all that Mrs. Hinch stuff." He wrapped his arms around her waist and consciously adopted his most charming smile. "And kids. You'll have your hands full then," he added, laughing at the expression on her face.

"You know what they say about 'behind every great man there's a competent woman,' or something like that . . ." he had said as he searched for a more convincing alternative to the word *competent*, which was possibly not the most accurate epithet in Imogen's case.

He had a point. Her stint as a temp at Nigel's office had been a disaster.

After meeting him once at Sally and Alistair's dinner party—where she admitted being sacked yet again—he had called her the next day, not to invite her out as she initially imagined, but to let her know about a vacancy for an admin assistant in the adjoining office to his own. Bemused by his offer, she telephoned the human resources manager as he instructed.

In the firm's Mayfair offices, she had been even more puzzled when he ignored her for the first few days. She was acutely aware of his presence, passing close by her desk in his impeccable pin-striped suits and shiny shoes, usually in conversation with a colleague or barking into his phone. He had been working in the commercial law division next door to Imogen's family law section that—as she had hoped—rewarded her yen for human drama with an almost daily sideshow of screaming divorcées. For pure entertainment, this was almost better than the reality shows she and her flatmates thrived on. They would wait for her arrival with chilled beer and peanuts in return for her regaling them with the dramatic events of the day.

Nigel had been right, of course. The pressure of her double life had started to show. At the time she was working all day and then up painting and drawing half of the night in her little room in the shared house. Despite taking twenty-minute naps in the staff room at lunchtime, she had one day fallen asleep at her desk. Exhausted by a particularly creative session of painting the night before, Imogen had let her head slump onto her hand—just for a moment—early one afternoon. She was lulled by the knowledge that her boss, a tyrannical older Scotsman called Hamish, had taken a well-preserved would-be divorcée to lunch. The woman had shamelessly flirted with Hamish, clearly under the impression that flattery of her solicitor and not her extremely rich ex-husband was the way to secure her the most favorable settlement.

Imogen had been woken by a deafening crash. Nigel, passing her desk and catching sight of Hamish emerging from the lift, had swiftly toppled a pile of heavy files onto the floor. As the noise woke her, she felt him tugging her down off her chair, giving her a chance to compose herself whilst pretending to pick up the files.

He stood up, apologized charmingly to Hamish for distracting Imogen with his clumsiness, and marched off, turning to give her a wink as he passed. From then, drinks to thank him had quickly progressed to lunch several times a week, then dinner, then weekends away, and—within months—she had accepted his proposal of marriage.

"THESE ARE THE facts," Imogen told herself briskly in the sunny orchard. "I am a dried-up old widow at thirty-two. I have a lovely, but definitely bonkers, and hands-off mother. I have few real friends and a family house with no family. I also have no job and, at most, a year of income to my name. To top it all, I am now living in the middle of nowhere, suggesting there is little chance of any of the above omissions correcting themselves."

Becoming the mad old woman who lives on the edge of the village in a decrepit, rambling house with about thirty cats, making herbal potions and frightening the local children, is an attractive option, she mused. However, at my age one does worry about peaking too soon . . .

She glanced at her watch. Nearly nine o'clock! She had been sitting in her tree for more than an hour. The early morning mist had burnt away now, the grass was dry, and the sun was shining hot onto her back.

She wanted another coffee. With milk. And a bacon sandwich, she decided, jumping down and brushing off her jeans.

Never mind life's huge questions, the smaller question was whether the ancient black bicycle, complete with basket in front of the handlebars, was still there. She had seen it tucked into a corner of the woodshed three months before. Given the state of it then, Imogen guessed it might have been left behind.

She was right.

"Yay!" she crowed as she disentangled it from a pile of firewood and dragged it out into the open. The tires were flat, of course, but there was even a pump clipped to the bike frame. She pumped the tires up and took it for a wobbly test run along the garden path. Embarrassingly loud brakes but otherwise, perfectly roadworthy.

Stopping only to put on some shoes and grab her wallet, she wheeled the old bicycle onto the lane and gingerly cycled off.

Middlemass was a picture-postcard village with expensive houses called things like "The Old Schoolhouse" and "The Old Bakery." There was a church with churchyard, which hugged the driveway to a grand old pile called Middlemass Hall—the Georgian mansion she could see from the orchard—and just on the other side of the driveway, on the road toward the market town of Portneath, was Storybook Cottage.

Her new home was about a mile from the center of the village, and she was soon cycling past the duck pond in the village center. She and Nigel had visited the house on a Sunday, and cricketers had been playing on the green, but on a weekday, it was deserted. The tiny selection of shops, the little village pub, and the primary school were all at the far end, near the duck pond and the cricket green. If any more serious shopping was required, presumably she would need to get to Portneath, which—according to the wooden road sign—was a bit further than she would like to go by bicycle.

No need to lock it up here, she thought, leaning her bike against the low wall outside the village shop. It was a combined newsagent, post office, and convenience store all packed into a short parade of shops, each with a Georgian bay window. The inside looked like a Technicolor version of the Old Curiosity Shop.

You couldn't swing a cat in here without making contact with half the product range, she thought—or is the term *retail line*? Not that I ever would *literally* swing a cat, she thought with a shudder, not even Tango, who sometimes deserves it. Actually, it hardly matters because there's probably some hygiene regulation that stops you from trying it anyway, she reflected idly as she wandered around the tiny interior, lobbing items randomly into her basket. The legislation would be something like, "page 217, Section C, Subsection 2 b forbidding the aerial perambulation of felines." Deliberating over spaghetti hoops versus baked beans, she was distracted by the shop's doorbell announcing a new arrival.

"Doctor, how lovely to see you," squawked the well-covered elderly lady behind the till.

"Hello, Mrs. Pinkerton, how's the knee today?" said the man. He was a tall, clean-cut, and strikingly handsome blond. He was also wearing an impeccable suit and tie despite the promise of a hot, sticky day.

"Ooh—'Muriel,' please—it's ever so much better now you've had a look at it, Doctor," she simpered.

"I'm sorry I haven't been able to do more than offer sympathy."

"But that's the thing, Doctor. I don't know what you did, but I feel ever so much better," insisted Muriel, breathless with admiration as she took the money for his newspaper.

"Well, I know we doctors have a reputation for thinking we're God, but I certainly don't make any claims for the laying on of hands." At this he caught Imogen's eye and gave her a wink.

She grinned conspiratorially back at him.

"Oh, you are a one," said Muriel delightedly as she watched him sketch a wave and go, running down the steps to the path. "Doesn't know how clever he is," she said to no one in particular, "and ever so handsome too."

Dumping her basket on the counter, Imogen smiled distantly at the older woman as she recovered from the excitement of the doctor's visit, still enjoyably flustered and pink in the face.

"Stocking up, dear?" Muriel probed, eyes burning with curiosity.

"Yep," replied Imogen, ignoring the implied invitation to explain herself.

"I think you'll find we have most things here," Muriel announced. "I always says to my husband, Ted, I says, 'You can hardly complain about people deserting the village shop if we don't provide what they want.'"

Imogen smiled distantly, hoping her lack of response would be noted as lack of interest. Which it was. No offense intended.

"Oh, yes," Muriel continued, oblivious, settling herself

more comfortably on her chair and launching into a well-rehearsed diatribe. "I've got no patience for them that say the supermarkets are taking over. It'll be a good long time before my ladies—because that's what I call them, 'my ladies'—have got to get themselves over to the likes of Portneath, if I have my way. Are you going to be in the area long, my dear?" she asked, her new train of thought following without her drawing breath.

Imogen smiled and nodded vaguely, her mind back at the house and on her list of things to do.

"I said, are you going to be in the area long, dear, or are you just here on holiday?" she persevered, speaking loudly and slowly like an Englishman abroad.

Imogen's eyes widened. "Oh, sorry! Yes, I moved in yesterday. Don't know how long I'll be staying, though . . ." She trailed away.

"You'll be the new owner of Storybook Cottage, then," Muriel proclaimed. "A lovely family house that, I've always thought." She looked at Imogen expectantly.

"Mm," said Imogen, not having the faintest idea what she was required to say. "I expect so," she added helpfully, as the woman clearly wanted more. When even this didn't do the trick, Imogen decided on a tactical retreat. She grabbed the bag of groceries and left with a cheery wave.

"Well, she's a funny one and that's for sure, isn't she, Paddy!" Muriel shouted across to the neat middle-aged man who was sitting behind the post office counter in the corner. He was methodically sorting notes and coins and keeping his head down. She pursed her lips, drew her pale mauve cardigan around her, and patted her matching hair, making a mental note to tell her sister Joan all about the strange new arrival. The satisfying thing about being back on speaking terms with her was that there was simply no one in Middlemass even half as interested in high-quality gossip as Joan was.

 *Chapter Three*

With her groceries stashed in the front basket, Imogen cycled slowly back along the lane. She felt strangely leaden again—an odd and profound fatigue that had made a habit of enveloping her with little warning.

Pedaling idly to save her strength, she basked in the sunshine. There was a fresh breeze and a soapy, washing-day smell from the cow parsley that foamed over the bank to her left. She was dimly aware of the rushing brook beside the road, the sound of the water getting louder and louder until eventually it was a roar, filling her ears and blocking out her thoughts.

Then she caught the sound of someone shouting through the din.

"Move, you stupid woman, for God's sake . . . Move!"

The sun went in. She glanced over her shoulder and saw the reason. Just feet away was a huge tractor, its massive wheels towering above her. One more half turn, and she would be dragged underneath them. Instinctively, she threw herself sideways into the cow parsley, landing with a thud that emptied the air from her lungs. Dazed, and with her bike and shopping piled on top of her, she lay on the bank, looking up at the sky. Suddenly, the sun was blocked out again, this time by an unshaven, dark-tanned face contorted with rage.

"What-the-bloody-hell-in-the-name-of-God-do-you-think-you-were-doing?" he bellowed in a continuous roar of fury, pulling the bike off her and flinging it into the hedgerow. She cowered, speechless and terrified. He crouched and ran his hands over her limbs gently, assessing, like she had seen people do with horses' legs.

"Are you hurt?" He didn't stop for a reply. "You bloody should be—it might teach you a lesson. Jesus Christ, have you got some sort of death wish?"

A thought obviously struck him.

"Are. You. Deaf?" he mouthed emphatically at her, looking intently at her face for signs of comprehension.

"No. I. Am. Not," she replied crossly, pushing him off and scrambling to her feet, relieved to discover that life and limb were still intact.

"Okay. You're not deaf. That leaves me with no clue at all why you didn't get the hell out of the way," he said, slightly less furiously than before.

"That's rich!" Imogen said, irritated at the hysterical squeak in her voice. She drew herself up to her full height and was even more irritated to find herself still only addressing the third button of the man's shirt. Tilting her head back to look him in the eye, she said, with an attempt at dignity, "I think I am perfectly entitled to ride my bike along a perfectly . . . perfectly . . ."

Horrified, Imogen realized she was going to cry; even

worse, her legs seemed to have suddenly turned to liquid and she was on the verge of slumping humiliatingly to the ground.

Clearly realizing this, the man grabbed her again, this time firmly around the waist, with both hands. She gasped and looked up into his face, her eyes swimming. For an insane moment, she thought he was going to kiss her. For an even more insane moment, she wanted him to. Very much. They stared into each other's eyes until Imogen, blinking back the tears, looked away, blushing.

"Come on," he said, giving his head a little shake as if to empty it of an unwelcome thought. "I'll take you home."

Without warning, he swung her off her feet and hoisted her into the tractor cab towering above them, seemingly without any effort at all. She scrambled away from him onto the far end of the bench seat and sat, sniffing and mortified, as he gathered up her shopping for her and then walked around to the other side and pulled himself up beside her. Wordlessly, he passed her the repacked shopping bag, followed by a surprisingly pristine cotton handkerchief.

"Not far to go," he said.

"How do you know?" she said, wiping her eyes. "I haven't told you where I live."

"I'm assuming it's Storybook Cottage," he replied. "I recognized the bicycle. Talking of which, I'll pick it up later and drop it back to you."

She sneaked a glance at him as they trundled the short distance to the house. He was tall—at least six foot two inches—and long-limbed. Late thirties, Imogen guessed, with dark brown wavy hair curling onto the collar of his frayed cotton shirt, sleeves rolled up to reveal surprisingly muscular forearms, out of scale with the rest of his lean body. He had heavy eyebrows and deep-set brown eyes and was still scowling thunderously. She didn't want to kiss him anymore, she decided.

Drawing up outside the house, and leaving the tractor blocking the lane, he took Imogen's groceries from her and, without glancing back, walked in through the unlocked front door, leaving Imogen to scramble down, which was fortunately easier than climbing up. Following him into the house, Imogen saw him disappear into the kitchen, where he dumped the bag on the table.

"You had better have a hot bath," he said. "You'll be good and stiff in a few hours if you don't."

"Fat chance with no hot water," she blurted, thrown by his familiarity with her and, obviously, with the house.

"What's the matter with the immersion heater?" he asked.

"What immersion heater?" said Imogen, feeling silly yet again. "I only moved in last night. I haven't really had a chance to get things sorted out."

"Right—well," he replied, with barely concealed impatience, "there's an immersion heater for the hot water in the bathroom cupboard. Mind you, you will need to switch it on," he said, giving her a scathing look. "Obviously that's just for the summer," he went on. "In the winter you'll probably be using the range," he said, indicating the hulk of black metal that Imogen had been regarding so dubiously that morning.

Like hell I will, she thought.

"It does the heating and the hot water," he explained.

"You can cook on it too, of course. You'll probably need to get in some more coal, but there's no rush. Anyway, if you're okay, I'll go. And for God's sake, keep your wits about you in future. By the way, my name's Gabriel—from Middlemass Hall."

With these words, he was gone, leaving Imogen feeling inefficient, foolish, and generally a bit dim. Had he realized she had wanted him to kiss her? Hopefully not. How embarrassing! What on earth was the matter with her? With that, she went upstairs with visions of long soaks in steaming hot baths, all thoughts of breakfast temporarily forgotten.

THE STILL-PACKED BOXES in every room seemed to multiply rather than diminish. Weeks after moving in, there was still a pile of them in the hallway that Imogen stubbed her toe on with monotonous regularity. One morning, Imogen had a word with herself and rolled up her sleeves. After two hours spent unpacking boxes, she looked a mess and itched with dirt. Her hair was escaping in corkscrew tendrils from its hasty ponytail, and her hands were filthy with newsprint from the old papers she had used for wrapping all the china and glass.

Nigel's Villeroy & Boch dinner service was consigned to the inside of the enormous dresser, at least until she had decided whether to bother having a proper dining room to put it in. The shelves on the top half of the dresser were stacked instead with tins and packets of food. Their bright colors looked quite jolly, she thought, and she had used the cup hooks on the edges of the shelves for a motley assortment of her favorite mugs plus her Denby jug collection, both of which had always been banished from display in their London flat.

Imogen's other kitchen improvements included a rag rug she had found upstairs and a Lloyd Loom basket chair which—with a couple of cushions—made a pleasant spot for Tango to sunbathe in and for Imogen to curl up in when she needed a rest, which was often. The rest of the rooms downstairs were still chaotic, even after a week in the house. Imogen was still retreating to the kitchen in the evenings.

Might as well get even dirtier, she thought, and started stuffing the wrappings and broken cardboard boxes into bin liners for transporting down to the wilderness at the end of the garden with the vague thought of having a bonfire.

After just two trips, it was time to stop for a breather. She was still feeling completely exhausted and weak, despite sleeping soundly through the night—courtesy of the diazepam. She had been horrified to discover the night before that she only had two left. Even though she had reluctantly accepted the prescription "just to get you through the worst," as her London GP had said, now she was dreading running out. She decided to phone her local surgery straightaway.

"I'm afraid you'll have to come in," said the pleasant female voice when Imogen explained what she wanted. "We always ask new patients to see the doctor when they join our list," the receptionist continued. "We have a cancellation this afternoon with Dr. Simon. Could you manage twenty past two?"

"That would be great," Imogen heard herself saying while silently cursing.

Damn. She would have to wash and put on clean clothes, maybe even comb her hair. She was in a right state. "If my mother could see me now, she'd have a fit," she said aloud, after ending the call.

It rang straightaway, the display announcing it was her mother.

"Darling, it's me," said the voice imperiously. Her mother still didn't understand about not needing to announce herself when she called.

"Bloody hell, Mummy, how did you know?"

"Language! How did I know what, dear?" June—Imogen's mother—said imperturbably. "How are you coping?"

"Yup, fine, fine!" barked Imogen, who said that every time—obviously not confessing she had been trying to score more drugs just minutes before.

"Anyway, I've decided it's about time I come down and make sure you are all right," she announced.

"But why?" said Imogen, horrified.

"Really, darling, don't be silly. I am your mother," she replied with finality. "Now, I thought I would come next week, after Gerald's Masonic dinner, and then I could just go on from you to my Using Yoga to Unlock Your Inner Child course in Totnes . . ."

Imogen accepted her fate and half listened, picturing her mother standing by the hall table in her gardening hat, glasses on a chain around her neck while she studied the pages of the leather-bound appointments diary she kept by the telephone. Even though they had long had a cordless phone, her mother still took all phone calls in the hallway, as if she was stuck in the 1930s. She had been an older mother, and Imogen—an only child—had long suspected she was an afterthought, or even a mistake, sneaking in under the wire when her mother's guard had dropped. That said, she had been actively campaigning for grandchildren since Imogen was barely in her twenties.

And that was another reason why Imogen was keen to avoid her at the moment.

Not that her mother had time in her life for grandchildren. Since her father's death from a heart attack twelve years ago, when Imogen was just twenty years old, she had watched her mother embrace the lifestyle of all women who have been left comfortably off and are terrified of finding themselves with nothing to do. The opposite of nothing to do was a breathless round of fundraising-event organization, visits to friends, and endless residential courses in everything from bookbinding to Balinese gamelan for beginners, as well as—in more recent years—organizing her boyfriend Gerald's life in a way he adored but Imogen would have found unbearable.

In other words, Imogen's mother was exhausting.

"SIMON, MRS. HEWITT TO see you. Shall I send her in?" said the receptionist into the intercom at the doctor's surgery.

The receptionist smiled at a response from the doctor and continued, "Two more after this one, and the kettle's going on."

Just a little bit of flirting, Imogen noted. I bet he's a crusty old git with an eye for the women in a misogynistic "do let me hold the door open for you to get back to the kitchen sink" sort of way.

"The doctor will see you now," the receptionist told her, with nothing like the warmth she had extended to her boss.

Slipping into the room, Imogen was surprised to see a familiar tall, blond figure standing at the window with his back to her. Was it? He turned, and she instantly recognized the handsome doctor she had met in the village store. Dr. Simon—of course.

He smiled and gestured toward a chair.

"Mrs. Hewitt, take a seat. Thank you for coming in. Do call me Simon—everyone does. Unless you would be more comfortable calling me Dr. Simon. A few of the older patients prefer it."

His handshake was firm but not the bone crusher that Imogen had endured from many men, and he was— Imogen decided dispassionately—definitely good-looking.

"I understand you've recently moved into the village. How are you finding it?"

"Er, fine," she replied, trying not to simper idiotically in the face of such physical beauty.

"And your husband, er, partner?" he continued. "Is he planning to sign up with us as well?"

"I, um, I don't think so, no."

"I'm sorry," said Simon. "You must forgive me, it's just the word in the village was that a couple had bought the house." He made a throwaway gesture to apologize for the imposition. "Is he not with you?"

"No," said Imogen.

"Er, or she, obviously," he added hurriedly.

"No."

"Separated? Divorced?"

"Dead, actually." This was awkward. "But really, don't worry," she babbled. "It's fine, I'm fine. I don't mind you asking. Honestly . . ." She trailed away, aware that Simon was silent, regarding her with quiet sympathy.

"I am so sorry," he said, when she had finally made herself shut up. "It must be terribly difficult for you."

He spoke so simply and calmly she felt her face flush and her eyes fill with tears. She blinked rapidly.

"Now, down to business, I think," he said, after a long moment. "We'll have your notes in a few days, I know, but until then, do you have any particular long-term health problems?" he asked.

She shook her head.

"How have you been feeling generally?"

"Okay, I suppose. Actually, I've been incredibly tired. I've been assuming it's down to the diazepam, although I was wondering if you could let me have some more. I can't bear to lie awake at night. Too much time to think about things," she blurted.

"It's not a good idea to take it long term," he said sympathetically. "But—in any case—I can't imagine it's responsible for the fatigue. How long have you been feeling like that?"

"I don't know. I suppose I was assuming it was since Nigel was killed." She swallowed hard. "But actually, I think it might have started a little bit before."

"Dizziness, fainting spells, nausea . . . anything like that?"

"No—well, no, not really—actually, maybe a bit—the

feeling sick thing, now you mention it. You don't think I'm really ill, do you?"

"No, no, I don't think so at all," he said slowly. "But I'll have a few tests done, if you don't mind. I'll arrange for you to see the practice nurse. She'll sort you out and then you can come back in a few days to see me for the results. In the meantime, I would rather not repeat your prescription for the diazepam." He looked sympathetically at her. "Can you manage without, do you think?"

She nodded meekly.

"Good," he said. "Now, what I would like you to do is try to get lots of rest, make sure you get plenty to eat—with most of my patients, I'd be telling them the opposite—and maybe cut back on tea and coffee. That can make a big difference to insomnia, you know." He stood to usher her out, giving her a warm smile. "I look forward to seeing you soon, Imogen, and don't worry—things will get better, I promise."

BY THE TIME she had got back to the waiting room, Simon had spoken to Mrs. Efficiency at the reception desk.

She smiled a little more warmly at Imogen and said, "The practice nurse can see you now if you have the time. I have also booked you another appointment with Doctor; here, I've written it on a card for you. Is that all right?"

The nurse took samples and asked questions with brisk efficiency. By the time Imogen got back to the house, it was just after five o'clock, the sun was low, slanting in through the high windows and flooding the house with golden light. After a cup of tea and some toast, Imogen, relieved at putting some responsibility for herself into the hands of someone else, felt overwhelmingly relaxed and even sleepy. She trailed up to her attic bedroom for a brief rest before supper, fell asleep immediately, and did not wake until the following morning.

 *Chapter Four*

With just three days' grace until her mother came, the pressure was on to get the house habitable. The combination of her tiredness and the heat meant the last week had drifted past with hardly anything to show for it. She made herself some coffee and, pursued nonchalantly by Tango, who gave the impression of having a number of better things to do with his time, she made a reconnaissance.

The kitchen was all right. The formal drawing room that led off the hallway to the front of the house was potentially beautiful. It had a pair of high arched windows to the front, with their original wooden shutters, and it ran the full depth of the house, with French doors into the garden at the back. The room cried out for elegant but comfortable sofas, a glossy grand piano, and jugs of roses from the garden. Unfortunately, what it had instead was twenty or more collapsing cardboard boxes of books with no shelves to put them on and a jarringly inappropriate selection of the fashionable contemporary furniture Nigel had preferred. The Eames chair looked distinctly odd by the faded green silk curtains the previous owner had left, and the starkly angular sofa and chairs looked brutal marooned in the middle of wide oak floorboards, which would be beautiful with polish and effort. The study, filled with Nigel's papers, and the dining room both led off the other side of the hallway and were even worse because they were smaller and seemed more cluttered.

She and her mother would just have to carry on living in the kitchen as Imogen had been doing.

That decision made, she felt more energetic. She went to tackle the upstairs but was soon glum again, making mental lists of urgent work to be done and wincing at the sight of electric wiring running along the skirting boards.

It looked prehistoric. She dreaded to think what an electrician would say. She imagined the ritual of tooth sucking and head shaking that plumbers and electricians seemed to engage in before announcing an estimate the size of a small country's national debt. "And that's just for the essential stuff, love," they always say, thought Imogen irritably, before going on to break down her resistance with sotto voce phrases like "death trap," "bleedin' cowboys," and "don't know why you didn't call me in earlier . . ." until Imogen had lost the will to live and sacrificed her annual holiday to pay for boring but essential things like new fuse boxes and damp-proof courses.

Off the galleried landing there was an airy, spacious bathroom with a huge claw-footed bath on a raised platform in the middle of the room. The view from the window was the orchard and the manor house beyond. So far there were no curtains, which hadn't bothered Imogen at all, but she could only imagine what her mother would say.

Oh well, thought Imogen. I'll just tell her I doubt the

sheep are interested in seeing anyone with no clothes on, and if the inhabitants at the manor are voyeurs with binoculars, then cheap thrills to them.

There were three bedrooms on this floor. The larger one looking out onto the front of the house had the same high arched windows and window seats as in the drawing room. She would have shared this one with Nigel. Another, they had immediately dubbed the nursery. She hadn't been able to bring herself to go in there since she arrived. Not much chance of playing happy family now.

Going into the master bedroom, she decided it would do perfectly well for her mother. It was lucky she had at least unpacked the bedding. She dug a set of clean white cotton sheets out of the huge airing cupboard in the bathroom—the same cupboard she had eventually found the immersion heater in, thanks to Gabriel's instructions.

With sheets and bedding sorted, she shifted ten or so boxes and bin liners of clothes to the nursery room and found a bedside light with a working bulb, which she stood on a wooden chest next to the bed. Then she cleared the junk from a little chest of drawers formerly in the spare room of their Wimbledon flat, and the room was ready. Luckily there were already thin curtains at the windows, not enough to cut out the light but enough to ensure privacy.

Apart from the cellar that Imogen—terrified of spiders—was too scared to explore, the only other rooms in the house were the attic rooms. One was currently Imogen's bedroom; the other room, leading off it, was slightly larger and flooded with light from the dormer window. She had secretly earmarked it as her studio, somewhere she could go to draw and paint. Tomorrow perhaps she would unpack her art materials and make a start.

AFTER SEVERAL DAYS of relentless sunshine that had left her feeling utterly drained, it had rained heavily overnight, and the stultifying heat of the last few days had finally lifted.

Tango had made his habitual early morning arrival on Imogen's pillow and was now curled up like a prawn on his side, instantly adopting the appearance of deep sleep to dissuade her from pushing him off. She prodded him experimentally. In response, he opened one eye and fixed her with a glacial stare.

After a hasty bath in water that was none too warm, Imogen pottered around the kitchen in her socked feet. Tango had followed her down and was howling piteously for food.

"You're awfully fat for someone who's starving," she told him. "Really, to look at you, anyone would think you'd already snarfed down a good half a tin of cat food as recently as last night," she said, knowing he had done exactly that.

She bent to scoop the remains of last night's tin into Tango's plate by the back door. She caught a whiff of the food, and her stomach lurched suddenly. She straightened up, taking a deep breath to fight the wave of nausea. It receded, leaving a faint dew of sweat on her upper lip.

"Honestly, I don't know how you can stomach the stuff," she said weakly as Tango abruptly stopped caressing her legs with his tail and tucked into his breakfast without a backward glance.

She sat for a minute in the Lloyd Loom chair by the stove

and tried some deep breaths. Feeling better, she put on the kettle and rinsed out the teapot, chucking in a couple of fresh tea bags from the open box on the counter. With Nigel, the thought of failing to decant the tea bags from the box into their own ceramic pot was more than shocking. At Storybook Cottage, Imogen would be the first to admit that standards had dropped.

Waiting for the kettle to boil, she peeped into the bread bin. The stale heel of the loaf was so impressively moldy, she thought fleetingly about donating it to science instead of chucking it out. Then she turned her attention to the remaining half loaf sitting on the bread board. It was stale but good enough for toast. She carved off a couple of thick slabs and chucked them under the grill.

A visit to the garrulous Muriel was definitely called for. Remembering her afternoon appointment with Simon, the doctor hottie, she made a mental note to do some essential shopping on the way home. She indulged in a few seconds' fantasy of Simon patting her hand and telling her charmingly what a gallant and brave woman she was, his face filled with admiration and concern.

Not that I could possibly be looking for romance, she added hastily to herself, remembering disturbingly how close she was to throwing herself at the grumpy tractor driver. It would be unseemly for such a recent widow to even entertain such a thing.

Grabbing the toast seconds before it burst into flames, she scraped off the worst of the carbon into the sink, plastered them with peanut butter and banana slices, and munched away contentedly. If my friends could see me now, she thought. Imogen had been famous for living—apparently for months on end—on coffee and her nerves while juggling her jobs and artistic ambitions in London. Breakfast had rarely happened. Despite the nausea, her appetite was not so much returning as introducing itself to her for the first time in living memory.

Hunger satisfied, Imogen settled to planning her day. She was getting used to a more relaxed lifestyle and was often surprised when she checked her watch how much time had passed without her having done anything. In London she had prided herself on guessing the time before looking at her watch, and she was rarely more than ten minutes out. She poured another cup of tea from the brown Denby teapot and marveled at the change. Success then had been measured by cramming more into the day, like finding Nigel's favorite olives from a particular delicatessen and then building even more insanity into life by making sure never to buy olives from anywhere else even if it meant a ridiculous detour to go there. A walk through a park, even with screaming roads on all sides, was a balm to the soul, and a treat was to stop for a flat white on the way to whatever job she had not yet been sacked from.

Now, let's face it, the treat is not having to go to work, she thought, but she sensed a creeping unease niggling at the back of her mind that was a bit more than the obvious problem of having to earn her own living pretty soon. Moving had been exhausting, so she had allowed herself a rest to recover, but now weeks had passed with little to show for it, and reality was going to have to return one day. Soon. It felt like one of those corny horror films where the children are playing in the sunshine, watched by smiling parents as the ominous music grows ever louder in the background. There was definitely a sense of unease. She even wondered if the house was haunted. She could be picking up the vibes of long-ago sorrow. Maybe a long-dead lovelorn serving wench was keeping watch in an upstairs room, longing for her dastardly lover to come and sweep her off her feet, only to discover that all along he had been double-crossing her with a woman of substance, leaving her to pine away . . . forever awaiting his return.

Or something.

With her overwrought fantasies, she was quite overcome, and reaching for her tea, she took a huge swig to restore herself.

"Aargh! Poison!" she choked. Spluttering and spraying the contents of her mouth everywhere she looked aghast at the mug in her hand to discover that she had grabbed the jug of salad dressing left on the table from her supper the evening before.

"Teach me to be such a slob," she said aloud, still gagging. "Sorry, Tango," she added appeasingly.

He was not quick to forgive and shot her appalled looks between licking the spray of oil and vinegar off his face and chest. Sitting on the table within strategic reach of the butter dish, he had received the full force of the explosion and was clearly disgusted.

At least it was a distraction from disturbing thoughts. Clearing up the mess proved to be a catalyst, and Imogen leapt into clean-up mode. She emptied the dishwasher and immediately nearly filled it again with the pile of dirty crockery piled up on the side. Then she poured lukewarm water over the washing up, and adding the remains of the kettle contents, she washed several days' worth of saucepans and baking tins. Finally, she rinsed out a cloth and wiped down the surfaces, including the scrubbed pine table that dominated the center of the room, scouring industriously at numerous unidentifiable sticky marks that had appeared only at the end she always used. The rest of the huge table was covered in a thin layer of dust, along with a pile of junk mail—mostly addressed to the previous owner—which was threatening to slide to the floor.

Filled with zeal, Imogen finished cleaning up the worst of the mess in the kitchen—although she knew she was only leaving it in a state where supercritical Nigel would have started. She even grabbed a dustbin liner and ruthlessly chucked away most of the junk mail, sternly averting her eyes from the intriguing piles of catalogues stuffed with indispensable items for the home. Imogen could never resist those "versatile nests of willow baskets" and "lovingly handcrafted casserole dish stands."

With the recycling bin only a quarter full of wastepaper, Imogen stood holding it, in the middle of the kitchen floor. She knew perfectly well where she should go to fill it up and—prodding her emotions cautiously like a tender bruise—she decided this was the morning to make a start on Nigel's papers in the study.

Apart from the policy documents and bank statements the solicitor's clerk had taken away to sort out probate, the contents of Nigel's office in London had been packed and brought down wholesale, because—until now—the thought of tackling old letters and photographs had been unbearable.

Feeling sick at the smell of oil and vinegar on her clothes, Imogen went upstairs to change. The washing was another thing that wasn't getting done too regularly, and she was out of any clean clothes that didn't feel hopelessly restricted around the waist, especially in the summer heat. She helped herself to one of Nigel's blue-and-white-striped office shirts, folding back the cuffs into a thick wodge at the wrists.

Before she got stuck in, she fortified herself with another mug of tea and another toasted sandwich. Then, with the tea in one hand and bin in the other, she headed for the study.

Settling herself cross-legged in a little space on the floor, she undid the flaps on the box nearest to her. Old bank statements and credit card bills were quickly consigned to the recycling, although she knew she should shred them, really. Perhaps she should burn them. The next box, filled with neatly filed mortgage paperwork on the Wimbledon flat plus old car Ministry of Transport certificates and garage bills, went the same way. Emboldened by the knowledge that Nigel's crusty old solicitor had any paperwork that might be vaguely important, she worked quickly through another couple of boxes filled with ancient tax returns and box files full of receipts.

She flattened the boxes as she went and took full bins to the bonfire at the end of the garden—she doubted the bin men would be thrilled with *that* much recycling—and the study soon started to look clearer. In fact, with its sweet little woodburning stove and window overlooking the garden, she was quite taken with the idea of turning it into a cozy sitting room. The main drawing room was beautiful, potentially, but sorting out a room on such a grand scale was still too daunting. This room, on the other hand, would be gorgeous at night with its dark-red-painted walls and its floor-to-ceiling bookshelves on either side of the fireplace. She was dying to unpack some of her art books and could think of nothing better than snuggling up in the evening with the roaring fire and a favorite book.

Opening another box, she whooped with pleasure. There, on the top of the box, was a thick pile of photographs she recognized.

Here was a picture of her at sixteen with Sally, nearly a year older, dressed up to go to a disco. They were posing in minidresses from Boohoo, Imogen's a catastrophe of pink ostrich feathers . . . What was she thinking? Sally's dress—a barely there sequined number that made her look like a hooker—wasn't much better. Both were striking what they had fondly imagined were sultry poses.

Memories of the night were suddenly so vivid she could even smell their body spray as they danced to Beyoncé and then—once they were drunk and maudlin—Amy Winehouse and Adele, leaning tearfully on each other as they promised to never ever lose touch after that long, hot post-exam summer had come to an end. Then, with a pang, she remembered the end of the evening, watching Sally clutched in the arms of the local heartthrob, Steve Winters, swaying to Snow Patrol's "Chasing Cars" while he investigated her tonsils with his tongue. All the while, Imogen had felt conspicuously alone as she wondered where her own date, his name long forgotten, had gone to after disappearing to the bar for more drinks nearly half an hour before.

Sally made life look easy in a way it had never seemed to be for Imogen.

She riffled through piles of photos showing nameless members of Nigel's family, with stiff little groups wearing rictus smiles, representing Christmases, weddings, and christenings past. There was one of their wedding in Nigel's parents' village, the photographer's pictures outside the church perfectly capturing maiden aunts with hurting feet and parents, rigid-jawed, trying to control overexcited children. Imogen had stood in the center with Nigel, beaming up adoringly at him, his hands around her waist as her mother-in-law looked on with a bitter smile.

Next she came across some older Polaroid photos. Her eye fell on a small, faded square print of a little boy around nine years old, standing by an open car door. He wore a school uniform too big for him, and one corner of his mouth was curved in an uncertain grin. Behind him stood a smiling younger version of Nigel's father, resting a hand on the boy's shoulder. She assumed this was him on the way to boarding school.

He looked so vulnerable in his oversized blazer and cap; she felt a stab of sympathy for the long-ago little boy, so different to the ebullient, loud, and confident man she later married.

No child of mine would ever be sent away, she thought, conveniently forgetting how she, gripped by Enid Blyton school sagas of midnight feasts and "jolly good eggs" trouncing the bad girls at lacrosse and life in general, had begged her parents to send her to boarding school. Then, within months of getting into a mild bit of trouble at secondary school, she *was* sent away. She had hated it, she remembered.

Imogen flicked rapidly through the remaining photos and, separating her own plus a few of Nigel as a child, she packed up the box again to offer to Nigel's mother. Groaning aloud at the thought of having to contact her, Imogen wondered if it would be too awful to get in touch with his sister, Anne, instead.

She decided on plan B. Anne was always civil and even sometimes quite warm. She could post them of course, but it would be so awful if they got lost. She should deliver them herself, and what's more, she could take a couple of days on a London trip, maybe stay with Sally and catch up with some old friends.

With this uplifting thought, she rallied her energy and opened the final box. This one was stuffed full of personal letters mixed up with old birthday cards and the correspondence sent by guests to their wedding. She quickly dispensed with the latter, slightly dispirited that—even only two years on—she could not put faces to the names on quite a few of the letters.

In an age of texts and messaging apps, it was a shame she and Nigel had never sent each other a single proper letter, she thought sadly. It would have been nice to have a little stack of love letters, all tied with a ribbon, but it just hadn't been that sort of relationship. They had decided—really, *he* had decided—to marry such a short time after meeting. Once she had moved into Nigel's flat, she was right there—and there had been no need to write down loving messages. Not then, and now it was too late.

Scooping up the pile of letters to shovel them into the bin bag, her eye fell on a piece of blue letter paper covered in thick black writing. Glancing mildly curiously at it, her eye fell on a phrase.

I hate having to keep our relationship secret, it said.

Picking it out of the pile, she sat back on her heels and read. As she did so, her hands started to shake and her heart to hammer so loud she could hear it thundering in her ears.

The date on the top of the letter was May that year, she noticed, just weeks before Nigel's death.

Dear Nigel,

It was so wonderful to see you last night. I can't believe how much we have in common. I have never found it so easy to talk to anyone before. It's almost like we've known each other all our lives, don't you think?

I hate having to keep our relationship secret. I want to meet everyone. The family, your friends—to feel like I belong in your life. I can hardly wait for the day to come, but I completely understand there are obstacles I have to let you remove before that can happen.

I know I shouldn't call you, but I really want us to meet again soon. Please, please try to get away as soon as you can.

Until then, with all my love,
Victoria

She felt sick.

Bastard, she thought. "Bloody, sodding bloody, bloody bastard," she said aloud. "Not only does he bloody get himself bloody killed within virtually minutes of me giving up my entire life to do his bidding, the bloody bastard wasn't even faithful. Not even for two years. Pathetic! Now I can't even confront him with it because he's bloody got himself out of it by dying . . ."

She sat, shaking, on the floor, great tears of rage and loss combined rolling down her cheeks and running together on her chin to drip onto the floor.

AFTER SOME TIME, she became aware that she was cold. Worse, her feet, trapped under her, had gone to sleep. Staggering upright, she waited for them to wake into an agony of pins and needles. Her nose was running too and, eventually, sniffing, she went through to the kitchen feeling lightheaded.

Blowing her nose on the kitchen towel and mopping her swollen eyes, she felt a little better.

"Sorry," she said to Tango, who had followed her—not out of concern, of course, but possibly curiosity. He was a sucker for drama.

Her eyes filled again, this time with self-pity.

Horrified, Imogen caught sight of the kitchen clock. She was supposed to be at the surgery twenty minutes ago. She was sure missing appointments was the height of rudeness in a small community like this. And also, although the last thing she felt like was a trip out of the house, the prospect of another conversation with the divine Dr. Simon beckoned seductively.

 *Chapter Five*

Pregnant?" said Imogen. "Oh my God! How?"

Simon cleared his throat and shuffled some papers, tactfully declining to comment. "We can work out roughly how long by the date of your last period, if you can remember," he said instead. "To be certain, a scan will help,"

"To be certain of what? To be certain that I'm pregnant?"

"No." He laughed. "There's absolutely no doubt about that. All I mean is that we might need to do a scan to see roughly when the baby's due."

"Oh my God . . . pregnant!" she said again, dazed. A tear welled up and spilled down her face.

Simon handed her a box of tissues from his desk.

"Obviously there's a lot to think about," he said gently. "These things take getting used to—especially if they are—um—unexpected," he continued. "You may want to . . ." He cleared his throat. "I mean, if you have a long think, and you decide that you are not happy with the situation, then—depending on your due date—there are still maybe things—"

"God, no!" said Imogen, suddenly realizing what he was getting at. "It's not that. I'm not unhappy about it at all, I just can't believe it, that's all. Sorry. I know I'm crying. I'm always crying nowadays," she said, blowing her streaming nose with an unladylike honk. "She's the best news I've had in months. Or ever, actually."

"So, it's going to be a girl, is it?" Simon said lightly.

"Yes, somehow I think it is," said Imogen slowly, and then, remembering the letter from the mystery woman: "God forbid that it should be a boy when there's a distinct danger he might take after his bloody father."

She looked up at Simon's shocked face and blushed.

"Okay," he said, "well, Morag will sort out dates with you and then, when you have your twenty-week scan, you can ask the sonographer to tell you, if you decide you want to know. Now, you will need to start looking after yourself," he continued briskly. "As I am sure you can guess, those pills are out of the question now." He reached for her notes and started to scribble as he spoke.

"You'll need to see Morag, our midwife. She's fierce. We doctors are terrified of her, but the mothers seem to get on all right with her. Also, you should probably start taking a good multivitamin for pregnant women plus a folic acid supplement. Morag will give you the details." He stood and handed her a referral note.

Picking up on the purposeful mood, Imogen thanked him and jumped to her feet. Swinging her scuffed black leather shoulder bag up from under her chair, the strap caught around the bottom and upended it, scattering the contents all over the floor. Blushing scarlet once again, Imogen scrambled around the surgery floor picking up keys, cards, mountains of loose change that spun off into all four corners of the room, tampons—won't be needing those for a while—plus an embarrassingly large number of random bits of paper.

Simon got to his knees too, carefully rounding up all the debris efficiently and without fuss. Amazingly clean nails, Imogen noted as she sat back on her heels and observed him. He really was very handsome. Goodness, first she was wanting to throw herself into the arms of a stranger, and now she was lusting after her own doctor. It must be the hormones.

Blushing, Imogen reeled out of Simon's office and went to the reception desk with instructions to organize a meeting with the midwife. The briskly efficient receptionist gave her a warm, knowing smile and handed her an appointment card for the next afternoon.

"COOEEEEE! ANYBODY THERE?" cried a voice faintly from the front garden.

"Oh, crap! I completely forgot," exclaimed Imogen, leaping to her feet and causing Tango to slither resentfully from her lap onto the floor.

"Where are you, darling? Oh, there you are at last," said Imogen's mother as she breezed into the kitchen, pushing her sunglasses onto her head and waggling a set of car keys aimlessly.

"Really, sweetie, is it all right just to leave the front door open like that? I mean, I know it's the country and everything, but I could have been anyone, couldn't I? A mad axe murderer or some ghastly salesman . . . Or don't you get them out here?"

"Mad axe murderers?" said Imogen, deliberately obtuse. "I'm sure there must be the odd one knocking about the place. No salesmen, though, as far as I know."

"Yes, well, I suppose it's all right, then," said her mother, vaguely. "I must say you've chosen terribly well. What an absolutely charming house! I think you will need to do something about this, though," she said, looking doubtfully at the cast-iron range. "It looks ancient," she continued. "Do you think it's safe? I'd be awfully worried about carbon dioxide poisoning."

"Monoxide," said Imogen automatically.

"What, dear?" said her mother.

"Nothing. Would you like some tea? The traffic coming out of London must have been awful."

They made and drank a pot of tea while Imogen's mother gave her the essential briefing.

Halfway through her acerbic opinions of Uncle Glen's two-week Caribbean cruise with his new third wife, "who can't be more than a couple of years older than you, darling," her mother gave Imogen a sharp look. "You," she said, "look more exhausted now than you did at the funeral. Why don't you go and have a nice lie down."

"Because it's two in the afternoon, and I'm not ninety years old," said Imogen defensively, feeling like she had *I am pregnant* tattooed on her forehead for all to see.

"Still," her mother said persuasively, now rummaging in Imogen's larder and speaking over her shoulder, "you could just take your shoes off and lie on the bed. While you're gone, I'll just pop down to the village with the car and get us something for supper. You've got absolutely nothing in."

Despite herself, Imogen gratefully trailed upstairs. Closing her eyes "just for a minute," she told herself, and then fell fast asleep.

By THE TIME Imogen woke up, the light outside was fading to dusk.

"Damn!" she muttered. "Eight o'clock. That's far too long to leave my mother to her own devices."

She found her mother in the kitchen, mashing potatoes.

"Darling, you're awake!" she exclaimed. "Good. Now, sit down and have a nice G&T while I finish cooking the supper. We're having cottage pie with peas, and I've got some cookie dough ice cream for pudding. I know it's your favorite."

She decided not to bother reminding her mother that cookie dough had been her favorite about twenty years ago.

"I didn't manage to find any ice in your freezer," her mother continued, "but there's a lemon here already sliced, and thank heavens the village shop stocks gin and even Fever Tree tonic water. Really quite civilized for 'the country,' isn't it? Pour me one too, would you, darling?"

Imogen braced herself to break the news. "Actually, Mummy, I think I had better pass on the booze for a while."

"It's not your liver, is it, darling?" said her mother, shocked. "You really aren't looking well, but I thought if it was liver trouble, you turned yellow. I wouldn't have said you actually look yellow, more sort of pale green, if I'm honest—"

"Bit harsh," Imogen interjected. "No, listen. I'm trying to tell you. I'm pregnant." She swallowed hard, staring at her mother beseechingly.

Immediately, her mother's mildly eccentric façade disappeared.

"Darling, that's wonderful," she said softly.

"Is it?" said Imogen, choked, not trusting herself to say more.

"Of course, it is," she said. "When Nigel died, I'm afraid the first thing I thought was, 'Will I ever have grandchildren?' This is an absolute miracle," her mother continued.

I wouldn't go that far, thought Imogen. It was hardly the immaculate conception.

"I couldn't be more delighted," said her mother, clapping her hands together. "But the point is, how do you feel about it?"

"I only found out a few days ago. It's just such a shock, I'm not sure if I even believe it yet," said Imogen. "We talked about it—me and Nigel—but not this soon, and now, with him gone . . ." Somehow, she couldn't think about the baby without remembering, with a wrench, the letter from the mystery woman. She couldn't bear to tell her mother about that.

"The last thing you should be doing is worrying, darling," said her mother briskly. "You'll be fine. I mean, here you are, you've got this wonderful house, and I expect you'll meet somebody fabulous. After all, you're barely into your thirties."

"Mother!" said Imogen, not sure if she was more shocked about her mother suggesting a new lover so soon after Nigel's death, or the wildly prefeminist idea that the only solution was to find a man prepared to keep her.

"Well, dear, I'm sure Nigel wouldn't ever have intended

you to keep his memory sacred, forever eschewing any chance of future happiness," she said dramatically. "Daddy and I were always quite clear that once one of us went, the other was to feel perfectly free to find another."

"Yes, but you didn't exactly go out and find a string of lovers," said Imogen, although, granted, she seemed to be getting very close to her current boyfriend, Gerald.

"How do *you* know, dear?" she replied simply. "I didn't say we agreed to get married again, just to feel all right about having a little fling or two."

"Whoa! Don't tell me, for heaven's sake. I don't want to know," gabbled Imogen.

"Talking of sex," continued her mother.

"We weren't!" insisted Imogen with a hint of desperation.

"I met one of your new friends in the village shop earlier. A lovely young man he was, and very handsome too."

Imogen was filled with dread. She couldn't really think of anyone she would consider a friend, except possibly the doctor, Simon. She blushed. He must already think she was a complete imbecile, crying whenever she saw him. Now he had met her mother, there was no hope he would *ever* take her seriously.

"You mean Simon?" she said at last.

"Is that his name, dear? I'm sure he told me, but my memory is so execrable nowadays. Anyway, I invited him to join us for lunch on Sunday, and he said he would be delighted. Isn't that wonderful?"

Embarrassed though she was at her mother's machinations, Imogen was not completely averse to seeing Simon in a more relaxed context than his surgery. She was prepared to admit, the courage to issue an invitation herself would have been a long time coming. Maybe her mother had her uses.

NEXT MORNING, IMOGEN found her mother marching around the garden, purposefully brandishing a trowel in one hand and a garden fork in the other.

"Morning, darling! This is a gorgeous garden, you know. At least it would be if it weren't quite so forlornly neglected."

"I know," Imogen agreed guiltily. "You can tell the previous owner looked after it beautifully. As you know, I have no clue about gardening. I think I'll go and get some gardening books out of the library. There's even a tiny one in the telephone box by the pond. I could try there first. Failing that, there's Portneath, but I haven't explored buses yet."

"Good lord, did I completely forget to mention it?" exclaimed her mother. "The car I came down in yesterday. It's for you."

"What? But I can't even drive," said Imogen, but then added curiously, "What sort of car is it?"

"Well, it's, um . . . It's a red one," said her mother finally. "You know what I'm like with cars, darling. The man said it's a perfect little run-around—you'll need it when you have the baby, living out here."

"Mummy, it's a perfect idea," said Imogen, cautiously thrilled, "but what about a driving license? I feel an idiot, getting to my age and not being able to drive,"

"Not silly at all. I didn't learn until my twenties. Actually, I took the test when I was vastly pregnant with you. I could hardly get behind the wheel. I think the examiner was too scared to fail me for fear the upset would bring on labor," she reminisced. "Anyway, lots of people in London don't drive, do they? Not when you've got the Tube, and there's never anywhere to park a car anyway."

"True," said Imogen. "And I must say, I would have hated to learn in London. Much better out here with fewer things to bump into."

"Not much more than the occasional sheep," agreed her mother.

"Can't imagine what Old Grumpy Features would say if I bumped into one of his sheep," said Imogen to herself.

"Who, darling?" said her mother.

"Oh, nobody, just the neighborhood's resident Heathcliff character, only without the charm," said Imogen. "He's a caretaker or something, up at Middlemass Hall. It's a conference center now, apparently. But there's farmland around it. I suppose he must be employed to look after that."

"Heathcliff, eh? Sounds rather intriguing. You know, the talent around here really isn't bad if you've got your very own wild romantic hero as well as that nice man I met at the shop—Simon—or whatever you said his name was . . ."

 *Chapter Six*

Scrubbing new potatoes in the stone sink, Imogen gazed through the window. Tango was lounging on a sun-warmed paving stone by the herb garden, and she could see the bees hovering lazily over the lavender hedge lining the path. The roses in the flowerbed under the window were so beautiful too. She had cut half a dozen blooms that morning and arranged them in a jug on the kitchen table. With the sunlight slanting in, they made a beautiful shot for her Insta feed. Mostly her content was focused on her drawings, but her growing band of followers loved to have little insights into her life in the country too. She always got lots of likes and follows when she shared anything more personal, and shots of Tango were a guaranteed winner, although she felt a little bad about exploiting him.

Imogen was mildly excited at the thought of seeing Simon for lunch. It was important for him to see her in a better light. A normal, relaxed lunch, with her mother on the strictest instructions to behave herself, would do a lot to rescue his image of her as the neurotic, sobbing patient.

Thankfully her mother had tackled the shopping. Plans for them both to drive to Portneath yesterday had gone awry when Imogen, yet again, was so exhausted she was forced to have another long afternoon nap. Being pregnant was very wearing. She felt permanently as if her brain had been replaced with cotton wool, which was not conducive to getting things done.

She had decided on a simple but hopefully elegant menu. It was high summer; the weather had turned even warmer and had the lazy summer glow that always felt as if it would go on forever. It was far too hot for a proper Sunday roast. Instead, they would be having poached salmon with mayonnaise, new potatoes, and French beans. Hardly any cooking involved, thought Imogen gratefully. She had already made the peaches in white wine for pudding. It was her specialty, mostly because it was easy, and also Nigel had thought it impressive enough for his smart friends. Her mother had even remembered the crème fraîche to go with them, and Imogen had dug out a pretty crystal bowl to serve them in.

"Good morning, darling!" exclaimed her mother, breezing in through the kitchen door. "Heavens, is that the time?" she exclaimed, staring transfixed at the kitchen clock. "Where on earth has that taxi got to?"

"Why? Where are you going?" said Imogen, puzzled.

"To see Amelia, of course," said her mother. "The train takes an hour, and she's picking me up from the station at midday."

"What on earth are you talking about?" said Imogen breathlessly. "Lunch is here. You invited Simon, remember?"

"Yes, I know I did, darling," said her mother, "but you remember my old school friend Amelia Westbury? No? Of course not, how could you—you weren't born. Oh well, anyway . . . She lives in Torquay now—she never married, you know—too fussy, if you ask me—and I promised I'd arrange to meet her while I was down in this part of the country. As for the day, well, would you believe, she's just about to go on a painting holiday in Bordeaux—can't imagine what she's going to paint—grapevines, I suppose. Actually, that might explain it, she's always been fond of the odd glass, if you know what I mean . . . I digress, though . . ."

Wearily, Imogen nodded her agreement.

"The point is," she continued, "I telephoned her last night."

"No, you didn't," challenged Imogen swiftly. "You didn't call anyone last night, I was there."

"Didn't I, dear?" said her mother, unconvincingly vague. "Well, I must have texted her, then."

"You don't know how to text." That would get her.

"Yes, I do, dear, Gerald showed me. And sexting too," she said with a wicked grin.

Imogen groaned and held a hand up in self-defense. Her mother won. Again.

"Anyway, I text all the time now," June added airily. "The thing is, she can only see me today, and she kindly invited me to join her for lunch."

A car beeped its horn twice.

"Ah, here it is at last," said her mother, checking her watch. "Must dash." With these words, she grabbed her bag and swept out, gaily waving behind her.

Imogen dumped the potatoes from the colander into their saucepan, muttering to herself about manipulative parents who always told you to tell the truth and then fed you a pack of lies when it suited them. But her mother was such a liability, maybe it wasn't a bad thing that it would be just Imogen and Simon for lunch.

Dithering as to whether it would be too breezy to eat outside, Imogen put knives, forks, and plates on a tray with the napkins and wineglasses. She would just have half a glass, to be sociable. Checking the wine was cooling in the fridge and sweeping the trimmed French beans into a bowl to keep by the cooker until she was ready to put them into boiling water, she settled down at the kitchen table to read the Sunday papers.

A LOUD KNOCK on the kitchen window made her start violently, the slew of newspapers under her elbow slithering onto the floor. Turning to look, she was dazzled by the sun and could only make out the silhouette of a tall figure with wild-looking hair. It definitely wasn't Simon. Suddenly, the figure disappeared.

"W-w-what do you want?" she called out tremulously.

"Lunch, actually," came a voice from behind the kitchen door, as it swung open. "If it's not too much trouble, that is. Your mother seemed to think it would be a nice idea for you to meet the neighbors," Gabriel continued. "I hardly liked to shatter her illusions and explain that we already had." He paused briefly as they both recollected their first encounter. "So I thought the easiest thing would be to just say yes."

"I know exactly what you mean," muttered Imogen, who had spent too many years doing "the easiest thing" when it came to her mother.

"I assumed you were in on the arrangement?" he said, looking at her bemused expression.

"Yes, of course," she snapped defensively and then, horrified in case he was insinuating she had put her mother up to it: "That is, I knew she'd invited somebody, but I had no idea it was *you*." The last word came out rather emphatically, so Imogen clamped her finger over her mouth to stop anything else spilling out before she had composed herself.

Trying to remember exactly what her mother had said about her meeting with the "friend," she had to concede that perhaps it was she who had first mentioned Simon's name, probably in a bout of wishful thinking. Mind you, she thought, Mummy was the one who said he was good-looking—hardly a description you'd apply to Gabriel. She eyed him doubtfully. With those deep-set brown eyes under heavy eyebrows, he had a disconcertingly glowering expression, presumably even when he wasn't cross, she thought, although Imogen hadn't yet seen him up close in anything other than a state of irritation at best. A major improvement since they had last met was a recent and thorough shave. With him standing just a couple of feet in front of her, Imogen could discern the faintest whiff of lemon balm in his aftershave. And those eyes, mesmerizing, hypnotic . . . Imogen swayed closer, transfixed.

"Do I pass muster?" said Gabriel quizzically, the corner of his mouth twitching upward at her lengthy appraisal.

"Yes, definitely," she blurted. "Sorry," she added, blushing deeply and taking the bottle he was offering her.

"Chablis," she said. "How lovely—and it's even chilled already. It'll go perfectly with lunch. I'll just put it in the fridge, or perhaps I should just open it, I've got the glasses out already, now where did I put the corkscrew . . ." she continued, hiding her confusion with a driveling commentary.

"It's a screw top, and where's your mother?" he interjected, cutting firmly across the waffle.

She stopped short, as if she had been slapped.

"Sorry," she said. "Erm, my mother. Yes . . . now . . ." Imogen gazed at a point somewhere over Gabriel's head as if searching for the answer to a particularly testing mental arithmetic question. "She's not here, actually," she admitted eventually.

"So I can see. Are we expecting her?"

"Erm, no," said Imogen, smiling weakly whilst mentally kicking herself, her mother, and anyone else who happened to be handy. It was bad enough that it looked like Imogen had put her up to asking him over without having to brazen out her absence, as if the whole situation were a ploy to get him on his own.

Which it totally wasn't. "We've been set up," she muttered weakly.

"We have," he said, looking pityingly at her. "Look, give the wine to me," he added. "You're just about to pour it all over the floor."

THANKFULLY, SHE WAS able to busy herself making the lunch after that, giving herself time to regain her composure as she plunged the beans into boiling water, sprinkled parsley on the new potatoes, and checked the salmon inside its tinfoil parcels. Gabriel had efficiently taken over the wine, offering no resistance to her request for just half a glass. He obviously thinks I've had quite enough already, she thought, slightly cross at the perceived judgment, given that she had been teetotal since she heard about the baby. Irritatingly, the hormones racing around her body made her feel permanently like she had had a few.

Without being asked, Gabriel had unearthed an ancient gateleg garden table and two folding chairs from one of the outhouses and set them up in the orchard. Leaving the bottle of wine in the shallows of the stream to stay cool, he had deftly laid the table, complete with tablecloth and finishing touches such as salt and pepper grinders, by the time Imogen carried out the food.

Facing each other over their laden plates, Imogen had despaired of keeping up polite conversation. Surprisingly, though, they talked continuously—or at least she did. Over the salmon, he prompted her for stories about her London life, and she found herself telling him all about her rackety single lifestyle with Sally. It was as if it was the same story on repeat, she realized for the first time. It was essentially Sally and her drinking pals in a London wine bar on more or less every Friday night from her early to mid-twenties. After graduating, the two women had shared a crummy rented flat in southeast London.

Imogen was permanently broke, she remembered that.

"I can't imagine you working in an office," Gabriel mused lazily.

"You're saying I'm unprofessional?" Imogen replied, nettled and deciding not to tell him how many times she had been let go.

"Not at all. I'm saying you're unconventional. That's different," mused Gabriel, stroking the stem of his wineglass as he tilted his head back and regarded her from under heavy lids. "Ever been sacked?"

"No comment," muttered Imogen.

"What kind of jobs?"

"All sorts," said Imogen airily, trying to think of a single job title she had held that might sound a little bit impressive. "Greeting card designer mainly," she added, on the strength of the fact she had sold a couple of her paintings to a stationery company once. "But my newest thing is I write and illustrate children's books."

"Really?"

"Well, no," admitted Imogen, "not yet, but I'm going to. I've started."

This response elicited a bark of laughter. "I like your honesty," he said.

For the sake of being entertaining—and somehow because it felt inappropriate to talk to this man about other men—she initially tried to skim lightly over her marriage to Nigel and his sudden death, searching her memory for funny anecdotes instead, but his quiet interest and probing questions found her telling him more than she intended. In particular, the expression of deep sympathy on his face when she told him of Nigel's accident made her eyes well with tears of self-pity, which she blinked away, embarrassed. Turning her head, she dabbed with her napkin.

This man knew loss too. She could see it in how his expressions mirrored her own. But he gave away so little of himself, and she didn't have the confidence to start interrogating him back.

No, this was a man who was driving the agenda, and his attention was mesmeric. Where most people made politely brief eye contact as they spoke to each other, Gabriel had a habit of fixing her with his gaze while he asked a question and then switching his focus from her eyes to her mouth while she answered. It was extraordinarily intense. Imogen found herself flushing and positioning herself slightly more sideways in her chair to present an appealing angle. Then she scolded herself silently. It was ridiculous to think he might be interested in her. The poor man had been suckered into having lunch with her, for heaven's sake. And this hyperfocus of his was clearly a tried and tested ruse. It might work on other women, but it wasn't going to work on her. No sirree.

She suddenly realized she had stopped talking for several long seconds and had been staring fixedly at the triangle of deeply tanned chest revealed by his open collar. She found herself wondering if the whole of his chest was that incredible chestnut brown color, and if the promise of his bulging arms was delivered on by equally well-developed musculature of his abdomen.

Raising her eyes, she met his inquiring gaze inviting her to continue.

God, she admitted to herself, it was such bliss to have someone to talk to. Tango was a rubbish listener. Before she knew it, Imogen found herself confiding her doubts over Nigel's plans, the move to the country, the bit about having lots of children, and his idea that she should give up her career plans as a children's book illustrator to be the perfect wife. She only managed to stop herself telling him about her pregnancy by physically biting her lip. That would have definitely been too much information at this stage in their acquaintance.

"You shouldn't give up on your talent," he said over the peaches and white wine. "It's a tough old life trying to make a career of art, but it's a crime to let a natural talent go to waste."

Imogen wondered what he could possibly know—as a caretaker—about making a career of art. "How do you know I've got talent?" she asked.

"I don't," he replied bluntly, "but nor do you unless you've got the guts to keep trying."

Fair point, thought Imogen, feeling slightly bruised by the directness. She picked up the plates, carried them back into the kitchen, and then put the kettle on to make coffee. They could have it in the orchard. With all her talking, lunch had taken more than two hours, but the afternoon was still warm, and the grass in the orchard was perfectly dry for sitting on if they wanted to stretch out.

Gabriel came in with another pile of dishes and cutlery precariously balanced and dumped them on the draining board. He went to make the coffee, confidently gathering mugs and coffee together as if he made coffee in her kitchen every day, she couldn't help noticing.

Granted, it was hot, but she felt ridiculously warm and flustered having him so physically near, particularly when he put his hands lightly on her waist. She froze, electrified at his touch, but he just gently moved her out of the way of the fridge so he could get the milk.

To put some distance between them, and regain her

composure, Imogen wandered out of the kitchen door to see whether anything else needed to come in. Walking past the dustbin by the door, her left foot nudged something soft and warm. Instinctively she stepped back.

"Tango, for God's sake . . ." she exclaimed, glancing down, expecting him to be walking infuriatingly an inch in front of her feet as usual.

What she saw instead made her freeze in horror. On its haunches in front of her was a huge brown rat, its fat tummy resting momentarily on her shoe. Twisting its head up to look at her, the rodent gave her an old-fashioned look before scampering across her path.

It whipped its naked tail behind it into the hedge, where it disappeared with a rustle, leaving Imogen rooted to the spot. Suddenly unfreezing, her heart pounding in her throat, she high-stepped rapidly back into the kitchen, flapping her hands frantically in the air and breathlessly emitting short screams of terror.

Gabriel was halfway across the kitchen, arms outstretched to catch her before she even came through the door.

"Rat!" she eventually managed to squeak, as he wrapped her in his arms. "Rat! Rat!" She gesticulated wildly in the direction of the open door and stared at him wide-eyed.

To her amazement and rage, he let go of her, threw back his head, and roared with laughter.

She glared at him, furious.

He caught her eye, made as if to speak, but then dissolved again into helpless laughter, wiping the tears of mirth from his eyes.

By this time, the adrenaline flooding her system had re-ceded like a tsunami, leaving her eyes filling with tears and her legs shaking.

Noticing her distress, Gabriel was contrite.

I'm sorry," he said, grabbing a napkin from the table. "Come here."

He tenderly wiped away the tears as if she were a child, and before she had a chance to know what was happening, he swept her back into a hug. "You're going to see the odd rat in the country," he explained. Of course he was right. She was being ridiculous.

It felt so wonderful to be held. Imogen's face was pressed against his worn flannel shirt, washed soft over the years, smelling of fresh air and humanity. With his arms around her, her legs no longer needed to hold her up, and she sagged limply against him. Mortifyingly, the tears, now they had started, refused to stop. Soon she was sobbing helplessly, feeling his hand softly stroking her hair, and hearing him shushing in her ear. He rocked her gently and, after a few moments, took her head in his hands, brushing her hair tenderly out of her face. Then he sank his lips straight onto hers. It was a melting, overwhelming, drowning kiss. He transferred one hand to the small of her back and held her securely as he explored her mouth delicately. He tasted of peaches, wine, and cool water. Imogen moaned and tilted her head further back to al-low him greater access, which he took—thoroughly and lingeringly.

Eventually, it was her blocked nose that forced her to

come up for air. She grabbed the napkin and honked un-attractively into it, not daring to look at him as she felt his eyes range over her doubtless shiny face and puffy eyes.

"Sorry," he said unrepentantly.

"I should think so," she snapped, trying hard to deny the melting passion he had just so carelessly evoked in her.

"I couldn't resist," he said, bobbing his head down to her level and forcing her to catch his eye. "You okay?"

"I hardly think it's appropriate for a woman so recently widowed to be snogging some bloke she's only just met," blurted Imogen, aware she was sounding hopelessly prim.

"You just looked—actually, look—so gorgeous."

"I bet you say that to all the girls."

"Just the gorgeous ones."

"Well, still, a widow," Imogen persisted, "and in my condition . . ."

"What condition?" said Gabriel, suddenly serious.

"The usual condition that women get into," said Imogen, still annoyed at his mirth.

Comprehension dawned visibly on his face.

"Wow," he said. "You have got a lot going on, haven't you. When's it due?"

"Not sure . . . New Year, more or less."

"That's quite a legacy," he said soberly, whistling low under his breath. "Assuming it's Nigel's, of course," he added.

"Of course, it's bloody Nigel's," she said. "What the hell are you suggesting?"

"You said you weren't sure about dates, and marriages aren't always exclusive, are they?" he reasoned.

"Well, this one bloody well was," she said hotly, before

remembering that, actually, as far as Nigel was concerned, apparently it wasn't. Her eyes threatened to well up again, and she sniffed defiantly.

"How about that coffee?" he said, calling a truce, "although I do wonder about whether you're supposed to drink it—'in your condition,'" he added, in a faintly mocking tone.

Mollified, Imogen sat at the kitchen table and allowed him to pour her just half a mug, adding milk for her and pushing the sugar bowl toward her.

"You've certainly made yourself at home," she remarked. And then, realizing she sounded rude, "That is, you look as if you've been here before."

"Yup," he said. "My grandmother lived here until last winter. Had done for years, it was my second home in the school holidays."

"Where does she live now?" said Imogen, keen to return the conversation to social chitchat.

"She's dead," he said bluntly. "I thought you'd have known that from buying the house."

"Sorry, no, I didn't. Nigel always deals—dealt—with that sort of thing," she said, feeling an idiot.

"Actually, that reminds me," Gabriel continued, "I had a note from the trustees saying that they needed me to sanction a letter to you about something or other. I said it was fine."

"What trustees?" said Imogen. "A letter about what?"

"Oh, you know, the whole Storybook Cottage, Middlemass Hall thing," said Gabriel. "Only clearly you don't know," he added, reading her expression. "It won't be anything interesting. It's probably some acknowledgment of the change of ownership of the house title or something equally dull. It would be going to your husband or—more likely—his conveyancer, if the"—Gabriel paused—"Well, if things were different."

"Oh, fine," said Imogen vaguely. "Death does seem to generate a lot of paperwork," she observed. "I'm sorry about your grandmother."

"That's okay. She was eighty-six, and she had a great life," he said. "And I'm sorry for *your* loss," he added.

"Thank you," said Imogen, not wanting to talk any more about Nigel. Especially not after what they had just done.

"Still," Gabriel said, trying to shake off the atmosphere of despondency, "with a baby on the way, it seems to me your life is more about new beginnings now."

Imogen nodded glumly. There had been altogether too many new beginnings recently. It was exhausting, and she was struggling to keep up.

"Whose is the car outside?" said Gabriel, changing the subject. "I don't imagine it's yours somehow."

"It is, actually. Why the hell shouldn't it be?" Imogen retorted, nettled at his assumption.

"I just assumed you don't drive, being a Londoner," he said. "Also, seeing your, er, 'road-sense' on a bicycle," he continued sarcastically, "perhaps I'm just hoping you don't."

"Well, actually, clever-clogs," flounced Imogen, "I do know how to drive—thank you very much—actually," she said, before remembering that, in fact, she didn't—and also that she was possibly failing to maintain the icy dignity she would have aspired to under the circumstances. Did she really just call him clever-clogs?

"Right. Well, that's all right, then," said Gabriel, smirking at her reddening face. "Perhaps you'd be kind enough to let me know when you're planning to hit the road so I can arrange to be off it at the time." He threw this last comment at her over his shoulder as, dumping his empty coffee cup in the sink, he made for the door.

"Thanks for lunch, by the way," he said, popping his head back around the door, and then he was gone, leaving Imogen squeaking with rage.

 *Chapter Seven*

"So anyway, sweetheart, don't forget . . . Is that everything? You are a darling . . . to put your feet up whenever you can," said Imogen's mother, alternately repeating her advice to Imogen for the fourth time that morning and directing operations as the bemused minicab driver loaded ridiculously large amounts of baggage into the boot.

After some minutes, watches were checked, gasps of panic about train timetables were uttered, and in a final flurry of extravagant waving through the window, her mother's taxi rounded the corner and was gone.

For over a minute Imogen stood listlessly watching the bend in the road where her mother had disappeared from sight. Giving herself a mental shake, she took another look at the little hatchback left behind in the driveway. I'll never be able to drive it, she thought. Gabriel's right, I don't even have the concentration to ride a bicycle at the moment. And then she groaned aloud. To top it all, she remembered, I told bloody Gabriel I already knew how to drive. He's bound to see me taking lessons and know I lied. God, how embarrassing! He thinks I'm eccentric enough as it is.

Energized by her irritation, she went back into the house and grabbed her laptop. Bugger, no battery. Rather than drifting off toward another, easier-to-achieve task, she went through the hall to fetch the cord from the study, but was distracted by a square white envelope on the mat, which had somehow gone unnoticed in the flurry of saying goodbye to her mother. The envelope was bare save for her name, written and then underlined in a strong, decisive hand. Opening it, she found a stiff white card with the address and phone number for Middlemass Hall printed across the top. In the same hand as the envelope was a brief message:

Sorry again about the kiss. Totally inappropriate. I am a good driving instructor though. First lesson 9am next Tuesday, no strings? It was signed *Gabriel* with a kiss.

Imogen took a deep breath and propped the card on the mantelpiece in the study, her heart pounding. She should get a proper driving instructor. As Gabriel implied, there could be—would be—nothing between them. That said, she didn't have his cellphone number, and there was no way she was going to call the landline to ask to speak to the handyman, so she couldn't even cancel. In all honesty, she was ridiculously excited at the thought she might see him again in just a few days. That was her hormones, she counseled herself. She needed to get a grip. Pondering, she was distracted by Tango, teeth chattering in excitement as he danced along the windowsill, chasing flies. Marveling at his ability to step around all the obstacles ranged across the sill at the same time as keeping his balance on his back legs, Imogen grabbed for a pencil and her notepad. Sketching furiously, she caught, with a line here and a smudge of pencil there, the shapes he made as he twisted and turned, thumping his front paws against the glass in an attempt to catch a noisy bluebottle. After a couple of false starts, he trapped it under his paw and transferred it to his mouth, crunching audibly, before licking his paws and washing his face with a fastidiousness completely out of keeping with his dietary habits.

"You are disgusting," she said resignedly.

Her voice caught his attention, and he wandered haughtily over, jumping onto the table and making to rub his cheek on her face.

"Ugh! Gerroff! You're not kissing me after what you've just done," she said, pushing him onto the floor, where he stalked off, affronted.

Turning back to the drawings, she impulsively sketched in a city skyline beneath the cat's feet, making it look as if he was dancing across the sky like Fred Astaire on acid. Rapidly penciling in some stars and a smiling moon overlooking the bizarre scene, she held the pad at arm's length and sighed. She should never have told people she wanted to write children's books. But—if not that—what on earth was she going to do to earn money as a single mother?

If there was any doubt Imogen was failing to grasp the reality of the situation, the scan to date the pregnancy cemented the news. Feeling exhausted, Imogen treated herself to a taxi to the hospital, which was a long, low 1960s building on the outskirts of Portneath. She managed to maintain her composure when she first saw the squirming little creature on the screen, but—when the sonographer told her she was having a little girl—the tears came.

"Dad not around?" the sonographer asked kindly as she passed Imogen a tissue. "It's a lot to cope with on your own."

A girl! Imogen hugged the secret to her as she stroked her tummy in the taxi home. For all his failings, this little girl had been Nigel's last gift to her, a miracle baby conceived in the final weeks before his death. This was now an irrefutable fact that was both terrifying and thrilling. The future was a challenge that was going to happen whether she liked it or not, but whatever it held, there was one thing that was in no doubt: Imogen was no longer alone.

AFTER A SERIES of sleepless nights, and desperately searching for a distraction to calm her racing mind, Imogen decided, after a few hours' work, to take herself for a brisk walk. She came out of the drive and followed the narrow pavement, heading for the green and for the village shop. She was so dazzled by the blazing sun, the first she knew of anyone coming the other way was when her right knee knocked into something solid. Looking down, she met the reproachful gaze of a fat chocolate-colored Labrador, his eyes rheumy and muzzle almost entirely gray.

"Sorry, old boy!" she said, bending down to pat his head. "I was miles away."

"You certainly were," said an amused voice.

Looking up, Imogen saw that the dog was attached to a woman apparently in her seventies, but possibly older, with sensible lace-up shoes and clearly a good-quality tweed skirt and jacket, their impeccable cut marred by a generous coating of dog hair and a paw-sized smear of mud on one sleeve.

"I am so pleased we have bumped into each other," the woman continued. "I really must speak to you about this fate of ours."

"This fate? Our fate?" said Imogen, blankly. It seemed a surprisingly existential concern for a woman she had never met to be raising with her.

"The church fate," the woman elaborated.

Imogen was still confused. What on earth could she be expected to know about the future of the church? Did the old lady mean the village church? Perhaps it needed a new roof or something. They almost always did, didn't they? Or, heaven forfend, was she referring to the future of Christian religion as a whole? In which case, what on earth could she possibly expect Imogen to do about it?

"The fate of the church?" she inquired, hoping for further clues.

"Well, if you want to put it that way," the lady replied, looking at her oddly. "Although I'm bound to say it's unusual to meet someone of your age who places such importance on syntax. Time is marching on. Of course, you have had to have some time to settle in, but there is always so much to do, one can never start too soon, don't you think?"

The lady looked hopefully at Imogen for signs of dawning comprehension, but her expression told a story of disappointment. Imogen could only imagine what story her own expression was telling.

"My dear girl!" the lady exclaimed. "I am so sorry. You must think me quite mad. Do let me start again properly. The first thing is of course to introduce myself. My name is Winifred Hutchinson, and this is Arthur, by the way. Please call me Winifred, but for goodness' sake, resist the temptation to call me Winnie. I'm not a teddy bear."

"I promise I won't." She could give her that, at least. "I'm Imogen."

"Yes, yes, dear, I know," said Winifred with a dismissive wave. "Now, the thing is, we don't need you to do very much yourself, but of course, we will need access to the kitchen for the teas."

"The teas?" said Imogen blankly, discomfited that after a promising flurry of proper conversation she had regressed to repeating Winifred's words with a stupefied expression on her face.

"Yes, dear, the teas," she repeated, seeing the clouds failing to lift from Imogen's expression, and starting to sound a little tetchy. "For the fête," she added, obviously feeling that repetition was a winning strategy.

"Ooh, the *fête*! As in fête? As in jam-making competitions, coconut shies, bunting, and . . . and . . . vicars . . ." Imogen declared, fully on point at last.

"Yes, dear, that's right," Winifred replied with relief. "What on earth did you think I meant? Now, I think the best thing would be for you to come home with me, and we can talk about it all over a cup of tea and a scone. Look, I've just picked up some lovely fresh ones from Muriel at the shop. She always keeps some back for me, the sweet lady."

Imogen noticed Winifred had an old-fashioned wicker shopping basket on her arm. A brown paper bag was sitting on top of several tins of dog food and a pint of milk.

By this time, the ancient Labrador had sized up the situation and had slumped onto the ground with a groaning sigh. At signs of movement, he staggered hopefully to his feet and began to plod along the pavement. Winifred was towed along behind him, throwing rallying comments to Imogen over her shoulder as they went.

After just a couple of minutes, Winifred and the dog turned suddenly through a low gateway. Following, Imogen found herself on a narrow path, flanked on both sides by a waist-high box hedge closing in a charmingly blowsy cottage garden, with geraniums and hollyhocks in abundance. The little path led to a perfect miniature thatched cottage complete with diamond-leaded windows and a heavy oak door.

Settling Imogen in the sitting room, Winifred went off to make tea.

The room was cramped with a large stone fireplace at one side, a low ceiling, and several oak beams. Two large sofas— one with horsehair poking out of a hole in the arm—were wedged at right angles along two walls; there was an exquisitely inlaid occasional table, an overstuffed armchair, and a beautiful but threadbare Persian carpet. The impression was one of someone who was used to living in grander circumstances having moved to a smaller house.

Imogen was standing, peering at a framed photograph on the mantelpiece, when Winifred returned with a laden tray.

"Is this you with your husband?" said Imogen, looking at an old photograph of a pretty young woman standing arm in arm with a man in flares.

"Gracious, no," said Winifred. "I was never married myself. That's me with my brother, Graham. He's no longer with us, sadly."

"I'm sorry," said Imogen, unsure whether she was expressing sympathy for the death of Winifred's brother or for her single state.

"Don't be, my dear. I did meet somebody around the time that was taken. He was in the army," she mused. "We got engaged while he was on leave at Christmas and agreed to get married the following summer, but I never saw him again. He was killed in a training exercise."

"Heavens!" exclaimed Imogen, appalled. "I'm so sorry . . . Was he . . . I mean, would he have been the love of your life?"

"Goodness no, certainly not," replied Winifred. "It was all very well at the time, but in retrospect, we were quite wrong for each other. Far too young, as well. Of course, we never did have a chance to marry and find out for sure, but I have always thought it would have been the most dreadful mistake if we had. Anyway, my lovely brother, Graham—he had a learning disability, you know—he could never have lived alone. I looked after him all his adult life, but then when he died a few years ago, I upped sticks and moved to Middlemass. Didn't need such a big house then, of course. Plus, I was keen to move somewhere less remote. It's good to be in the middle of a village. There's lots going on, and it keeps me busy."

All the while, Winifred was deftly pouring tea and milk before handing Imogen cup, plate, and knife, and offering the plate of scones.

"Are you married?"

"I—no—I'm not," Imogen stuttered, wondering when, if ever, it was going to get easier to tell people. She took a deep breath and broke the news.

"Goodness, my dear. How absolutely awful for you," said Winifred. "So now you are all on your own," she continued with calm compassion.

"Not for long," said Imogen, and found herself telling Winifred all about buying the house just before Nigel was killed and moving in after the funeral. She finished by telling her about the baby.

"My dear," she said in dismayed concern. "Although I must say I hold modern women like you in absolute awe. In my day it was never dreamt of that a woman would have to juggle work with having children, and then one had a nanny to look after them anyway. Really," she said wonderingly, "I just can't think what women of my generation used to do with their time.

"Have another scone, my dear. If you don't mind my saying so, you do seem awfully slight for someone who is having a baby."

"I'm stronger than I look," said Imogen automatically. "I'm so sorry to have gabbled on like that," she added, feeling she was making a habit of it. "I don't think I like people to know about Nigel on the whole, because I hate the thought of people being embarrassed and then feeling they have to behave differently in some way."

"Quite right," said Winifred robustly. "In my day, everyone said they were sorry just once and then turned a blind eye and expected you to buck up and get on with it. I just can't see the point of all this navel-gazing everyone seems to go in for nowadays. It seems to me people do no more than stub their toe, and they have to have four years of counseling to recover from the experience.

"Now then," Winifred continued briskly, pouring Imogen another cup of tea. "Back to the fête. It's been held at Storybook Cottage for years, you see, and now that your predecessor has sadly died, the general assumption is that the new resident will continue the tradition."

"Right," said Imogen, "but wouldn't the church fête usually be held at the vicarage?"

"Of course, it would be, but the vicarage was turned into a home for mad old dears absolutely years ago—there but for the grace of God go I—then we held it for several years at Middlemass Hall. That worked very well until the family leased the place to this ghastly conference center company. We went to book the date, and this flibbertigibbet child in a cheap red suit with a short skirt had the audacity to start talking about hire charges and in-house catering—made the whole thing totally impossible. Thank goodness we had Storybook Cottage to turn to, and of course the gardens plus the lovely orchard make it absolutely ideal. We have the tea tables and the cake stall in the kitchen garden, put the bric-a-brac, white elephant, plant stall, and tombola in the main garden, and then the orchard is free for the children's games and the tug-of-war."

"It all sounds wonderful," said Imogen cautiously. "And, of course, you are all more than welcome."

"Excellent, my dear. I knew you would agree."

Just then, Imogen's mobile tweeted loudly. "I'm so sorry," she apologized as she reached for her bag. "It's my phone, I'd better just check . . ."

There on the screen was a text from her mother:

Darling, it read, *All fine here. How are you? Big jugs, Mummy xxx P.S. Told you I could text!*

"It's from my mum," she explained to Winifred, swiftly tapping a reply. *I think you mean "big hugs" mum! :) Predictive text can be a minefield, can't it?*

"Sorry," she told Winifred as she pressed send. "I must introduce you. I think you two would get on."

IMOGEN WAS SERIOUSLY thinking of ditching her landline phone as—yet again—she found herself thundering down the stairs from the attic to answer it.

"Er, hello?" she said. Silence. Just as she was about to hang up, a tight little voice said, "Imo?"

"Yes? Who is this?"

"It's me," stronger now, but cracking slightly.

"Sally! My God, what's the matter?"

"Hi! Oh, nothing. Just a bit tired actually, you know how it is. Unrealistic deadlines, impossible clients, staff crises, and now—to top it all—my bloody husband's behaving like an alien. Last night he got pissed and told me he loved me, but he wasn't sure if he was still *in* love with me," she rattled, her voice rising and breaking into a mirthless laugh.

"That's not like Alistair," she said. "He's devoted to you."

"Believe it, honey," said Sally, a little steel returning to her voice. "Anyhow, I completely overreacted. Made a massive tit of myself, and we had a big row. Ridiculous. Long story short, he's gone off camping with Ed in Devon, and I stupidly insisted I needed 'me' time. Which means I'm now stuck here alone in an empty house, bored rigid."

"Come and stay," Imogen said. "You can have 'me' time with me. Sounds like you need a break, and I'd love to have you here."

She could tell Sally about the baby.

 *Chapter Eight*

Dressing rapidly, Imogen ran her fingers cursorily through her hair and trotted down to the kitchen, with Tango in close pursuit, for her early morning fix of peanut butter and banana sandwiches.

Surveying the kitchen guiltily while she ate, Imogen decided she just had time for a quick tidy up in Sally's honor. When it came to interiors, Sally was hard to live up to. Her kitchen permanently looked like a room set for *Elle Decoration* magazine with the obligatory—and never used—KitchenAid stand mixer along with a state-of-the-art espresso machine—constantly used—both displayed on expanses of spotless granite worktop. Imogen's kitchen, on the other hand, boasted the latest accessory in knife-scarred wooden bread boards—surrounded by asteroid clouds of crumbs scattered across somewhat sticky, not-very-scrubbed oak worktops. To complete the coveted lifestyle effect, there were teetering piles of washing up arranged rather too artlessly for art in and around the deep stone sink.

In a blast of inspiration and energy, Imogen tackled the washing up—plenty of hot water for a change—and was wiping down the surfaces when she was interrupted by the clang of the doorbell. Averting her eyes from the floor that needed a sweep at minimum, and ideally a good mop, she ran to open the front door.

Standing in front of her was Gabriel, his face arranged into the closest thing to a smile she could remember seeing.

Could it really be Tuesday already? She had become totally distracted by the Sally emergency.

"You good?" he said, rubbing his hands together briskly. Imogen nodded, still mute.

"Car key?" he queried. "Unless you want me to teach you to hotwire your own car?"

Thankfully, her mother had left it hanging on the key hook next to the front door, and she jiggled it in front of his face in a confident manner she definitely didn't feel.

"Hang on," he said, suddenly freezing in mid-turn. "I forgot to ask. Tell me you've got a provisional license?"

"Of course," said Imogen, breathing a sigh of relief that she had applied for it years ago. At the time, it was only because she looked so ridiculously young—it had been a handy proof of age. It beat having to produce her passport whenever she wanted to buy a bottle of wine.

Walking to the wrong side of the car and then staring blankly at the passenger door wasn't a great start.

Gabriel smirked as she scuttled back around to the driver's side, striking her forehead with her palm in embarrassment.

Sliding into the driver's seat, her nerves were not improved by Gabriel's five-minute lecture on the main controls, starting with the gear stick. There was so much to remember.

"Just work your way through the gears to start off with," he suggested.

She began to sweat slightly as she rammed the gear stick from one gear to another, taking her hand off repeatedly to look at the funny little diagram on the knob. Of all the stupid places to put it. As if she had an eye in the palm of her hand, she thought with irritation.

"It seems a bit stiff," she said.

"You might want to put your foot on the clutch," Gabriel suggested with what—she suspected—was a facetious tone.

"Ah, that's much easier," she admitted, dreading to think what damage she had just done to the gearbox.

Gabriel remained implacably calm, even after she checked with him for the fifth time which pedal was the brake and which the accelerator. Setting off, Imogen negotiated the driveway entrance, which seemed impossibly narrow, and was soon bowling down the lane toward the village, feeling dangerously out of control, even with Gabriel as a steady presence beside her.

He gave a running commentary, calmly observing that she might want to change up from first gear now they had gone a hundred yards and later gently mooting the idea she should accelerate a little. Glancing down, nervous of her eyes leaving the road, Imogen saw she was only going fifteen miles an hour, with her fists clutching the wheel so tightly her knuckles were white. She decided this was quite fast enough for the moment. Coming into the heart of the village, she felt even less confident. They were trundling along the road running beside the village green when she fumbled with a gear change, panicked, braked sharply, and then stalled.

Despite Gabriel's amazingly calm guidance, Imogen found it impossible to muster the coordination to set off again. Starting the engine, first she forgot to take the car out of gear and stalled, then she accidentally set off in second gear and bunny-hopped alarmingly for a few yards before stalling again.

By the time she finally managed to draw away, she was nearly in tears with mortification. To Gabriel's credit, he was sitting patiently and implacably beside her. A lesser man would have been terrified, especially if she had—at any point—approached the speed limit.

For the remainder of the lesson, she was hopeless, miserably certain she would never learn to drive. Her confidence was barely restored by an uneventful trip along picturesque country lanes back to the house.

"Same time next week?" said Gabriel as she climbed out, knees trembling now the ordeal was at an end. She felt utterly exhausted.

"You must let me do something to return the favor," she said, turning to him. "This is so kind."

"Purely self-interest," he said. "I'd rather be in the car with you than at risk of being run over by it."

Rude, thought Imogen, taking a breath in to berate him, but then good manners prevailed.

"Anyhow, I just want to say, it's extremely kind, and I'm very grateful," she said tightly.

"Noted," he replied, with a little bow.

DECIDING IT WAS about time she mastered the local buses—clearly passing her driving test was going to take a while—Imogen decided to head into Portneath to meet Sally from the train.

The bus stop, with its little wooden shelter, was near the telephone box library on the green, and the walk in the golden late summer sunshine was a welcome chance to let her mind drift. Disconcertingly, though, whenever it did, memories of kissing Gabriel filled it on repeat. Safely on the bus and trundling into Portneath, her daydreaming continued. Mainly it was the kiss itself she re-created in her head, sometimes allowing herself to imagine what might have come next. Less promisingly, she would usually move on to wondering first how on earth she could have allowed herself to do it, and then—shamefully—how soon they would have the chance to do it again.

ARRIVING IN PORTNEATH with a couple of hours to spare, Imogen allowed herself a leisurely browse in Portneath's brilliantly stocked art shop, where she loaded up with supplies. She was desperate to start the children's book that was taking shape in her head. By the time she had finished, she had spent a fortune, and the train was imminent. She had just enough time to dive into the supermarket near the station and pick up essential supplies for supper.

Hauling the heavy basket to the nearest open checkout, Imogen shifted from foot to foot impatiently, glancing again at her watch. An improbably dark-haired woman with a scarlet slash of lipstick bleeding into the lines around her mouth was making a fuss of searching through the money-off coupons in her purse while Imogen idly wondered if the hair was a wig or just an overdose of hair dye.

Smiling vaguely at the checkout woman, Imogen eventually loaded her booty into two carrier bags, but she noticed the woman casting significant, pursed-lipped looks at her wine and then at her bulging tummy. Resisting the temptation to run back for a large bottle of gin and a packet of cigs to wave in the woman's censorious face, Imogen paid demurely and left.

AT THE STATION, she quickly checked the screen showing arrivals without even breaking her stride. Just her luck, the train was on time. She arrived at the platform as the train was drawing out again. There were perhaps a dozen passengers heading for the exit. A second later, they saw each other. Sally waved exaggeratedly and then ran the twenty yards toward Imogen in comic slow motion, arms outstretched and a daft grin on her face. Even clowning around, Imogen thought, she looked lithe and elegant in her white skinny jeans and butter-soft suede jacket, cut off at the waist to make her legs look endless. Her hair was shorter than Imogen had seen it before, curling softly at jaw length with expensively applied color enhancing the natural coppery tones. Sally made it all look so effortless. Would Imogen ever be able to achieve such a nonchalant, glossy style? Stupid question.

Close up, though, Imogen saw her eyes were red-rimmed and her skin pale.

"Hello, sweetheart," she said, clutching Imogen in a too-hard hug. Releasing her after several seconds, Sally put her hand between their two bodies, puzzled at encountering Imogen's bulging midriff.

"What's this!" she shrieked, eyebrows disappearing under her artfully streaked fringe.

"Wind," deadpanned Imogen. "Plenty of time for that later."

"And over a bloody glass of wine," Sally shrieked again. "For me, anyhow."

ALL THE WAY back to Middlemass, Sally kept up a flow of chitchat—the scenery, the house when they arrived, the gardens, her bedroom. It was all very much in the manner of "how charming, my friend has chosen to move to a countryside theme park": cute but—essentially—inexplicable.

An hour later Sally was showered and changed, and they were pottering over their supper preparations, Imogen drinking tea and Sally making inroads into the first of the bottles of Chablis.

"Some fresh basil and buffalo mozzarella would absolutely make these pizzas," said Sally, ripping the plastic wrapping off the chill-cabinet pizzas Imogen had chosen earlier.

Imogen reached up to the spice shelf and handed Sally a jar of mixed herbs. "Cheddar's in the fridge," she added.

"Oooh, sorry!" said Sally, not sounding the least bit repentant. "I'd forgotten the Nigella experience has bypassed the countryside."

"Actually, you're wrong, there's apparently an excellent deli in Portneath. I just didn't have time to go there today. Also, I'm told there's a farmers' market every Saturday and it's pretty good. I'm going to use it quite a lot when I can drive, I think."

"Planning to stay, then?" said Sally, giving Imogen a piercing look.

CURLED UP IN armchairs either side of the woodburning stove in the study, they watched the flames in companionable silence. Full of pizza, and with the initial urgency of news sharing over, Imogen was well aware Sally had so far avoided the big Alistair discussion. Instead, supper had been spent exclaiming over the baby to come, sharing her own birth experience with Ed. "Bloody undignified and hurts like hell. Make sure they give you lots of drugs," had been Sally's advice.

"So," Sally announced at last, pouring herself another glass, "he says he still loves me, a hundred percent, but he's not sure if he's 'in love' with me," she continued. "I mean, please! And then, as if that trite rubbish wasn't insulting enough, he 'reassured' me there wasn't anyone else!" She laughed mirthlessly. "I swear to God! He actually said, 'I just want you to know that there isn't anyone else,' as if that's supposed to make me feel better. As if, somehow, the fact that I've become boring and irrelevant—even though he *isn't* even screwing his secretary—makes it less horrible." She sighed shakily. "I mean, since when was 'complete celibacy is preferable to sex with you' a positive thing to hear?"

Tango, sensing negative energy, uncurled himself from the rag rug in front of the stove and slunk out of the room, the end of his tail twitching in annoyance.

Imogen searched for something comforting to say. "I'm so sorry, Sal, but . . . he's only saying how he feels, isn't he? I mean, all marriages get a bit stale sometimes, don't they? Don't they?"

"Not yours," said Sally bitterly. "Widows get the sympathy, not potential divorcées. At least you know he died loving you!" And then, "Sorry. That's a completely horrible thing to say," she added, stretching out a hand in apology. "It's appalling to lumber you with my problems now with what you're going through."

"What are friends for?" said Imogen. "Anyway, he didn't."

"Didn't what?" said Sally, peering at her blearily over the top of her glass.

"Didn't die loving me. I thought he did . . . but I was wrong."

"No." Sally was certain. "Imo, you mustn't think that. For all his faults . . ." She paused, clearly running through a long mental list of them. "I mean, he completely adored you, Imo. Put you on a pedestal, really . . . even if I did think he was a bit of a pompous twat. I never doubted his devotion. Nor should you."

Staring into the flames, Imogen remembered how Sally had described Nigel before they had met. He had been invited to one of Sally and Alistair's dinner parties. Then a last-minute dropout had left Sally on the phone to Imogen an hour before the guests were due to arrive, begging her to make up the numbers.

"There's this boring old fart of a solicitor Alistair has to suck up to," Sally had told her. "He's about thirty-five going on sixty, but he's the only unattached man there, and it'll look so obvious if the numbers are wrong. Please come, Imo."

Racing across London from her digs in Camden to Sally and Alistair's house, Imogen had arrived after a hasty shower and change of clothes into the only thing she could find that was clean and didn't need ironing. Unfortunately, this meant wearing an elasticated minidress in startling black and red horizontal stripes. It had made her look like a tart even when it was new. Since then it had shrunk in the wash, so wearing it meant hauling the skirt down to less X-certificate levels every few minutes. Sidling into the drawing room after giving the dress a hefty hoick south in the hallway, Imogen had discovered the other guests, including Nigel. Nigel, in a pin-striped suit, was standing in front of the fireplace drinking whiskey. He was rocking on his feet, one hand in his pocket, the glass in the other, proclaiming on capital punishment (he was in favor) to Alistair, who was standing with his head on one side. Rather than looking at him while he spoke, Nigel's eyes were fixed on a point above Alistair's head in the way of people who are not particularly interested in other people's views and dislike being interrupted to listen to them.

Sitting opposite Nigel at dinner, Imogen had felt herself being cursorily assessed. He had asked the routine questions about her job—nonexistent at the time—and her interests, for which she shyly mentioned her ambitions as an artist. She remembered how he had weighed her answers briefly and then seemed to dismiss her, turning to the advertising executive on his left to share his views about the property market.

She had been amazed when Sally reported the next day that he had asked for her number. Granted, it was only to offer her a job, but that had at least demonstrated he had remembered her telling him about her unfortunate— and quite unfair—dismissal the week before. He later admitted that setting her up with a job had given him the chance to keep her close while he planned his next move. The rest—as they say—had been history.

"He pursued you relentlessly," said Sally, poking the fire and chucking another log on, diverted from her own problems and reaching for the bottle of wine for a refill. "He was so besotted I don't see how he could *possibly* have been having an affair. What makes you think it?"

Getting up, Imogen produced the mystery woman's letter from the desk drawer. She handed it over, then went back to sit down, watching Sally's face as she read it.

Casually puzzled at first, Sally quickly froze, only her raised eyebrows giving away her surprise. Reading it through again, she muttered extracts from the letter aloud.

"*So wonderful to see you last night . . . I completely understand there are obstacles I have to let you remove before that can happen.*" Here she snorted in outrage, giving her friend a sympathetic glance. Finishing the letter, Sally paused reflectively.

"Bloody hell!" she said at last. "Do you know who this woman—this Victoria person—is?"

"No idea. A secretary? Another lawyer he met somewhere? Who knows . . . Actually," she added slowly, weighing up whether to mention it, "it ties in with something I overheard at Nigel's funeral. You know Richard, Nigel's boss?"

Sally nodded.

"I overheard him talking to a retired partner of the firm at the reception after the funeral. The old man was talking about a blond woman he had seen Nigel with. Said he had assumed that she was Nigel's wife. I asked Richard about it afterward, and he was obviously embarrassed. He didn't want to talk about her at all."

"Probably because he didn't know anything," said Sally reasonably. "Still, the fact is, I just can't imagine Nigel doing this. You know it takes a lot for me to say something nice about him, but honestly, Imo, if I had to choose, I'd make him the least likely person I know to have an affair." She brightened. "Maybe it's an old love letter from before you were married."

"I thought of that," said Imogen, "but look, the date on it is just a couple of weeks before he died. Anyway, what about the 'obstacles that have to be removed'? I take it that refers to me."

"Are you going to do anything about it?"

"Like what?"

"Well, I mean, are you going to try and find this Victoria person? See what she looks like?"

"Would you?" said Imogen.

"Yeah," Sally said. "I think I damned well would."

"I CAN'T POSSIBLY give her this," Gabriel protested, handing back the letter.

"Why ever not, dear boy," said his uncle Godfrey, who was the one nominated by the other trustees to come up with the plan of action over the whole difficult business.

"Because she isn't expecting it. She has no idea, and it'll be devastating."

"That's as may be," said Godfrey, who was pretty uncomfortable about it himself, "but let us not forget, the estate needs this money very badly indeed. I would go so far as to say it's our only hope."

"It can't be," Gabriel argued. "We've just had a massive cash injection from selling Storybook Cottage in the first place. We can't need to impose this on her as well."

"Death duties, dear boy," Godfrey reminded Gabriel, who sighed.

"Middlemass Hall can't afford to lose its relationship with Cavendish Conferences," Godfrey went on, "and there are some very worrying mutterings from them. I've constantly got that Louise woman on the phone about one thing or another—if you ask me, she's an absolute harpy . . . I only wish I could afford to ignore her, but someone has seen fit to put her in charge. We need to carry out these repairs, or they will take their business elsewhere. And *then* Middlemass Hall will be in a pretty pickle."

Godfrey, looking quite red in the face, took a long drink of water and then slapped his glass down on the table with a little more force than was necessary.

"I say," piped up the family solicitor, "it does seem a bit—well—odd. After all, this thing dates from when Storybook Cottage and Middlemass Hall were all owned by the same family. It's a pretty opportunist thing to have in the Storybook Cottage deeds now, expecting the owner to pay a fortune for repairs at the Hall."

"There is nothing opportunist about it," Godfrey protested, stung at the criticism. "The liability is there, fair and square, and it's something I am bound to say they should have brought up during the conveyancing. It's too late now. 'Caveat emptor,' as they say."

"'Buyer beware' is all very well," said Gabriel, "but this woman—who is recently widowed, by the way—is alone and expecting a child. I can absolutely assure you, she is not expecting a massive and ruinous bill from an estate she doesn't even have a stake in. I mean, who would?"

"You should consider your priorities," said Godfrey. "If you seriously think you owe a greater obligation to this woman than you do to your own family and estate, then fine. Remember, you are not alone in the decision-making, Gabriel. Your father appointed us all to help you, and help you we will, even if we are not always in agreement as to how we do it.

"I am passing this letter to the new owner of Storybook Cottage and propose that it be dealt with before our next meeting in a month's time," he went on, with a glare of finality. "Now, if we are quite finished, the next item on the agenda is the issue of persistent rent arrears from our tenants in no fewer than three of the estate cottages, which is the last thing we need in our financial situation . . ."

 *Chapter Nine*

Sally and Imogen talked by the dying embers of the fire until nearly two in the morning. When the knock at the door came at nine o'clock, they were far from ready to face the day.

"I'll go," shouted Sally, trailing wearily down the stairs.

Imogen, meanwhile, was dawdling in the bathroom. She was feeling less sick, as predicted by Morag the midwife, but early morning was her worst time. She was debating whether to brush her teeth straightaway, which would almost certainly make her vomit. It was either that or leave it until after breakfast, when being sick would definitely be more horrible.

Curiosity about who could be at the door made her mind up.

She found Sally leaning seductively against the wall by the open door. Unfortunately, her come-hither manner was let down by smudges of mascara on her white face and by the disgracefully ragged old dressing gown she had found on the back of the bathroom door. She was chatting to a pleasantly smiling man in his early thirties. He had a neatly controlled short back and sides, glasses, and khaki gabardine shorts that were a little too long.

"Hi," he said, over Sally's shoulder. "If this is Sally, then you must be Imogen."

Imogen nodded, smiling encouragingly.

"Gabriel sent me to do the garden."

"You're a gardener?" asked Imogen, puzzled, although the real puzzle was why Gabriel was sending staff to do anything with her house.

"Actually, strictly speaking, I'm a forester," he said. "I do quite a bit of work for Gabriel on the estate, and he gave me a call. He said I should come and get the garden sorted for the fête. I'm sorry I've not come sooner."

"Heavens, I forgot!" wailed Imogen. "It must be practically now, and the garden is just a complete jungle, and there's loads to do and . . . How long do we have?" she said, regaining control with difficulty.

"It's tomorrow, actually," said Peter apologetically. "But don't worry! Gabriel specifically sent me round, so you don't have to do anything at all." He glanced involuntarily at Imogen's tummy. Clearly, he knew the score. "I need to just have a bit of a go at the garden today and then the teams are all set to move in early tomorrow morning. It'll all be fine, honestly." His reassuring grin was enthusiastically returned by Sally.

"That's so kind," said Imogen with relief.

After settling Peter in the garden with whatever tools the house had to offer from one of the spider-infested sheds—luckily, he had also brought some things of his own—she and Sally retreated to the kitchen for breakfast.

"Excellent!" Sally exclaimed. "I love village fêtes."

"It's the church fête, actually, and since when, exactly, have you attended either sort?"

"Never, as far as I can remember," she replied happily, "but I must say, if that's the talent that's available, I am going to dedicate the rest of my life to attending as many as possible."

"He had socks on under his sandals, for heaven's sake," Imogen told her, waving an arm in the direction Peter had disappeared.

"Yeah, but he had a lovely smile."

"And probably a lovely wife and children too," said Imogen repressively, "as, indeed, you have yourself," she added, not entirely accurately.

"Maybe that's the problem," said Sally, suddenly serious. "If Alistair was a bit more masculine and dictatorial about everything, there might be more of a spark."

"You wouldn't have married him if he was."

"Yeah, but I didn't know what I wanted then."

They both sighed sadly.

"Let's not think about it," said Sally, clapping her hands. "Our unconscious minds will work on it while we do country things. Now, what's the plan? I want it to involve welly wanging, cream teas, and coconut shies."

THE DAY OF the fête dawned as warm as the days before, but this time the sky had turned from azure to a heavy gray-white. The atmosphere was unbearably oppressive, washing Imogen with waves of sweat as she rifled through her clothes in the search for something to wear. Or, come to that, anything to wear. Her wardrobe was shrinking as her tummy expanded. Too hot for the long-sleeved shirts and trousers she had been wearing to cover her bump, she plumped for a skimpy T-shirt and an ancient Indian cotton skirt with tiny flowers all over it. Thankfully it had an elastic waist. The T-shirt stretched uncompromisingly over her newly swelling tummy, but the skirt was quite pretty, and her face, flushed with the heat, at least had a healthy glow. She added some silver disc earrings she had bought in a little hippie shop in Portneath and grabbed a scarf to tie back her hair.

Coming down the stairs with Tango at her heels, she felt a little nervous to see what Sally was up to. She needn't have worried. She found her friend in the garden, next to Peter the forester. Peter and Sally were clearly overseeing operations as hordes of small boys in scout uniforms scurried to and fro in the garden and over the bridge into the orchard, all carrying folding trestle tables.

Distracted by feeding Tango and making tea, Imogen glanced out again a few minutes later. Miraculously quickly, the tables had been set in two orderly rows across the lawn. Now the boys were carrying immaculate, folded white tablecloths to each table. Imogen noticed Arthur, the fat chocolate Labrador, lying on the grass under the yew tree, panting laboriously in the heat. As she looked around to find his owner, there was a rap at the door.

"May I come in, my dear?"

"Winifred, how lovely," said Imogen, unconsciously raising her hand to check her hair was staying neatly within the scarf. Winifred Hutchinson tended to have that effect on her. "Would you like some tea?" she added, holding up the pot she had just made.

"That would be splendid," Winifred replied, "and may I

say how well you are looking, my dear," she added, glancing approvingly at Imogen's gently curving tummy.

"Er, is everything okay for the fête?" said Imogen anxiously. "It is all looking rather tired, I'm afraid. I've not really had time for gardening."

"That's not surprising," replied Winifred. "At least we have the roses in bloom. The collection you have in the rose garden includes quite a few very special plants, you know. The lady who lived here before you was quite a collector and expert on the matter."

"Really?" said Imogen, thinking guiltily of the greenfly- and black-spot-infested bushes, straggly with neglect. "I don't really know what to do about roses—"

"In the autumn, I'll come over and show you how to prune them back for the winter. Once as soon as the flowers have faded, and then again in December or January. As for today, my dear, your only responsibility is to do exactly what you have done so far and then to waft around the stalls for a bit and let people have a jolly good look at you. There are lots of people who are awfully curious about the new owner of Storybook Cottage, you know."

IMOGEN FELT TOO hot and uncomfortable to eat lunch, and Sally, looking hungover, did little more than pick at the salad she had prepared. Relieved to clear it away, they both joined the throng congregating around the podium in the orchard. Winifred was thrilled to have engaged the services of the local radio DJ, but Imogen was unimpressed. He looked suspiciously orange.

Several of the village's middle-aged women felt differently. They clustered around him as soon as he arrived, fawning and politely jostling to be by his side. Mrs. Muriel Pinkerton, in particular, lived up to her name by becoming quite pink in the face, giggling skittishly whilst patting him on the arm.

Bounding heavily onto the low podium, narrowly avoiding treading on Winifred's toe, he grabbed the microphone from the stand and waited for the smattering of applause to die down.

"Not exactly irresistible, is he?" said Sally, appearing at Imogen's side and making her jump. "Although looking at this lot, they wouldn't be more excited if Elvis Presley rocked up."

"They'd be surprised, though," whispered Imogen. "He's obviously a bit of a local hero. Look, even Winifred is flushed with excitement." Although it could be the weather, she told herself, retying her scarf to take the hair off the back of her neck.

Not only was the heat becoming more oppressive but the gray-white skies were regrouping, with black clouds now stacked onto the horizon behind Middlemass Hall.

After a good five minutes of talking about himself, the man declared the fête well and truly open. Scuttling back to their respective stalls, the ladies of the village prepared to do battle.

Meanwhile, clearly concerned that their local celebrity would be harassed by members of the public wanting to do inconvenient things like paw him and ask for his autograph, a small group of advisors formed a shield around him and hustled him off. Looking on with an expression of mild amusement on her face was a pretty woman with a short, shaggy brown bob. She was holding a lead with a handsome black Labrador on the end of it, with her other hand on the shoulder of a cross-looking blond-haired little girl. "But Daddy said I could!" she protested.

"Eilish?" the woman said warningly. "Daddy's not in charge now. I am. Now, you go and choose a cake from Miss Perkins at the cake stall." She tucked a five-pound note into the little girl's hand. "Off you go," she added, raising an eyebrow to brook no argument. "I think I saw a lemon drizzle one there earlier, but you'll have to be quick."

Imogen watched them with longing. They looked so comfortably as if they belonged. Even the dog had an air of confidence. That would have been her with Nigel if things had gone as planned, she thought wistfully, wondering if she and her baby would ever feel as at home in Middlemass as this woman clearly did.

Wandering around the stalls, she gave the villagers the "jolly good look" at her Winifred had said they wanted. She was very aware of her shiny nose and the tight T-shirt stretched over her bump.

"I think you'll find that's a size eight," said a lady at the secondhand clothes stall to Muriel, who—with her round face glowing red in the heat—was examining a skimpy slip dress.

"Oh, good," Mrs. Pinkerton replied before adding to a pursed-mouthed woman behind her, "It'll fit my niece Stella a treat, then. There's nothing of her, you know."

"It'll certainly cover 'nothing of her,' that's for sure. Why young girls go around with hardly a stitch on them nowadays is a mystery to me," she replied sourly, apparently irritated that her love idol had been hustled away from her so abruptly.

Imogen wandered on past a stall selling plants she couldn't begin to identify. The initial buying frenzy over, it was already nearly as empty as the cake stall, with only an elderly man she knew by sight chatting to Muriel's husband, who was obviously in charge. They stood at right angles to each other, both staring—eyes narrowed—into the middle distance, hands in pockets rattling change. Occasionally one would allow a brief comment to escape the corner of his mouth and the other would nod economically in response. Thankfully being ignored beyond the initial 'ow do? and cap-touching, Imogen carried on.

Feeling compelled to buy something, she stopped at a stall selling jams and chutneys, most of them with handwritten labels and frilly gingham caps. She was dithering between gooseberry jam and a delicious-looking chunk of honeycomb crammed into a jar, when someone tapped her on the shoulder, making her jump.

"Check out that gorgeous hunk," said Sally.

"It does look rather irresistible, doesn't it?" Imogen replied. But Sally wasn't looking at the honeycomb.

Turning to follow Sally's gaze, Imogen sighed. "You need to raise your standards, woman. Since I got here I've not seen—bloody hell, you don't mean him!" she exclaimed, as she realized her friend was very obviously and indiscreetly pointing at Gabriel.

Oblivious to their examination of him, he was loping moodily toward them wearing grubby cream cricket flannels, an open-necked shirt, and about three days' worth of beard. He looked hungover, exhausted, bad-tempered, and stomach-meltingly desirable.

"Who else?" sighed Sally appreciatively.

"Well, he's a grumpy, oafish yob for a start," said Imogen. Who kisses women, takes the piss, and then makes as if it never happened, she added to herself.

"Ah, a Mr. Rochester sort of character," said Sally understandingly. "All injured machismo and charisma. Yum. What does he do anyway?"

"Some sort of caretaker at Middlemass Hall."

"Ooh, good with his hands too, eh?"

"It's more managerial from what I can gather," Imogen said crushingly. "And he laughs at me," she added, feeling disloyal at not mentioning his kindness offering the driving lessons.

"So important to find a man with a sense of humor."

"And he nearly killed me once," said Imogen, remembering the tractor.

"Gosh, how exciting! I wish he'd nearly kill me," Sally purred, giving him a come-hither look. But she was too late. Just then, an excessively glossy and manicured-looking woman in a floaty dress came up to him and put her hand on his arm. He stopped, seemingly reluctantly, and turned to her. She was chatting animatedly, a girlish laugh ringing out again and again as she repeatedly tossed her hair back before looking coquettishly at him from beneath a shiny blond fringe.

"And what do you reckon to *her*, then?" Sally added, nudging Imogen painfully in the ribs.

"I reckon she'll give herself whiplash if she keeps doing that flicky thing with her hair," said Imogen sourly, only slightly reassured that Gabriel appeared to all but ignore her, whoever she was.

SUDDENLY EXHAUSTED, IMOGEN snuck back into the house. Ten minutes later, she was curled up in the Lloyd Loom chair in the corner of the kitchen with a big mug of tea. Half hidden by the range, she escaped the notice of the ladies doing the teas as they bustled into the kitchen with stacks of dirty cups and saucers en route to the sink.

"What on earth possessed Mrs. Rudge to offer up her Victoria sponge for the teas I will never know. In my book, you've either got a way with sponge cake or you haven't," said one of the women.

"She'd have been better off doing flapjacks, same as last year, Joan," Muriel added. They both nodded in smug agreement.

"This sink could do with a spot of bleach," Joan went on.

"You'd never have seen stains like this when you were doing for her ladyship," said Muriel, rolling up her sleeves.

"No, you wouldn't," agreed Joan. "There's plenty has changed since she died, that's for sure," she added. "Who would have thought there'd be a young single woman living in a big family house like this, for a start?"

"Well, them career girls with their money can do every-thing they like, can't they? And I do mean *everything*. There's the house and the car, and you've not failed to notice there's a little stranger on the way, if you please—all that, and not a husband in sight!"

"And," continued Joan, working up to her pièce de résistance, "what I want to know is, how exactly has she earned the money for it all?"

"She's no better than she ought to be," concurred Muriel sanctimoniously, pursing her lips. "You needn't think it'll take long before she spots Lord Havenbury and makes a play for him, you mark my words."

"She'll have a hard job," replied Joan. "I hear that toffee-nosed girl from the conference center company has him in her sights already, and she looks like a one who gets what she wants."

"In my opinion," said Muriel weightily, "she's a brazen hussy—that's what!" not bothering to clarify if she was referring to the conference center girl or Imogen. Both probably.

Imogen used the noise of clattering cups and water splashing into the sink to sneak out of the open kitchen door. Head down, she crashed into a male chest clad in a striped shirt.

"My newest patient. How nice!" exclaimed a voice as, mumbling an apology, she stepped back to see her dishy doctor, Simon.

"How are you?" he said, noticing Imogen's flushed face.

"No better than I ought to be, apparently," said Imogen.

Catching sight of Muriel and Joan through the kitchen door, he quickly summed up the situation. "Really? How exciting!" he said with a wolfish grin.

She smiled back ruefully.

The moment was broken by a pretty young woman running up and grabbing Simon's arm.

"There's no escape, darling," she said, tugging at him. "I've promised you in the stocks for the wet sponges, and the mob are accepting no excuses."

"This is Genny," he said to Imogen, as she tried to tug him away, "my chief torturer and fiancée. You'd think she'd plead for clemency on my behalf, wouldn't you?"

"Certainly not," Genny said, acknowledging Imogen with a smile. "My class still remembers their last lot of inoculations from Dr. Simon here, and they're not prepared to forgive and forget."

"Genny's a teacher at the primary school," explained Simon. "If there's bedlam in the playground, you'll generally find her in the thick of it. Crowd control isn't in it. It's more like incitement to riot if this one's on duty."

He grabbed her fondly around the waist, and Imogen had to admit, they made a lovely couple, both blond and blue-eyed, Simon classically handsome, and Genny like a nymph—with her delicate, makeup-free face. Artlessly elegant, she was barefoot, with faded jeans and a loose denim shirt that complemented her pale, clear eyes.

"Simon mentioned you'd just moved into the village," said Genny easily to Imogen. "You should come for supper soon."

"I'd love to."

"Good! How about the end of next week?"

Arrangements discussed and confirmed, Genny and Simon shot Imogen matching wide grins and sauntered arm in arm to the orchard, where the children were noisily playing some organized games. A little bit disappointed to discover that Simon was taken—and by a woman she had no chance of living up to—Imogen wandered after them. She came across the still-grumpy-looking Gabriel on the little bridge over the stream. As she was already on the narrow path, there was nowhere to escape, and he had seen her. In fact, with the black cloud over Middlemass Hall visible behind him and his glowering expression, he looked like the wrath of God standing squarely in Imogen's way. Right on cue, the first clap of thunder crashed and then rumbled lengthily through the heavy air.

"*There* you are," he said accusingly, rather as if Imogen had been avoiding him, which she might have been, she had to admit.

"Gosh, so I am," she exclaimed, looking down at herself and pretending to be amazed. "I thought to myself, 'You know what? I haven't seen myself for ages. I wonder where I've got to.'"

"Does your friend always behave like that?" he said, cutting across her witterings and jerking a thumb over his shoulder. "That is, assuming you're prepared to admit she is a friend of yours?"

Imogen followed his indication.

Sally—her feet bare and her skirt tucked into her knickers—was whooping with excitement as she whacked the rounders ball into orbit and then launched herself toward the first base with half the children pounding after the ball and the other half screaming their support.

"Actually, no," said Imogen, meeting his gaze, which had nothing of the melting warmth she had seen in his eyes before. "Most of the time she's really quite grown-up. However, as a well-balanced person, and as a mother, she is occasionally capable of letting her hair down to play with children on their own terms—unlike you, apparently."

"Apparently so," he echoed. Still, he barred her way, staring intently at her.

"Is there something the matter?" she said at last, noticing a tiny quiver in her voice and hoping he hadn't.

"Yes," he replied.

There was another silence.

"Is it because I'm a rubbish kisser?" she blurted.

He made a sound that might have been a laugh. "No," he said.

Imogen saw his eyes drop to her mouth, and her stomach flipped with longing. They were so close, nearly touching on the narrow bridge, she imagined she could feel the heat from his body. "Well, what is it, then?" she persisted, flushing under his gaze.

"Nothing for you to worry about," he replied, wrenching his eyes from her face at last. "I . . ." he hesitated, clearly deciding how much to tell her. "I'll sort it," he concluded, moving out of her way so she could pass.

She noticed, confused, that he pressed himself against the handrail of the bridge so there was no chance of their touching. She thought she felt his eyes boring into her back, but when she looked back, a few seconds later, he had gone.

WATCHING THE GAME, Imogen felt a heavy drop of rain plop onto her bare arm. Another splashed on her cheek and then a brilliant flash of lightning rent the purple-black clouds apart. The crash of thunder that followed hard behind coincided exactly with a sudden and violent deluge that sent the remaining stall-holders scuttling to the house.

 *Chapter Ten*

wish you didn't have to go," said Imogen a few days later, as she sat on the bed, picking fretfully at a loose thread on Sally's beaded cardigan.

Unlike Imogen, Tango, who was lounging on top of Sally's cashmere scarf, was truly content with his lot. He was dribbling steadily as he purred, something he only did when extremely happy, she noted fondly.

"Honey, I wish I didn't have to go. If it weren't for the mud and the complete absence of coconut chai masala, I could really get into this country-living stuff." Sally was at the dressing table, tossing makeup into a soft black leather bag. "More than anything, it's the—good God, do you mind!" she exclaimed as she turned back to the bed. Batting both Imogen and Tango away, she scooped up her damp scarf and cardigan, now with a rather long thread trailing from it where several beads used to be. "That cardigan's vintage, for goodness' sake . . ."

"Sorry," said Imogen. "Still—like you said—at least it's not new."

"Now, where was I?" Sally continued, briefly examining both garments, and chucking them resignedly into the open case on the floor. "I'm just dreading talking to Alistair. He's making it clear the ball's in my court, but what does he want me to do? Before he and Ed left to go camping, he just kept looking at me, like he was observing me for a psychological experiment. He probably thinks I'm perimenopausal or something."

"Hardly, at your age," Imogen observed. "It's good that he wants to communicate," she went on encouragingly. This was the first time Sally had voluntarily referred to the subject since her first night at Storybook Cottage.

"Yeah, yeah I know," admitted Sally. "I knew things weren't going brilliantly, but—well—frankly, I still think the problems are with Al, not me. Maybe *he's* menopausal? He's older than me, after all, and I've read that the male menopause is actually a thing."

"You just need to talk, both of you."

"Hmm," said Sally, unconvinced. "We could do with an umpire. When are you coming to London?"

"But it's nicer here. You said so yourself. Apart from the chai thingie, which I personally don't miss, because I don't even know what you're talking about."

"Not to live. I mean, when are you going to come and see me, to say nothing of finding yourself some work to keep the little one in mashed banana and nappies when it arrives?"

"But what's the point of looking for work in London if I'm not planning on staying?" replied Imogen.

"There's more than just the nine-to-five on offer. Anyway, I think we both accept that office life isn't exactly your forte. No, I've been thinking a bit more creatively than that."

"Uh-oh."

"No, no, listen, would you? The answer's definitely in your artistic talents—if you could just rustle up a bit of confidence in yourself—but, as you said yourself, never mind birthday card designs and stuff. I think you should do those books for children. I mean, I read the other day the bloke who did *Spotty the Dog* or some old nonsense, apparently he's a multimillionaire now, and then there's the Harry Potter phenomenon . . ."

"But I imagine you mean illustrating, not writing? Oh, Sally, no, don't make me," pleaded Imogen, who hated the idea of putting herself out there, even though—after Gabriel's pep talk—she had been thinking more seriously about it. She preferred to imagine the author ambition as a kind of gentle, future dream. "I tried all that before, for goodness' sake. I toted my *Aesop's Fables* illustrations around every children's book publishers in London. There were two that actually acknowledged my stuff—and even they told me to bog off in the end."

"I don't recall you being told to 'bog off,' as you so charmingly put it. I seem to remember one of them being extremely complimentary."

"Well, yes, there was the old bloke with the glass eye and a scary penchant for cravats. He said I had a fresh, charming approach."

"Well, there you are, then," said Sally comfortably.

"Hmm, the trouble is I'm not sure he meant my work. He's the one who took me out for a drink and kept putting his hand on my knee. I never heard another peep out of him after that one time, although I suppose I ought to be grateful he didn't send me the dry-cleaning bill. I'm not sure you can even get Beaujolais stains out of a tweed suit."

"I know you took a lot of knocks," said Sally, not without sympathy. "But you've learned so much since then, and anyway, I don't think you should just illustrate existing stuff on the off chance. I think you should do something new. Your own thing."

"Create a whole new concept, you mean—the next Postman Pat?"

"Well, why not?" said Sally.

Imogen was too shy to mention that she had already begun working on the outline of a book for preschool children. She didn't feel ready to show anyone yet, not even Sally, but it was exciting to be working on something bigger than individual designs. She had felt inspired to let her imagination run free with so much time on her hands at Storybook Cottage.

"I'll tell you what." Sally broke into Imogen's thoughts. "I've got this business card knocking around in the office somewhere. It's a literary agent—a senior one. I met him at an awards dinner a couple of months ago. He's not in children's books himself, but I'll bet he knows someone who is."

AFTER WAVING SALLY off in the taxi, inspired by her encouragement, Imogen went up to her attic studio. There, laid out, she had all her art stuff from London plus the new paints and pastels from the art shop in Portneath. Untying the strings of her portfolio, she shuffled through the most recent sketches she had done. Starting with little more than doodles, she had been pushing herself hard, giving her imagination and her pencil free rein. As well as local landscape sketches, a pair of characters had consistently emerged. There was Tango, a marmalade cat with more elegance and charm than his real-life inspiration could muster, and a little girl with bobbed black hair who Imogen had tentatively called Ruth. Spreading them out on the floor, using the deep windowsill as well, Imogen began to see how the one-off sketches and the tiniest scraps of storylines could be developed.

GETTING READY FOR supper with Genny and Simon, she put on the same Indian cotton skirt she had worn for the fête. With its elasticated waist, it was rapidly becoming the only thing she could get over her nearly five-months-pregnant bump, apart from a couple of pairs of seriously disreputable tracksuit bottoms. She should check out some maternity clothes when she went to see Sally. Somehow the thought of shopping for elastic-paneled trousers and vast floaty tunic tops alone made her feel glum. Not that Nigel would have been a good shopping companion, she told herself quickly; it was just that losing him and then moving out of London had utterly finished her social life in two fell swoops. Now there was no one available for girly lunches or shopping sprees, cooing over baby clothes, and debating the relative merits of fleece versus cotton cot blankets.

Although she knew a handful of people in the village well enough to stop and discuss the weather, this supper with Genny and Simon was her first proper invitation, and Imogen saw it as a significant step forward in finding herself a local social life. Genny and Simon were kind. She was sure they had lots of lovely friends too, and Imogen hoped one or two of them would be there for her to meet tonight.

Thinking that bringing wine would look a bit silly since she was not drinking, she had made some flapjacks instead. Then, going out into the rain-soaked garden, she cut the last roses she could find, gently shaking the heavy drops out of the flowers and wrapping them in a fat cone of news-paper.

Laying the flapjacks and roses carefully in the wicker basket of her bike, she wheeled it past the little red Fiesta parked in the drive, giving the car an affectionate pat on the bonnet as she passed.

It took just five minutes to reach the village green and a minute more to reach the little lane Simon had told her to look out for. Turning in, the road immediately deteriorated from tarmac to a hard-packed stony drive with deep ruts either side and a tuft of grass and weeds running down the middle like a Mohican haircut. The rain, which had been almost continuous since the thunderstorm at the fête, had turned the potholes into pools of water stained almost the color of blood by the red Devon soil.

One hundred yards along, as promised, Imogen came across a long, low cottage with a straw-thatched roof and small windows set deep into the thick cob walls.

Despite being just half past seven, the daylight was already turning to dusk. A wisp of woodsmoke drifted up from one of the leaning chimneys, adding to the autumnal mood.

Leaving her bike against a shed, Imogen gathered up her offerings and her nerves and knocked at the front door.

"Imogen?" a female voice cried seconds later from the other side of the door. "I need you to come to the back door, actually, just go round to the left, could you?" Imogen started uncertainly in the direction she had been told.

"So sorry!" Genny appeared as Imogen wandered tentatively around the corner. "Gosh, are those for us? How gorgeous," she added, sniffing the roses Imogen handed over. "We can't open the front door because—frankly—we've lost the key and we dare not confess to the landlord. There's a big chest against it actually, absolutely full of rubbish, we just didn't have anywhere else to put it and, as we never use the door anyway, we just thought . . ." Genny grabbed Imogen's arm, chattering warmly as she swept her along the little brick path to the back of the cottage.

"Here she is," announced Genny as she ushered Imogen through the stable doors into a roomy and comfortable terra-cotta-floored kitchen. A collection of freestanding wooden cupboards and a dresser were ranged around the walls of the room. Attractively worn, they were clearly old, providing a sharp contrast with the gleaming stainless-steel range cooker that dominated one wall. The center of the room was filled with a huge pine table, its top scrubbed nearly white, and a mismatched selection of pine chairs. The only thing on the table was a striking candelabra holding six slim candles, already lit.

"Imogen!" said Simon warmly, giving her a hug and peck on the cheek. "How lovely to see you. Do you know Gabriel?" he continued, detaching himself.

Just my luck, thought Imogen, consciously suppressing an eye roll. I come here hoping to meet like-minded people and end up with Attila the Hun—the man of few words and even fewer smiles. At least when he was teaching her to drive there was no need to chat. She suspected this evening was going to be heavy going.

"We know each other," said Gabriel, emerging from a little room off the kitchen, which Imogen, glancing behind, could see was the larder. He met her eye briefly and then turned to Simon.

"Will this do?" he said, waving a bottle of red wine.

"Couldn't have chosen better myself," Simon said, dumping four wineglasses onto the table.

"Are you all right with wine, Imogen?" said Genny solicitously.

"Half a glass won't hurt," said Simon.

"Great, well, you're the boss. Yes, please, then," replied Imogen, grateful for the distraction of wine opening and pouring to see them over the awkwardness of the moment. She didn't know if Gabriel was as surprised as she was by the meeting, but either way, he didn't look particularly thrilled to see her, and there was no sign he had resolved whatever problem was troubling him the last time they met.

"This is wonderful," said Imogen, sitting at the table.

The candelabra really was extraordinary—and very beautiful. Made from wrought iron, its surface was left unpainted, a silky brushed silver finish that gleamed in the candlelight. The six candles were held, each at a different and apparently random height by a complex of sinuous metal lengths. The rods twisted and coiled in and around one another, before tapering to fine tails that—although they looked entirely natural and random—balanced one another miraculously to hold the main body of the piece off the table. Reaching out to touch it, Imogen almost expected the sculpture to wrap itself around her fingers like the tentacles of an octopus, it looked so full of fluid movement and life.

"It's amazing, isn't it?" said Genny, noticing Imogen's interest.

"It's absolutely beautiful," Imogen replied reverently.

"Our Gabriel's a clever lad," said Simon. We're always trying to persuade him to push these original pieces a little more. He's got a good reputation locally for the more mundane stuff, fire grates, garden gates, and so on."

"You made this!" said Imogen, sounding, perhaps, a little too amazed, she thought in retrospect. She looked at Gabriel, wide-eyed.

"It was an engagement present for Simon and Genny," said Gabriel.

"It reminds me of Medusa," said Imogen.

"Who's he?" said Simon.

"She, stupid," said Genny affectionately. "She was a Gorgon, a monster with snakes for hair who was so ugly anyone who looked at her was turned to stone," she continued. "That's right, isn't it, Imogen?"

"Gives a whole new meaning to the term 'bad hair day,' doesn't it?" she replied, relieved to see that Gabriel was regarding her a little more warmly now. Even if there was some problem with the two of them having a romantic relationship—as Gabriel had made all too clear—surely, they could be friends. Or at least be civil to one another.

"Most people think that wrought iron is limited to curtain

poles and garden gates. Anyway, I'm glad you like it. Knowing you're an artist yourself, I value your opinion," he said pleasantly. Clearly Gabriel was keen to make an effort too.

She was ashamed that she hadn't found out more about Gabriel when they had lunch or even during their driving lesson. In hindsight, she had dominated the conversation. Not to put too fine a point on it, first she had talked endlessly about herself, then she had behaved exactly like the "brazen hussy" Joan and Muriel had referred to.

"It's lamb, potatoes, and salad, if anyone's interested," said Genny from the sink, where she was rinsing lettuce.

"Sounds delicious, darling," said Simon. "Can we do anything?"

"Actually, no, you are excused, you will be glad to hear," replied Genny. "I was planning for us to barbecue these"— she pointed to the thick, juicy-looking chops on the side— "purely on the basis that it gives you boys something to do while us girlies drink all the wine, but sadly, autumn has decidedly arrived."

She said this gazing out at the rain, which was now lashing against the windows in waves.

"I'm sure it will all be delicious anyway," said Imogen encouragingly—and it was.

The lamb chops were impregnated with garlic and rosemary, blasted quickly under the grill until deliciously browned on the outside but still pink in the middle. Crunchy-skinned baked potatoes with floury insides and lashings of butter were accompanied by a green salad, with yet more garlic in the dressing, topped with bacon, croutons, and crunchy toasted seeds. It was simple comfort food, and completely delicious.

Conversation was light and entertaining with lots of bad jokes and laughter. Imogen was amazed at how relaxed Simon and Gabriel were with one another. They teased and traded insults in a way that told her they knew each other very well indeed. Genny sparkled too, wearing faded jeans and what looked like one of Simon's shirts, her perfect skin glowing in the candlelight. Not just a pretty face, though. Imogen was impressed to hear more about her work at the school.

"She was absolutely brilliant last week," Simon told Imogen proudly. "They had their school Ofsted inspection—a huge big deal for everyone—with a ton of extra work leading up to it over the last few months, although no one knows exactly when it's going to be. Anyway, the headmistress, Mrs. Marshall, has been off sick for most of the term, so Genny just had to steam in and take over."

"Yes, well, not just me." Genny flushed pink at Simon's praise. "Anyway, we'll see how big a disaster it was when we get the report back next week." Looking at Imogen, she continued, "We're desperate to get a good report from the inspectorate. It could be just the leverage we need to get the Local Education Authority to cough up for the renovations. The truth is, the whole school is falling to bits. We think it's great, and the children are fantastic, but it needs money spending on it, and—with funding so tight—the LEA are always looking for an excuse to cut costs. It's central government, not local, who do the Ofsted reports, but if we get a negative one, it could be just the excuse that our LEA need to 'rationalize,' as they call it."

"What would rationalizing mean?" Imogen asked.

"Well, I'm not saying it would happen, but there were rumors a year or so ago that they were looking at merging our little school with the one in Latchfield. It's bigger, newer, and a longish bus journey away for the Middlemass children."

"But we want our own school," said Imogen, amazed at her own passion. She had walked past the little red-brick Victorian building often and had daydreamed extensively about how her bump would one day be hand in hand with her on the way to their first day.

"We certainly do want our own school," said Simon, smiling warmly at Genny. "Anyway, like you said, it probably won't happen," he reassured her, squeezing her hand, "but it does crank up the anxiety when it comes to an inspection, doesn't it, darling? As if you needed more stress!"

Seeing Simon look adoringly at Genny, Imogen blinked rapidly. Nigel had never sung her praises or regarded her with that kind of pride.

She caught Gabriel watching her, and his expression of deep compassion and—what else was it?—pity?—took her breath away. And then, just as their eyes met, he looked away and took a deep swig of wine, newly paying rapt attention to what Genny was saying.

"Have you been teaching there long?" asked Imogen. "You seem so committed."

"Of course, I am. It's a fabulous job—and then, of course, it's my old childhood school too. It seemed like fate when the post came up just as Simon and I had decided to move out of London. The job at the surgery clinched it, of course—"

But Imogen interrupted, not at all interested in the local GP practice. "You mean you were a pupil there? How long ago was that?" She loved the idea of the school having been there forever. The thought made it seem all the more important that it should stay open for many years to come.

"I'm thirty, " said Genny. "So, it's been nearly twenty years since I left . . . Mrs. Marshall was our headmistress—she was Miss Butterwick then. And now here I am, as her right-hand woman. I couldn't be more thrilled. She was probably my biggest inspiration when I was thinking about training to be a teacher." Her expression darkened. "It's just so sad that she's ill and we've got all these things going on."

WHEN SIMON AND Gabriel had been instructed to get on with the washing up, Imogen and Genny took their mugs of coffee and the flapjacks into a cozy sitting room. The long, low room had small lattice-paned windows, oak beams, and a huge brick fireplace. Two squashy sofas covered in multi-colored throws, polished floorboards, and a wall of books made it a comfortable, relaxing place to be.

Settling herself into one of the sofas, Imogen asked, "Have you and Simon known Gabriel for long?"

"Absolutely ages," said Genny. "Simon's known him longest of all. They were at boarding school together. I sort of knew Gabriel from living here since I was tiny, but well, he was older, and we moved in different circles until I met him when I was working in the pub. It was my holiday job.

I met Simon through him, and here we are, married." She plonked her mug on the table and reached for a flapjack. "And now Simon is a GP at the local surgery. With any luck, he'll be offered a partnership soon. That's when we'll think about family. No rush. We both want to get established in our careers first, buy a house, all that jazz."

She took a huge mouthful and chewed ecstatically. Considering how much Imogen had seen her eat already, her appetite was impressive.

"He's lovely, isn't he?" she said, shooting Imogen a piercing look.

"Simon? Yes."

"Actually, I meant Gabriel."

"Er, yes," said Imogen more doubtfully. "Well, at least I am sure he's very nice when you get to know him. Unfortunately, when we first met, he hated me so much at first sight he tried to run me over with his tractor. After that, I thought we had started getting on quite . . . well." She paused, blushing a little. "But—just recently—I seem to have done something to upset him again."

Genny made comfortingly disbelieving noises.

"No, honestly," Imogen continued. "He's been reasonably all right tonight, but when I saw him at the fête last week, he looked as if he wanted to kill me."

"Ah, that. You mustn't take it to heart," said Genny. "He does seem to have something on his mind, I agree, but I'm sure it's not about you, and if there's a real problem, Simon will get it out of him. And then, of course, this is a bad time of year for Gabriel. Late summer always is."

"Oh?"

Genny sighed and smiled sadly.

"That summer," she began, staring into the fire, "it was the year after Simon and I met—he was worn out with the pressure of work and the long hours. When I finished my teacher training, I was just freewheeling before my first teaching job, and we both decided to take the summer off."

She gazed into the flames, remembering. "We came back to the village to hang out for a couple of months. Of course, Gabriel and the rest of the crowd were here for the summer too. You can imagine why, can't you? Those long, lazy days at the Hall or down by the river, drinking wine and chilling out . . . We were making the most of our lack of responsibilities—only young once, and all that."

She sighed. "Gabriel was different then too. He was so funny and carefree—lush, too. I tell you if I hadn't already fallen for Simon . . . Well, he wasn't available anyhow. There was this beautiful girl called Annabel—she and Gabriel were totally besotted with each other—always together, always laughing and sharing their private jokes. Everyone expected them to be the first to marry from the group. In the end, it was Simon and me."

"So, what went wrong between them?" said Imogen.

"She died."

Imogen gasped.

Genny paused, choosing her words carefully. "So . . . there was a huge fuss—a scandal, really—we had to have an inquest of course . . . And there was a police investigation."

"What on earth happened?" said Imogen, shocked.

"We were down at the river one boiling hot day. A long summer it was that year. Lots of us were jumping in off the side of the stone bridge. You know the one? On the way to the school, on the road to Portneath?"

Imogen nodded.

"So," continued Genny, staring into space as she recalled the scene, "we had all had a couple of glasses of wine, except Annabel. We weren't drunk, though, just relaxing and lounging around on the bank. We suddenly realized that Annabel had dived in and hadn't come up again. There was a huge panic. It was like time slowed down, like we were all in a nightmare. The trouble is the water was terribly cloudy, with all the silt stirred up from the bottom, and we just couldn't see a thing. The boys all searched for her. Gabriel was completely frantic, but by the time he found her and brought her to the surface, it was horribly clear that she was already dead. Gabriel tried to revive her. Simon was trying to help, but Gabriel wouldn't let anyone else near her. He kept on and on at it way after we all knew it was useless. The ambulance men had to drag him off her in the end." Genny gazed into the fire unseeingly.

"Anyway," she continued with a sigh, "it turned out she had dived too near the edge. The water had dropped so much over the weeks of hot weather. It wasn't as deep as we thought. She'd broken her neck. She would have been paralyzed instantly, and—because we didn't realize she was under the water, caught in the weeds—she just drowned immediately."

"How awful," Imogen said softly.

"Yeah," agreed Genny with a twisted smile. "The police were insistent that she must have been drinking or taking drugs, even though we kept telling them she hadn't. In the end Gabriel went completely mad. He screamed that she couldn't have been drinking because she was pregnant. It turns out they'd found out just days before and were planning to break the news to their parents and then to announce their engagement. The autopsy confirmed it. It was all unspeakably horrific."

"When did all this happen?" said Imogen.

"It's getting on for ten years ago now. He never stopped blaming himself for—oh, I don't know!—not taking better care of her, not finding her sooner, not making a good enough job of reviving her . . . Take your pick. And then of course he was absolutely devastated at losing the baby too."

"And still no new relationship after all this time?" said Imogen.

"Nothing much. He's not a monk, mind you, but there's been nothing more than the odd no-commitment fling with girls we often don't even get a chance to meet. I think there's someone in the picture at the moment—that girl working up at the Hall. Louise is her name, I think—but she's nothing special to him as far as we can tell. We've all given it a go—dangled wonderful women right under his nose, but it's like he can't find anyone else to measure up. Mind you, he doesn't even want to look—that's the real problem. It's like he's thinking, 'If you don't love, you don't lose.' He just slogs away, working his guts out trying to keep the Hall going all day and then working at the forge for half the night. When he's really bad, we don't see him for weeks at a time. Frankly, it's amazing he's even here tonight."

Poor, poor Gabriel, thought Imogen, her eyes filled with tears of empathy. She and he were the same. They had both loved and lost. Then she remembered the letter from the mysterious Victoria woman. No. It was not the same. Nigel had not died loving her. She knew that, of course. Knowing didn't make it any easier.

In a somber mood, Genny and Imogen consoled themselves with the flapjacks, both of them on their third by the time Simon and Gabriel reappeared.

"Whoa, I'm glad to see you're both keeping your strength up in the face of all our hard work," said Simon, grabbing a flapjack and throwing himself full-length onto the sofa that Genny was on so he could rest his head in her lap.

Gabriel, more decorously, sat in the wing chair by the fire.

"These are fantastic, Imogen. You'll have to give us the recipe. Genny never makes stuff like this," Simon said, pulling a soulful face.

You'd eat too many and end up diabetic or something, that's why," said Genny mock sternly. "And what sort of an example would you be to your patients then?"

"Imogen needs the extra calories, though," observed Gabriel.

"So true!" exclaimed Genny. "It's all incredibly exciting, Imogen. When's it due?"

"Just after Christmas, apparently," said Imogen. "The first week of January, to be exact, but I'm a bit worried the poor mite will arrive early and be condemned to a lifetime of being given joint Christmas/birthday presents rather than one for each."

"I shouldn't worry," said Simon. "In my experience, first-time mothers tend to have their babies late."

"Just as well," said Gabriel. "Imagine all the poor boys born on Christmas Day, landing up being called Chris. Or Noel."

"I think Noel's a lovely name!" said Genny. "Anyway, there must be lots. I suppose you couldn't really call him Jesus, though, could you?"

"Plenty of people in Spain and Brazil would disagree with you," observed Gabriel.

"Girls are easier," said Imogen. "You could call her Carol. Or Holly."

"Or even Ivy!" chipped in Genny. "Ivy's a beautiful name."

"I think we had better hope the child sticks to his or her due date, don't you?" said Gabriel. "Anyway, I've got a big conference delegation arriving at the Hall tomorrow. It's going to be a long day, so I think I'll make a move."

"Oh, but it's early!" Imogen said, reluctant to see the evening break up.

"Sorry," he replied shortly. "You'd better get your coat. I'll give you a lift home."

"I don't need a lift, thanks," said Imogen, nettled at his patriarchal manner. Then she felt bad, remembering the sad story she had heard tonight. Maybe it was no wonder he wanted to take control, having learned that—if you don't— truly awful things really do happen.

"You absolutely *do* need a lift," he said, cocking a thumb at the window. "You're not riding your bike home in that."

He had a point. The rain was still lashing down relentlessly, and the thought of negotiating water-filled potholes in the dark did not appeal.

"I don't want either of you to go," said Genny, pouting,

"but I suppose we should all hit the sack. I've got a stack of marking to do, so I'll be up horribly early."

WITHIN WHAT SEEMED like seconds, Imogen was strapped into Gabriel's car, hitching a lift again. At least it wasn't the tractor this time.

"Rains a lot in Devon, doesn't it?" she said inanely, nervous at his closeness in the dark as he skillfully negotiated the potholes.

"Wouldn't be green if it didn't."

There was an uncomfortable silence.

"You know, I never received that letter you said was coming from the trustees," said Imogen, more to make conversation than anything else. "The Middlemass Hall trust thingie you talked about . . ."

"I know. I went back and told them not to send it until I spoke to them."

"Why?" she said, beginning to be concerned.

"Because I've got some stuff to sort out, and—until I do—you don't need to know," he snapped impatiently, suppressing further discussion on the matter.

She was relieved when, a moment later, they drew up at Storybook Cottage. He got out to open the car door for her while she was still struggling with the seat belt. Sighing, he leaned in and undid it, causing her to press herself backward in the seat.

In two minds about whether to extend their scintillating conversation about trust administration over coffee, she considered inviting him in as he helped her out of the car like some precious, fragile creature.

Their eyes met in the dim light from the porch and held for a long moment. Surely a kiss, she thought longingly, staring at his mouth, her arm still burning from his touch.

"Good night, then," he said with finality.

"Good night," she answered, clear that she had been firmly dismissed. Nonetheless, he waited, car engine purring, for her to fumble with her keys and go inside. She heard the car pull quietly away as she shut the door behind her.

 *Chapter Eleven*

Gabriel was as good as his word with the driving lessons and took her out twice that week. Nervous in his presence, Imogen did a terrible job, the second time in particular, and started to despair about ever passing her test. They were awkward with each other too, with Imogen feeling there were so many topics off the table for discussion, she was terrified to open her mouth. At the end of each lesson, she would arrive back home exhausted and relieved it was over, but then—within hours—felt herself strangely looking forward to the next one.

After several days of wet, blustery weather, Imogen woke early to find the rain had stopped overnight, leaving the sky overcast and the air clammy. It was oddly warm for so late in the year, the weary summer heat seeming reluctant to release its grip, despite the shortening of the days. Imogen felt sweaty again immediately after her shower and was shedding layers of clothing before she had even finished her breakfast.

Of course, the cessation of the rain needed to be exploited, Imogen decided. Her encounter with Gabriel had left her too restless to settle herself in her attic studio. She needed to be out. Plus, she reasoned, she didn't know how much longer she would be able to easily plan an outside sketching day. She still had to draw out a final double-page spread for her autumn Tango and Ruth book. She decided to walk down into the village to choose a landscape and make a start.

There was no need to lug all her art kit—she only really needed her big sketchpad and her pencils, along with a picnic blanket she often used. It had a waterproof layer on the back. Everything would still be soaked after the rain and sitting on the wet ground did not appeal. She would take some photos too, and do all the color painting back at home, she decided, packing a satchel with the essentials. A water bottle would have been nice, but Imogen didn't fancy adding any more weight to what she was carrying. Anyway, it wasn't *that* warm.

By the time she had strolled down into the village with her gear, it was past nine o'clock. The commuter traffic had ceased, and the morning flurry of activity around the little village school had settled down too. All was quiet and peaceful except for the white duck at the pond who quacked territorially at her as she approached. The pond—although picturesque—was not her destination today. Instead, she followed the little stony path running between the road and the stream, which headed toward the cricket ground and village hall. The stream quickly widened and slowed along this stretch, transforming to a small river as it continued its journey toward Portneath and the sea. The rushing of the water over the boulders on the riverbed was soothing and hypnotic. Imogen was glad she was alone with her thoughts.

She had explored most of the paths around the village now, and she knew there was a sweet little corner where the path led down the bank and under a pretty stone bridge, popping up and rejoining the road on the other side. She wondered if this was the spot Genny had been talking about at supper the other night. What an awful story that was.

Arriving at the spot, Imogen sized up the scene, looking for a pleasing composition. The bridge was definitely the centerpiece, and she could picture, in her mind's eye, Tango sitting, neat and smug, on the wide stone balustrade, looking down into the river, perhaps watching the fish casting shadows in the water. Most of the wildflowers on the grassy bank were looking tired now, worn out by a long, hot summer, but the daisies were still sprightly, and the bindweed smothering many of the taller plants on the bank was studded with fresh pure-white trumpet flowers. It was perfect, she decided, laying out her blanket and making herself comfortable with her sketchpad propped on her knees and her little stash of pencils fanned out beside her.

Imogen was soon engrossed, using broad swipes of the pencil to approximate the composition. In the background was the row of elegant, upright poplars—the trees lining the drive to the Hall—then there was the arch of the bridge with a scribble in a softer, darker pencil to approximate the texture of the stone, and then—in the foreground, the river itself with its reed bank, giving way to the grassy verge in the foreground. There was lots of detail she would put in later, and she thought about this as she sketched—the reeds were begging for a water vole to be in evidence, building its messy nest, and there could be butterflies around the wild buddleia, with its arching purple flowers. Imogen adored cramming detail into her paintings, with something new to find every time someone looked, from a tiny, scarlet ladybird on a leaf to perhaps even a stork here on the left, peering into the river for fish.

Time passed. Imogen was oblivious as she hyper-focused on her work.

Feeling warm and sweaty again for the second time that morning, she looked up to notice the heavy, gray cloud had been replaced with blue sky and brilliant sunshine. She wiped her brow and started to wish she had bothered to bring a water bottle after all.

Oh God, seeing as the sun was out, she supposed she should take a picture of the scene for her Insta feed. It wasn't that she didn't love her growing band of followers, and she knew she needed to post regularly, but selfies made her feel painfully shy. Perhaps she could just get away with taking a picture of her sketchpad with the bridge in the background . . . People loved to see all the work in progress.

She was faffing about, propping her sketchbook on her rucksack and contorting herself to see if there was an angle where she could get it all in the shot. No, damn, it was going to have to be a selfie so she could hold up her sketchbook.

She was holding the phone up as high as it would go and trying out insouciant grins, which were mainly coming across like something out of a face-pulling competition, when suddenly her eye was caught by an addition to the background. A horribly familiar face.

Imogen spun round and blushed scarlet.

"Strange time of day for a picnic," said Gabriel, looking

at her oddly as she dropped her sketchbook in a flurry of pages onto the picnic blanket.

"It would be, if I was," she said, smiling nervously at him as he strode sure-footedly down the bank toward her. Goodness, it was actually quite difficult to speak with her tongue glued to the roof of her dry mouth. Her eyes lighted on his right hand, which was holding an aluminum water bottle, wondering if it was full.

"Want some?" he said, noticing immediately and proffering it.

"Actually, yes, please," she said, with relief. Unscrewing the lid, she drank deep. It was cold and refreshing and sweet. She took several huge, delicious gulps and then, worried about him having none left, wiped the top and offered it back to him.

"Have it all," he said. "You shouldn't be out here in the blazing sun without water. Did you not bring any?"

"Wasn't expecting it to be so hot," she muttered, chastised.

He was gazing transfixed at her morning's work, his face unreadable.

"It's just a sketch," she said, shyly.

"Is it all right to look?" He glanced at her apologetically.

"Yes, of course! Sit?" she offered.

He folded himself down onto the other half of the picnic blanket with unconscious grace, gazing all the while at her rough pencil sketch of the scene. There was no real detail yet, just some scribbly place markers where she pictured some of the extra bits she loved to include. The sketch of Tango was full of majestic attitude, though—she was pleased with that—and the little girl, Ruth, was standing beside him, hanging over the parapet of the bridge, staring into the depths of the river below.

"Phew, isn't it hot?" Imogen commented inanely, fanning herself performatively to cover her self-consciousness as he studied her work, at close quarters. It didn't help her to remember that he too was an artist. "You'd never think it was September. I could just dive off the bridge into the river, couldn't you?" she gabbled. "I mean, I don't know . . . I wonder how deep it is, after all this r—" She gasped and clapped her hand over her mouth.

"Oh God, I'm *so* sorry, this is where . . ." Imogen was horrified. How could she have been so crass? He would never forgive her. She would never forgive herself.

If she thought for one hopeful moment she had somehow got away with her faux pas, a single glance at his face told her otherwise.

He was stark white, lips pressed together and brow furrowed. For a nanosecond their eyes met, and Imogen gasped at the agony she glimpsed before he closed his eyes tight and turned away.

"Promise me you'll never . . ." But he couldn't finish. He hung his head, seemingly drained. "How did you know?" he said at last, looking back at her.

"Genny told me at supper," Imogen gabbled. "I'm so sorry. I'm just so desperately sorry for your loss. Genny said Annabel was an amazing person."

"An angel," he murmured, "she was perfect."

He sighed, staring at the horizon for so long Imogen wondered if he had forgotten she was there. "But you know this stuff," he went on at last. "Losing your husband?"

"I wouldn't say Nigel was an angel." Remembering the letter from Victoria, she added, "Actually, he *definitely* wasn't."

"But losing someone you love like that?" he went on.

He was clearly unwilling to let it go. Unfortunately.

"It was an accident too, wasn't it?" he pressed her. "A car crash, you said?"

"Yes, a stupid accident that should never have happened," Imogen agreed. "It just feels so senseless, doesn't it? Like you've suddenly been handed a completely different life to the one you expected. I don't think you ever get rid of the sense of instability that comes with that, do you?" she went on. "That idea that a whole lifetime with that other person can disappear in a split second. It's kind of insane."

"It certainly makes you *go* kind of insane," agreed Gabriel. "I was lucky to have such good friends." His voice was stronger now, his strength and resolve being slotted back into place through a sheer act of will.

"I'm just really, really sorry," Imogen said again, tears flooding her eyes in a wave of empathy. She blinked and looked back at the bridge, kicking herself for her stupidity.

"Life goes on," said Gabriel briskly as he stood up and brushed himself off. "Keep the water bottle, and don't stay out here too much longer, okay? It may be September, but you'll still burn."

"That would be good. Maybe my freckles will join up," said Imogen, feeling that he must now be comparing beautiful Annabel with her in her jogging pants and her bare, sweaty face.

"Take care of yourself, Imogen," he said over his shoulder as he climbed effortlessly back up the bank in just three giant strides.

It was only when he had disappeared from view that Imogen remembered she should ask about the trustees' letter. Oh well, she would find out soon enough. Apart from her faux pas about Annabel, he seemed in a better mood. Maybe everything was okay now.

SEVERAL WEEKS PASSED, where Imogen neither bumped into Gabriel again nor received any correspondence from him and she was too shy to make the first move. She ached for contact with him—any contact—but dismissed her yearning as a general need to get out more. Winifred seemed to have gone to ground, Simon was frantically busy with autumn flu vaccinations, and Genny, of course, was flat out at the beginning of the academic year. Even Sally barely seemed to have time for her, and Imogen's last text to her had gone unanswered for days.

For the first time since moving to Middlemass, Imogen felt stifled by her little life in the village. Trapped, almost. Things would be different when she had her driving license.

Gabriel had offered no more lessons, at least for now, and Imogen hadn't asked. She felt like the two of them needed some time apart to recover from her distressing habit of only opening her mouth to change feet whenever she was with him.

AUTUMN ARRIVED ABRUPTLY with the damp, brackish chill of October. In response to the darkness crowding in by early evening, Imogen had started going to bed straight after supper, curling up with Tango and a good book, lights out by ten. Her sleep had been restless, though. She woke again and again to unfamiliar sounds, many made by Tango crashing around flat-footed—and many not. The previous night Imogen had been woken suddenly, sitting up with a thudding heart in response to chilling screams coming from the woods between Storybook Cottage and Middlemass Hall. She managed to rationalize them as the cries of a fox, but shaken, she had lain awake for over an hour listening to the house creaking around her.

She was no good at being alone.

Arriving in the village on her bicycle early next morning, Imogen was craving human company. Squinting against the low sunlight, she saw two figures in conversation on the edge of the green and spied a dark brown shape at their feet. It could only be Arthur, the long-suffering chocolate Labrador. She was delighted. The no-nonsense approach of Winifred Hutchinson was the perfect antidote to nighttime terrors.

Getting closer, she was even more pleased to see that Winifred was talking to Genny.

"Imo, hi!" hailed Genny cheerfully.

"Hello, Genny . . . Winifred," said Imogen, arriving at their side and panting only slightly.

"Should you still be riding that thing in your condition?" said Winifred, eyeing Imogen's very large bump doubtfully.

"Apparently there's no harm in it," said Imogen. "In any case, I don't have a lot of choice until I pass my driving test."

"Oh yes, how is that getting on?" said Genny.

"So-so. Gabriel's been teaching me on and off." Imogen pulled a face. " I don't think he's terribly impressed with my driving," she admitted. "But he's very patient considering . . . He didn't even shout when I drove into the ditch, not realizing there *was* a ditch."

Winifred raised an eyebrow.

"Oh, it wasn't a problem," Imogen rushed to add. "He was diplomatic enough to agree it did look a lot like a solid verge because it was so overgrown. I've applied for a December test date now. I'm just waiting for it to come through." She really needed to get in more practice before then; she must get on with it and start looking for a professional instructor.

Winifred nodded approval. "My old schoolfriend Madge learned to drive as a land girl during the war. I'm older than I look," she added, noticing Imogen's expression of surprise. "I'm bound to say a few proper lessons wouldn't have gone amiss with her—she was probably an absolute whiz at driving tractors, but she was a bit rough. I remember her offering to drive my car when I sprained my wrist a few years ago. She went to turn left and broke the indicator stem clean off." She chuckled. "Anyway, as Genny and I were just saying, we need help. Could you rustle up a few apple pies, do you think?" she said to Imogen.

"Oh, er, well, to be honest, my pastry's not the best," Imogen admitted, thinking of her last gray, leathery efforts.

"All right, well, if you can't do pastry, what *can* you do?" fired Winifred impatiently.

Imogen winced. Her self-esteem was already a little bit

fragile without Winifred writing her off. Making good pastry wasn't everything, surely?

"Winifred means, what else do you think you could do to help us raise some money for the school?" explained Genny kindly.

"I see!" said Imogen, feeling a little less crushed. "Why? What's the matter with the school?" For the first time, she noticed that Genny was looking tired, her eyes pink-rimmed as if she might have been crying.

"It's all been going a bit pear-shaped since I saw you last." Genny smiled bravely, but the corners of her mouth twitched down, and she blinked rapidly.

"That blasted Education Authority," exploded Winifred. "I don't think I've ever seen such a display of pettifogging bureaucracy masking the kind of insane decision-making that we have here." She drew a calming breath, looking to Genny for permission to continue. Genny nodded gratefully, so Winifred went on. "The situation is, despite having always received absolutely superb inspection reports, the gray suits"—she nearly spat the words—"have turned down the school's application for improvements funding."

"But if it's a brilliant school as it is, why do we need funding for improvements?" asked Imogen, trying to remember what Genny had said at supper. Admittedly, she had been too distracted by Gabriel to listen properly.

"It's a bit more complicated than that, unfortunately," said Genny with a sigh. "You should come and see. It's amazing how much *hasn't* changed in the last fifty years or so. The building we have is lovely, but it is Victorian. There are some big repairs that need doing, mainly to the roof, and there's rising damp in half the classrooms. The funding was supposed to cover that too. Worse still, the improvements aren't just 'nice to have,' they are essential. We're still using the outside loos in the playground, for instance, and regulations mean we *have* to install proper plumbing in the main building soon or they'll close us down. We're talking somewhere around eighty thousand at best for the whole lot."

"Hang on, though," said Imogen, clutching her head. "Aren't the 'they' that want to close us down the same 'they' that won't give us the money?"

"Yes, basically," said Genny gloomily. "They want us to merge with Latchfield school, and this is a pretty good way of making sure it happens. They've got us, all right."

"They most certainly have not," said Winifred stolidly. "As soon as news gets out, the whole village will be up in arms about it. It's not just the ones with children, you know," she said, glaring at Imogen.

"Er, no," Imogen agreed hastily, worried her rapid calculations on the average age of the village—surely fifty plus?—showed too clearly on her face.

"No, it is not," Winifred continued, punching out each word. "I don't think there's a family in this village that doesn't either have a child at the school now or remember going there themselves. It's part of the soul of this village—has been for the last hundred years and will be for the next hundred—at least," she said, jaw jutting intimidatingly.

"Fighting talk," said Imogen admiringly, stirred at the

thought of her own little girl tumbling through the school gates in years to come, chattering with her friends and dragging a satchel on the ground.

Letting the school close was unthinkable.

"We need a village meeting," said Winifred. "To tell everyone what's going on. Make a plan of action. Tomorrow night, village hall, and, Genny, you can tell everyone just exactly what the situation is. We'll co-opt a committee there and then." She stopped briefly, eyes ablaze with the challenge.

"Don't you have to sort of . . . book the village hall with someone?" said Imogen timidly.

"Yes. Me," said Winifred.

Genny caught Imogen's eye and grinned.

"Now . . . it's supposed to be the Mothers' Union meeting tomorrow, but they'll just have to rearrange," Winifred was muttering to herself.

"Won't they be awfully cross?" ventured Imogen.

"Heavens, no!" she exclaimed. "They'll pretend to be, of course. Probably even say something silly about finding an alternative venue, but there wouldn't be a soul there if they did. Every one of that crowd will be at our meeting, because they wouldn't miss a scandal like this for the world,"

Winifred eyed Imogen. "You're an artist, aren't you, my dear?"

Imogen shrugged modestly, eager to make up for her failures as an apple pie baker.

"Good, you can do the posters. No time like the present, I say. I've got a box of marker pens and a roll of art paper at home. Come with me, and I'll make you some tea while you work."

 *Chapter Twelve*

Ensconced in Winifred's crowded dining room with Arthur lying heavily on her feet, Imogen felt like a ten-year-old, coloring in contentedly and waiting for tea to be brought.

She heard the door being nudged open with a foot and jumped up to help.

Winifred put down her loaded tea tray and leaned over.

"That's awfully good. You are clever, my dear," she said, admiring the posters Imogen had already produced. Choosing a simple design, easy to reproduce quickly, she had spelled out *Save Our School*, boldly emphasizing the first letter of each word so, from a distance, it read *SOS*, with the time and venue filled in below. She had already managed to finish three.

"We need one at each of the bus stops, then there's the noticeboard outside the church and the other by the village hall, plus the one for the door of the shop—that's five," Winifred said. "Of which, the one in the shop is the most vital."

"Because more people will see it there?" said Imogen.

"Well, yes," said Winifred slowly, "and, perhaps more to

the point, so many more people will hear about it there, thanks to the communicatory zeal of Mesdames Joan and Muriel," she added with a wry smile.

Later, Imogen and Genny went around the village with posters and drawing pins, gratified to see little knots of chattering people were gathering around the notices before they had even finished putting them up.

THE SLITHER AND flop of the post arriving through the letterbox made Imogen jump.

Taking the post through to the study, she leafed through, tossing the junk mail into the wastepaper bin.

Setting aside a boring window envelope from the gas supplier, doubtless a bill, she laid the two remaining letters on the desk side by side. Still nothing that looked to be from Gabriel's Middlemass Hall trustees. One was an expensively midnight-inked scrawl that she delightedly recognized as Sally's. A handwritten letter is a beautiful thing, thought Imogen, turning over the thick vellum envelope appreciatively and then putting it to one side to enjoy later. The other was a plain brown envelope with a Swansea postmark and what felt like a piece of card inside. Ripping it open, she whipped out the card, thrilled to see the DVLA logo at the head. The note read, *We are writing to inform you that Mrs. Imogen Hewitt has been allocated a driving test at 10.00 a.m. on 23rd December . . .*

She whooped with glee and was rewarded by a hefty kick in the kidneys from the little one, her heart thudding quicker with nerves. It might only be mid-October now, but that only really gave her a couple of months. She suddenly felt hideously unprepared. She needed Gabriel to let her do a bit more practice over the next few weeks. It was awkward for her to ask, with his attitude toward her at the moment.

She tapped it into her online calendar both as a timed event and as an all-day, relieved to see that it was the day after a checkup with Morag the midwife and not clashing. She had forgotten the previous one, and Morag had turned up at the house within an hour of the appointment time, breathing fire but clearly relieved—underneath her brusque manner—that Imogen was just forgetful and not somehow so ill she couldn't leave the house. Her brain had turned to mush with the pregnancy and, with no job other than her art to mark off time, she had got scattier than ever. Constantly mislaying her phone, she sometimes needed to turn on the radio or television for a clue about what day of the week it was, let alone the date.

Pausing to savor a little fantasy about bowling up to London in an open-topped sports car, hair blowing in the wind, one hand insouciantly on the wheel, she tore open the letter from Sally. The combination of flamboyant, right-sloping scrawl and the relative brevity of the letter, exclamation marks scattered generously throughout, was the personification of Sally as sure as a photograph would be.

Read your email occasionally! was the first exhortation. *And switch on your mobile* was the second. She had a point, admitted Imogen guiltily. *Who does letters nowadays when you can scribble and launch into the ether in seconds? I can't be doing with all that scrabbling around for stamps and carrier pigeons,* it continued impatiently.

Hope you and the little (big?) bump are well. Hectic at work so keep forgetting to call, except in the evening but then don't, assuming you country folk go to bed with the sun.

Mentioned the scarlet woman to Alistair—hope you don't mind—but nice to talk to him about something other than how dysfunctional our relationship is. Al actually came up with a good idea! He suggested you get a private detective on to it to find out who, what, and why. Personally, didn't know they existed IRL but apparently, it's not just detective novels and 1950s movies. Anyway, just a thought because personally I never would have thought the old fart (dear, dear Nigel) would have had it in him but am thoroughly intrigued, aren't you?

Imogen thought *intrigued* was probably not quite the word. Since the stomach-lurching discovery of the letter from the mystery blonde, she was ashamed to admit she had thought about his apparent betrayal less than she would have anticipated. Her brief married life with Nigel was beginning to feel like something that happened to someone else a long time ago. Coming alone to Middlemass, waiting for the baby, she was cocooned, existing in limbo between the past and the future. The letter from Sally was an intrusion into the calm, a shocking blast of cold air from the real world. Disturbed, Imogen read on:

Real reason for note being, found the business card for Quentin Barker-Williams (that literary agent bloke I mentioned—met at party, v. boring but influential apparently . . . no telling by appearances). Anyway, he works with an agent who's THE big noise in children's books. Left them at work so call me in the office for her details ASAP!!!!

Wiping the sludge of dead wet leaves from their feet, the rain-sodden crowds filled the village hall. Condensation ran down the windowpanes as the temperature quickly rose inside. The smell of sheep from wet woolen coats was all-pervading, and voices, sharing scant information and rumor, rumbled around the hall.

Imogen pressed herself against the wall. She had been pleased when Genny had offered to give her a lift to the public meeting. Ulterior motives had quickly become apparent, though, and she found herself making promises with a confidence she no longer felt in the five minutes it took them to arrive at the hall. She could hardly have refused to help when Genny was so nervous. The headmistress, Mrs. Marshall, had cried off the public meeting with a flare-up of the ill health that had kept her away from the school for much of the term. Genny had reluctantly agreed to brief everyone herself. Imogen noticed with sympathy that Genny was now trembling with nerves at taking on such a high-profile role.

"Frankly, stopping a class full of six-year-olds from killing themselves and each other every day would frighten most people a lot more than talking to a bunch of adults," Imogen had said encouragingly, but Genny had just given her a wan little smile.

"Thanks so much for agreeing, though, Imo," she had said. "If we've got people like you pitching in, I know we'll be fine."

Imogen didn't like to point out *she* wouldn't feel fine if she had people like her on side, but she was flattered by Genny's faith.

She was amused to see the Mothers' Union contingent fussing with coats and capacious handbags as they claimed seats in the front row. Winifred had been right. They may have had their meeting venue snatched out from under their noses, but nothing would persuade them to miss such a potentially dramatic event as this.

Her eyes were drawn to the door at the back of the hall just as the flicky-haired woman from the fête—who must be the Louise that Genny mentioned—swept in, simpering at someone behind her who was holding open the door. It was Gabriel. Of course, it was. Imogen watched as he returned Louise's smile and solicitously helped her take off her coat—as if she had lost the use of her arms, thought Imogen sourly. The vibe was entirely of casual, happy intimacy as Imogen watched her reach up to pick a piece of fluff off his collar, smiling up at him winningly.

"Sit near the front, won't you, Imo?" pleaded Genny, interrupting her thoughts. "I don't want just those old gasbags in my sight line," she said, indicating the Mothers' Union ladies, who were now firmly installed, chatting and passing around a bag of humbugs.

"Of course, I will," Imogen assured her.

"Good, you can sit between me and Gabriel, then," said Simon, materializing at Imogen's elbow. She saw Gabriel looking stony-faced, now following behind having offloaded Louise at the back of the hall, where she seemed to be queuing to sign the petition.

"There's strength in numbers, and that way we can shout down the hecklers together," Simon added, grinning reassuringly at Genny.

"Hecklers?" she quavered, turning a shade paler.

"Okay, no hecklers, but we can lead the applause from the front," amended Simon.

"Not much to applaud, sadly," said Genny.

"There will be," said Simon. "People always rise to a challenge. Just tell 'em what needs to happen, and we'll all make sure it does."

"I'm surprised Winifred isn't here," observed Imogen, having scanned the crowds thoroughly. "She's been right behind this whole thing."

"Ah," said Simon. "Sadly, I think I know why. Her old dog died last night. I bumped into her just this morning . . . She was being terribly brave, but you could tell she was very upset."

"Oh no!" Imogen gasped. "I only saw him yesterday . . ." Her heart ached for the older woman. The creaky old chocolate Labrador had been her constant companion. She must go and offer condolences.

"I think we should start now, darling," said Simon to Genny encouragingly, shooing her and the others toward the front.

"Er—oh—okay," stammered Genny. "There's quite a lot of noise," she added nervously when they got to the top of the room, turning reluctantly to face the crowd as the stragglers slid into their seats.

Imogen, keen to have Simon sit between her and stony-faced Gabriel, tried to maneuver as far away as possible, but Gabriel swept in next to her at the last minute, along with Louise, who had popped up again, giving Imogen a basilisk stare before taking the seat Gabriel was offering on his other side.

Simon squeezed Genny's arm reassuringly and raised a hand. "Let's all hear what Genny has to say, shall we?" he said in a voice that seemed barely raised, but the authority was absolute. The noise immediately died to a murmur and then stopped.

"Th-thank you all for managing to come along tonight, I know we are all very busy—" Genny began quietly.

"Speak up, love," shouted a male voice from the back.

"S-sorry," said Genny, louder. "I—er—Mrs. Marshall sends her apologies to you all. She isn't too well, as many of you know, but I'll try to explain what's going on at the school as best I can, then we need to see how we can all get together to sort it out." Genny's color and confidence returned as she spoke.

It took ten minutes for Genny to go through the details. Voices tutted and gasped as the scale of the problem unfolded, and outraged chatter burst out briefly when she explained the Education Authority's plan to merge the school with Latchfield. She had come well prepared, and Imogen was touched at how people cooperated, listening carefully and asking questions to clarify points as they were raised. A community with such a range of ages and characters all unified in a common quest. It was a community she felt proud to belong to. She stroked her bump, feeling unaccountably moved.

As Genny waved the builder's eighty-thousand-pound quote for the essential repairs and restructuring work, voices murmured, "Where's Bill?" and "What about Bill taking a look, that's never going to cost that much, surely . . . especially if Bill would take it on."

Bill Cromer was sitting toward the back of the hall, a ruddy-faced man in his fifties, solid rather than fat, with huge, rough hands, Imogen noticed, and an air of quiet authority. He put out his hand to look at the paperwork that was eagerly passed back by those sitting in front of him.

"Give me a minute, my love. I'll need my glasses . . ." he burred, waving at Genny to carry on and then reaching into his shirt pocket for a pair of wire-rimmed glasses that he put on ponderously.

Imogen sat, armed with the paper and Biro that she had brought to take notes of who had volunteered for what. She had already assiduously written down that the Mothers' Union en masse had volunteered to organize a cake bake. Muriel would chair the first committee meeting to plan it next week.

A desiccated, bespectacled man volunteered to manage correspondence with the Local Education Authority, including the delivering of the petition against the merger with Latchfield. Murmurs of approval throughout the hall greeted this news, and those sitting on either side patted him on the back.

Gabriel touched Imogen on the arm, making her start violently.

"That's Mr. Fielding, the solicitor," he said, regarding her strangely.

"Yep. Right," replied Imogen in a whisper, trying to sound alert and efficient.

"So, you might want to write it down, then," he continued, pointing at the paper.

"Right," said Imogen again, blushing and bending her head to the page.

After that, she drifted off a little, lulled by the warmth and the drone of voices as they talked back and forward about the best approach to take with the Education Authority.

Dreamily twiddling a lock of hair with her Biro, perusing in her head the sketches she had done that morning for a new Tango and Ruth storyline, Imogen suddenly realized Genny had said her name.

"It's just so brilliant we have all these people with the skills and the will to help," Genny was saying. "Imogen, who hasn't even been in the village for long, has really kindly promised to help us decorate the school with some brilliant new murals, haven't you, Imogen?"

Imogen nodded, tugging frantically where the pen had got snarled up in her hair.

"I know there are a couple of things Imogen needs, and also, you may not all know her by sight," Genny continued, not noticing the struggle. "Imogen, would you like to just introduce yourself?"

Giving the Biro a last abortive wrench, Imogen stood up and turned to face the crowd, Biro dangling just below her ear. She felt Gabriel and Louise looking up at her. She didn't dare to catch Gabriel's eye.

"Er, yes, hi, everyone, I'm Imogen, and I just thought it would be really nice to do some colorful murals in the school once we've finished the refurbishment. It should be good fun, and I hope lots of people will get involved." She shifted from foot to foot nervously. "We're going to need quite a lot of emulsion paint, doesn't matter what colors because we can tint them to get what we need. So, if anyone has any cans of emulsion left over that they don't need—pale colors are the most useful—it would be great to have them. Also, the more brushes we can get—all sizes—the more people can give me a hand if they'd like to," Imogen said with a shy smile, ducking her head and sitting down.

"That would be a great way to get the kids involved," said a voice.

"Don't talk stupid," said another. "They'd just mess it up, wouldn't they?"

"Not at all," replied Imogen, half standing up again. "I could easily do a sort of 'painting-by-numbers' system. It would be wonderful to have the children's help."

Imogen blew a sigh of relief when attention turned to the next matter on the agenda.

"I think you've lost an earring," hissed Gabriel, shoving another Biro at her. "At least, this looks like a match for the one on the left."

"Oh, ha ha," she muttered mirthlessly, finally managing to wrench the pen free and taking a chunk of her hair with it. She could see Louise out of the corner of her eye, smirking delightedly. "So, what do you think, Bill?" said Genny, looking hopefully at the builder raising his hand for attention.

Slowly, he got to his feet.

"Well, my love, from the look of this quote—and I'd have to see the job for myself—there's quite a bit of work to be done," he said. Genny's face fell.

"Yes, there is, of course . . ." she said sadly.

"Now, now, I'm not saying it can't be done, mind," he continued. "I'll tell you something, you can knock about fifteen grand off the materials costs, there's healthy profit built into this quote by the look of the quantities involved. No, with the discounts we can get for buying at trade prices, there's no need to worry about us taking profits on that."

Murmurs of support filled the hall, a buzz of optimism beginning tentatively to build.

"The other big cost is the labor, of course," he continued. "Now, we're going to need some skilled workers for this, but a heck of a lot is just humping and carrying. It'll be hard work, but if a few of the lads in the village don't mind workin' up a sweat, then I don't mind bossin' them about a bit. We can cut out a few thousand on that alone, and I can ask my own lads if they can give a bit of time for free in the evenings an' that."

"It all sounds absolutely wonderful, Bill," said Genny, her eyes beginning to shine with hope. "When do you think we can get things underway? Money allowing, of course."

"Oh, don't you worry about money up front, my love," said Bill. "If we can be startin' a bit of the groundwork as soon as the kids break up for the holidays—just a bit in the evenings, like—we can schedule the main stuff for the break between Christmas and the New Year, I reckon—that's always a dead time for us, see."

"Perfect," Genny breathed. "If we could get it done before the start of the new term . . ."

Bill held up a restraining hand. "That's assuming we can sort out the bodies to help," he said, looking expectantly around the hall.

Several of the men put up their hands, and Imogen noticed a lot of stern-faced women elbowing spouses to volunteer. Gabriel stood to see who was offering and fed names to Imogen for her list.

"And me, of course," he said finally when she got to the end.

"Didn't have you down as the bottom cleavage type," joked Imogen.

"Didn't have you down for the type that went weak at the knees at the first whiff of a bit of manly sweat."

"Well, I'm not, actually," said Imogen hastily. He obviously assumed she was flirting. Perish the thought.

"No, of course not, it's a pinstripe man that turns you on, isn't it? Just one hint of a city salary and an expense account, and you're anybody's, I should imagine—as long as he's called something like Jeremy or Rupert, and he's prepared to deal with everything, so you don't have to," said Gabriel, leaving Imogen breathlessly searching for a crushing reply as he wandered off to say something to Joan. She felt like she had been led into a silly flirting game and then immediately slapped sharply across the face for falling for it. That wasn't going to happen again. Gabriel was disappearing toward the rear of the hall now, his back view radiating his bad mood. Imogen was too far away to hear, but she noticed with irritation that both Muriel and Joan immediately simpered archly at him and that Louise was prowling beside him, deflecting anyone who got too close.

She wondered what the hell was eating him. Whatever it was, he seemed to think it was her fault. If this was the mood he was in, she was glad he had not mentioned offering any further driving lessons, despite his earlier promises. She sure as hell wasn't going to bring it up herself. And then she remembered his terrible loss when Annabel was drowned. It was hardly surprising he got down at times. And maybe his taking it out on her was a compliment of sorts. He felt comfortable enough to let out his feelings with her. Or something. Or maybe it was because he actually cared? No, that couldn't be it . . . If he wasn't making it obvious himself, then that Louise woman was clearly keen to communicate she had some sort of hold on him.

IN THE INTERESTS of discipline, Imogen stopped herself from calling Sally about the literary agent first thing. Instead, she stuck with her recently established routine. First was a bike ride to the village shop for milk, bread, and a newspaper. Then, it was back to the house to post something—anything—on her Insta. Usually shy about showing her artwork, she had—as a discipline—got into the habit of uploading her work, or perhaps a photo of her daily walk, to her @Storybook_Ending Instagram account every single morning without fail. She was now watching with amazement as the likes and followers climbed from one day to the next.

The truth of it was, social media made her feel exposed, and she hated carrying her phone everywhere, pinging away and destroying her concentration, so once she had posted in the morning, she generally switched it off. No wonder poor Sally had been complaining about her being incommunicado. Once the social media chore was done, Imogen would settle down to drawing and painting in the crooked little attic room next to her bedroom. Later she would have lunch, and the afternoon usually involved a walk.

Ruth and Tango had taken on an existence of their own,

occupying her thoughts throughout each day. They even gate-crashed her dreams with snatches of storylines and vivid, detailed images that made her want to grab her pad and pencil as soon as she woke.

Today, she was determined to finish a demanding double page of illustration, and when she finally laid down her brush, it was already two o'clock. After cheese on toast, Imogen even thought about delaying her call to Sally until the following day, keen as she was to set out on her walk without wasting more of the precious late autumn daylight. She could spend the time when she was walking mentally planning out the mural for the school. But then, realizing further prevaricating would make her look ungrateful for the trouble Sally had gone to, she put down her post-lunch coffee and reached for her phone.

 *Chapter Thirteen*

'm afraid Ms. Armitage is in a meeting," the secretary said briskly. "May I ask who is calling?"

"It's just Imogen, tell her," said Imogen.

"In connection with . . . ?" barked the secretary.

"Erm, I'm a friend," she added, remembering punishments meted out to her in the past for taking personal calls at the office.

"Imogen?"' parroted the secretary, clearly enunciating for an unseen audience.

There was a brief pause.

"Ah, yes, it appears Ms. Armitage has finished her meeting, I'll just put you through."

"Imo, honey! Where've you been?"

"Sorry! Busy, actually, you know how it is," said Imogen. "That Rottweiler you've got screening your calls is a bit fierce, isn't she?"

"God, yes, she scares the hell out of me, but she keeps the baying hordes off. My office has been transformed from Piccadilly Circus in the rush hour to a Zen temple of serenity and mindfulness."

"Sounds like hell," said Imogen, knowing perfectly well how much Sally thrived on chaos.

"Yeah, well, it's just one of the things that one must put up with when one attains the heights of senior management—like what one has," said Sally loftily if ungrammatically. "Anyhow, about that funny little guy I was telling you about. Hang on, I've got him on LinkedIn."

Imogen listened to an extended period of keyboard tapping.

"Here!" came Sally's voice triumphantly. "Now, it's not actually him, it's this woman he's in partnership with who's massive in children's publishing. Wait, there's a link . . . yeah, so it's Rowena Plummer-Jones. Ring a bell?"

"Actually, yes," said Imogen, in awe. "But she'll never take me on. I'd never dream—"

"Well, he said he can't—obviously—promise she'll take you on. She has to like your stuff. But, he said, call him before you submit, and he'll smooth the way."

"This is really very sweet of you," said Imogen, her heart pounding with nerves at the thought of laying herself open to scrutiny. Instagram was one thing, but having the temerity to send her portfolio to Rowena Plummer-Jones was something else.

"Not at all. I just can't bear the thought of you sitting in that lovely house piddling about with the odd bit of drawing when you could be slaving your guts out like me," said Sally uncharitably.

"Are you actually slaving, though?"

"Yup. At least, I thought I was being a thrusting, successful, high-powered businesswoman, but according to Alistair, I'm just another rat in the rat race and a neglectful mother too," she said lightheartedly, but unable to prevent the bitterness seeping through.

"I'm sure he didn't say exactly that."

"Maybe not exactly, but still," said Sally. "He said he'd love to see you, though. You should come up and stay sometime. It's tough finding friends he's prepared to be polite to, but he's always been fond of you, for some reason."

"I'd love to come," Imogen told her. "Maybe if this Rowena Plummer-Jones does actually agree to see me and my work, I'll be up sooner than you think."

"Well, make sure it's this side of Christmas, anyway," replied Sally, "God help us, that's not far away now—nightmare!"

Making whatever promises were required, mainly around eating properly, sleeping properly, not talking to strange men—which ruled out most of the men she knew in Middlemass— Imogen persuaded Sally to let her go on the promise she made the call straightaway.

Checking her watch again and looking at the fading light outside, Imogen dialed the number nervously.

She was fully expecting to have to, embarrassingly, remind him of his conversation with Sally, explain who she was, and then listen to him sighing and regretting having offered to help. She was relieved when he immediately said, "Ah, yes! Sally said you would be in touch—a very impressive woman. In every way," he added thoughtfully, as if to himself.

Imogen suppressed a smile. He was obviously another sucker for Sally's charms. Many times Imogen had watched

Sally use her considerable feminine powers to manipulate men, leaving them broken in her wake as soon as she got whatever business advantage she was after. Imogen couldn't imagine ever behaving like that. Of course, that was because—in her case—she doubted it would work.

Returning to her call, Imogen heard Quentin Barker-Williams—just the sort of name a literary agent should have—telling her something she could hardly dare to believe.

"Spoke to Rowena about you—she's the children's books specialist, you see. As you probably know, Barker-Williams and Todd is fully committed usually, but—as it happens—Rowena has just lost one of her authors to an archrival. She's spitting about it, of course," he mused, "but I expect they'll live to regret it. Obviously, we haven't seen all your work, but Sally steered me toward your Insta account, and I loved what I saw. A not unimpressive number of followers you have too, by the way. It all helps. We are both intrigued," he went on. "Rowena told me to tell you to speak to her PA about making an appointment with her for some time next week if you're free?"

He paused, waiting for a response that Imogen was too stunned to give.

"Is that all right?" he prompted.

"All right? It's amazing!" she crowed, her tongue finally unsticking as the brain caught up with the good news. "Yes, please," she added, more calmly.

"Great," Quentin said, sounding relieved to have discharged his responsibilities. "Well, I'll put you on to Rowena's secretary, and we look forward to seeing you soon."

Appointment booked for the following Tuesday, Imogen put down the phone and blew out her cheeks.

"What on earth did Sally say to him?" she asked Tango, causing him to lazily raise one eyelid. "Whatever it was, it could end up keeping you in that fancy gourmet food you insist on for a very long time."

Refusing to be impressed, Tango stretched languidly and then went back to sleep.

Imogen could not help a skip of excitement that turned out to be more of an elephantine thud now her pregnant belly dictated her center of gravity. Beaming inanely, she pulled on her coat and boots and headed out belatedly for her walk.

In her first few days at the house she had gathered up some bricks and stones and improvised a little step to help her climb over the wall into the field from the orchard. She was intrigued to discover, as she started her walk that afternoon, that someone had replaced the wobbly pile with a properly constructed wooden stile. It could only have been done for her to use. So, who was it that was watching over her?

Setting off in a daze, she fantasized about her meeting with Rowena for the first half mile. She would need to prepare a portfolio, a roundup of the work she had to show. There were an awful lot of possibilities, perhaps including the illustrated *Aesop's Fables* from forever ago, but eventually, she decided on the first fully illustrated Tango and Ruth story, plus the two further stories she had finished sketching out, even though only a few of the illustrations were fully drawn and colored. She chewed her lip anxiously.

Surely not having finished them wouldn't be a problem? She didn't want to waste the biggest break she had ever had.

Dismissing her preoccupations for now, Imogen stopped and took a deep breath, enjoying the rich, fungus smell of the recently plowed earth. She was on her favorite walk, a track that followed the perimeter wall of the estate, taking her through fields, skirting woodland of several acres that wrapped around the rear of the manor house, then back, eventually, through the woods and over the river to the cottage. She was walking around the edge of a field where she remembered wheat had been growing when she had first visited Middlemass, last spring with Nigel. It felt like a hundred years ago now as she plodded through the mud, already thinking of hot cups of tea and maybe buttered crumpets.

Reaching the brow of the hill, Imogen paused briefly to drink in the view. The early sunset was already flooding the skies with a wash of pink and orange streaks like hand-painted silk. Glancing at her watch, Imogen scolded herself for setting off on the longest route she knew—maybe not such a good idea after her delayed start. She should crack on. As soon as she entered the woodland on the narrowing path, the canopy of branches intensified the gloom of the fading daylight. Although she was still able to see ahead of her clearly enough, the shadows deepened and encroached ever closer. Pondering the wisdom of retracing her steps, she came to a little rabbit track she had noticed before. Knowing vaguely that it must cut through to the path in the valley below, saving probably about fifteen minutes' walk, she decided to give it a try. Her bump was starting to ache, and her legs were already tired and heavy. Plus she didn't much fancy stumbling into Gabriel or one of the other estate workers in the pitch-black, which was what would happen—knowing her luck—if she didn't get home before darkness fell. Also, she admitted to herself, she always felt a little like she was trespassing when she walked on the estate. That said, she reasoned, Storybook Cottage was sheltered, just inside the high brick estate walls that ran for miles around the perimeter. In her mind, that made them an extension of her own garden—at a push.

Groping ahead of her with both hands to save her eyes from the whippy low branches, Imogen soon found herself unable to discern the track beneath her feet. Instead, the steep incline was thickly covered with dead leaves over stones and treacherous tree roots that threatened to turn her ankles at every cautious step. Surely the path must be not far below. She pressed on, sliding down the steeper slopes on her bottom at times, sorry her inelegant and noisy approach was frightening the squirrels and rabbits she usually saw. Their presence was only indicated now by skittering, scurrying sounds all around her. At least she assumed it was squirrels.

A loud crack off to her left made her stop dead. Was it a deer breaking a branch? It was too loud, surely, she thought, her heart pounding as she peered into the shadows beneath the canopy of branches. Another crack, louder this time, followed hard by a bloodcurdling scream, set the hairs on the back of her neck crawling. Frozen, Imogen listened intently. It must be a fox, like the one she sometimes heard at night. They could sound like banshees, couldn't they? Staring wide-eyed into the gloom, Imogen listened with increasing confusion.

Then, a crashing sound much closer and coming closer still. She spun around toward it, catching her foot under a tree root and staggering forward with a tearing pain in her left ankle.

Next, a series of what felt like slaps on the chest. Spinning around, Imogen glimpsed a neon-bright plastic gun held below a terrible, screaming face before she crashed onto her back, all breath leaving her body as she hit the earth.

Hours seemed to pass. Imogen gazed at the sky, through a lacy canopy of branches. The birdsong had ceased. There was no sound beyond the ringing in her ears. This is what it must be like to die, she thought serenely. For some reason, fate has decreed that my life should end at the hands of a screeching madman rampaging through the Devon countryside with a pink plastic machine gun, mowing down everyone and everything in his wake. And that is completely fine. In a minute, I will look down and see my life's blood pumping out onto the ground. I have not breathed for what seems like hours, and I know now that I will never breathe again. This is not a problem. Dead people don't have to breathe.

Although, weirdly, her chest didn't hurt.

Eventually, she lifted her head a couple of inches and peered down at where the shots had landed. Bizarrely, her shabby green waxed jacket was covered, not with blood as she had expected in her worst imaginings, but with some strange, viscous substance that was bright, luminous yellow. Imogen winced at the appalling color. And then she winced again as the first wince sent a bolt of pain shooting up her left leg, reminding her that her ankle was still pinned by the tree root in a place it would not have chosen to be in relation to her now horizontal body.

"Rupert, you wanker!" hollered a voice to her left. "You've bloody gone and shot a peasant."

"Christ, so I have," the madman with the machine gun exclaimed mildly.

"Are you all right?" he inquired solicitously, but spoiled the effect by breaking into a loose-mouthed grin. "I really got you, didn't I?" he crowed, pointing at the luminous mess on her chest.

"You bloody idiot," said the voice that now presented itself as belonging to another young man, dark-haired and kitted out in the same combat gear as the first. "Everyone else has been dead for bloody hours. We're due back in the conference center in precisely eight minutes."

"Conference center . . . Debrief, eh? Yah, yah," said the lunatic excitedly. "Better crack on then, eh?" He shifted impatiently from foot to foot.

"Can you get up?" said Dark Hair to Imogen, holding out a hand.

"Yes, I . . . Ow!" she squeaked as her ankle violently objected to even the thought of movement. Imogen sank back again, biting her lip.

"I've really hurt my foot," she said, fighting not to sound as pathetic as she was beginning to feel. Remembering how far away from home she was, with the sky rapidly deepening to indigo and only two posh-boy idiots to assist, she felt impossibly daunted at the thought of the immediate future and close to tears.

Dark Hair looked perplexed and not a little bit irritated. "We'll lose automatically if we miss the return deadline," he said distractedly.

"You'll lose a bloody sight more than that if I ever see you on my land again," boomed a stern voice out of the darkness.

They all jumped violently, Imogen immediately regretting the answering stab of pain.

"Who the hell are you?" said Dark Hair.

"I might ask you the same question if I gave a damn about the answer. What I really want to know is what the bloody hell are you doing trashing my property?" said Gabriel, marching toward them and scowling thunderously.

Imogen was astonished. How was it that she should see him now? There she was, yet again, failing to be in command of the situation—and there he was to witness her indignity. She couldn't even fathom how he could have got so close without them hearing his approach. Surely he hadn't been trailing her? Standing with his back to the remaining light, he loomed above her, reassuringly solid but unnervingly cross.

"I might have known you'd get yourself involved in this idiocy," he snapped at her.

Relief was replaced with outrage at the injustice of it all. "What?" she said, affronted. "I'm out for a leisurely afternoon stroll when I get stalked and leapt upon by a khaki-clad idiot with a paint gun and splattered with gunge right here"—she indicated her chest area entirely unnecessarily—"and I've also really hurt my foot and now I can't walk and I don't know how I'm going to get home . . ." She trailed off, her voice beginning to crack. She was blowed if she was going to cry with Gabriel watching.

Kneeling in front of her, he threw her an exasperated look but examined her ankle, still trapped in the tree root, gently enough. Cutting through the root with a penknife and then through her laces, he eased off her boot.

"Ow, ow, ow," Imogen moaned through gritted teeth.

"You shouldn't walk on it," said Gabriel, feeling her already swelling ankle. "We'll have to carry you back to the Hall—it's nearer than Storybook Cottage."

"Look, I just want to go home," she muttered ungratefully.

"The Hall *is* home. It's my home. It's also where my car is, and—believe me—I'll be wanting to get rid of you soon enough, I'm too busy for all this nonsense."

"Righto—everything seems to be under control, so we'll be off, then," said Dark Hair hopefully, glancing pointedly at his watch.

"No, you won't," said Gabriel. "It'll take at least two of us to carry her over this terrain without jolting that ankle too much."

Crestfallen, the two gunmen fell into step, taking turns to link hands with Gabriel as Imogen clung embarrassed to their shoulders. Ungainly enough with her huge tummy obscuring her view of her own feet, she was made even clumsier by such awkward close proximity to Gabriel, who glowered indiscriminately at them all, occasionally stifling oaths as they stumbled over the uneven ground.

 *Chapter Fourteen*

Although it felt like forever, it only took around fifteen minutes for the strange little party to come across the path to the rear of Middlemass Hall. Eventually they were there, relieved to see the lights streaming comfortingly from the windows, illuminating the stable yard and throwing the surrounding woodland into pitch-blackness.

"Not that way," snapped Gabriel as Dark Hair made to follow the branch of the path that led to the Hall front, nearly unseating Imogen in the process.

"Stop here," he added, sliding Imogen gently to the ground, where she stood swaying on one foot as he grabbed a bunch of keys from his waxed jacket pocket. Selecting a large key from a bunch—even in the semidarkness Imogen could see it was a beautiful object, slim and elegant with an elaborate head of wrought iron in the shape of a clover leaf—he slipped it into the lock of an arched oak door set into the outer wall of the stable block and swung open the door into a room of echoing blackness.

"You had better push off now," he said over his shoulder to the two men, who looked relieved to make their escape.

"And I hope I never see your ugly mugs again," he added to their departing backs.

"Can you hop if I support you?" he said gently.

"I'll try," she said, keen to impress, although admittedly it was a bit late for that.

Leaning heavily on his arm and gritting her teeth, she half hopped, half lurched inside. Gabriel slammed the door with a clanging crash and reached behind him to flick a switch. As the interior flooded with dazzling, bright light, Imogen gasped. It was a huge space, only around twenty feet wide but perhaps sixty feet long, making up what looked like a whole wing of the old stables that Imogen had previously glimpsed in daylight—a quadrangle of two-story buildings enclosing a square cobbled yard.

Glancing down at the floor, Imogen saw that they were standing on flagstones, dark and slick with age. The ceiling was beamed, with great rough-carved and smoke-blackened oak studded here and there with giant iron hooks. And what was hanging on the hooks made Imogen gasp again. For dangling from the beams and resting on the long steel-topped bench along the wall was a mind-boggling selection of pincers and tongs, all blackened metal and fearsome-looking. Stacked in the corner was a pile of metal bars of all widths, and—most chilling of all—Imogen's eyes settled on a stained leather apron hung casually on the back of the door alongside a pair of thick black leather gloves with elbow-length gauntlets.

Panting with fear, Imogen assessed her situation. Here she was in the most chillingly well-stocked torture chamber she could have ever imagined. The door to freedom was closed, and her throbbing ankle meant that she could only hop—not a good mode of transport with an enormously swollen tummy. Weighing up the odds, though, flight was the only option. She took a deep breath and lunged for the door.

"Whoa, there! Steady!" said Gabriel, solicitously grabbing her elbow. "Where are you going? The stairs are over here, in case you thought I was just going to dump you on the floor of the forge."

Ah, thought Imogen, consciously slowing her breathing and looking again with new eyes. Forge. As in, blacksmith's forge. Relieved she hadn't made an even bigger idiot of herself and intrigued that she was in the space where he created the iron candlestick she had so admired at Simon's house, she relaxed. A little.

With her arm firmly tucked into his, he propelled her—hopping—to a narrow flight of wooden steps leaning against the rough brick wall, linking the workshop space to an upper floor. It was obviously once the hayloft or perhaps the grooms' quarters. The steps were too narrow for them to go up together. Gabriel paused, weighing the options.

"Up you come, then," he said, unexpectedly sweeping her off her feet and into his arms.

"No," she squeaked. "You'll strain your back. I weigh a ton."

"You're not kidding," puffed Gabriel ungallantly as he clumped up the stairs. Imogen was relieved when he dumped her—fairly gently—on a fat teal velvet sofa with generous feather cushions.

"Wow!" she said, gazing around. If the forge had taken her breath away for all the wrong reasons, this room did it for all the right ones. Acres of polished oak floor swept the length of the room, a lofty arched ceiling with bent oak beams dividing and supporting its structure like the hull of an upturned ship. Several large skylights along both sides of the roof framed a star-studded sky. The light now was supplied by dozens of low-voltage spotlights set almost invisibly into the beams, casting sunshine into every corner. The décor was restrained but luxurious, with thick wool rugs on the floor, a brick fireplace big enough for Imogen to stand upright in (if only she could stand at all), and yards and yards of books lining the walls.

"Hi, Simon, it's me . . ." she heard Gabriel saying on his mobile as he stood out of sight in the kitchen area at the far end of the room.

"So, you'd better come . . ." he continued. "Bloody idiot" and "yeah, you'd think so, wouldn't you?" were the only other phrases she caught during the brief call.

She tried to persuade herself the unflattering stuff referred to the two young men. Then she saw the set, irritated expression on his face when he returned.

"Sorry," she muttered.

"So you should be—charging around the estate in the dark in your condition."

The two of them sat in awkward silence for several minutes, waiting for Simon to arrive.

Imogen suddenly became aware that she had remembered no squirming and kicking from the baby. Surely the fall hadn't . . . Mind you, she reasoned, with all the excitement and the pain from her ankle, if the baby had turned somersaults, she might not have noticed. She lay very still and concentrated. A kickstart of caffeine would give the little one a bit of a jolt, she reckoned, hoping this apparent ability to sleep through chaos would continue after the birth. "I'd love some coffee," she said.

"I bet you would," he replied forbiddingly, but got up and went to the kitchen.

She heard cupboards opening, the fridge door, and a glass being put down on a hard surface. Downstairs the heavy oak door opened, and Imogen heard, with relief, the sound of someone running lightly up the stairs.

He and Simon arrived back at the sofa almost simultaneously.

"Imo, you poor old love," exclaimed Simon, "what have you been doing to yourself?"

Kneeling by her side, he took her foot in his hands, feeling gingerly around her now impressively puffy ankle that was already streaked an attractive shade of purple.

"Anywhere else hurt?"

"No. Ow!"

"Sorry."

"Ah, coffee," said Imogen sniffing appreciatively at the steam spiraling from the cafetière and trying to take her mind off the throbbing pain made worse by Simon's gentle manipulation.

"That's for Simon," said Gabriel bluntly, handing Imogen a tall glass of milk instead.

"And you'd better have one of these," he added, handing her a plate of obviously homemade chocolate chip cookies.

"I didn't have you down as a cookie man," she said.

"I'm not."

"Or a baker, actually."

"I'm not."

Fortunately, Simon interrupted this vibrant exchange. "I think you've got away without any serious damage," he said. "Basically, I'd be amazed if there are any broken bones, but it's a nasty sprain. You'll have to take it easy for a few days, keep off your feet, that sort of thing. How's the baby?" he added.

The blob, enlivened by the milk and cookies, launched into what felt like a brief flurry of running on the spot, topping it with a breathtaking uppercut to Imogen's left kidney.

"Fine," she gasped, tears pricking again at her eyes with relief at the unspoken fear being dispelled. "The thing about keeping off my feet might be a bit tricky, though," she added. "I'm planning a trip to London, seeing friends and stuff . . ." She didn't want to mention the literary agent—not before she had something to announce.

"Well, as long as the friends can help out a bit. I'll strap it up for you, make it a bit more comfortable. Genny was saying the other day that she'd love to see you, by the way. She's on half term at the moment, so why don't I ask her to come along and give you a hand getting packed?"

"That would be lovely."

"Good. Also, you might find it helpful to use a walking stick for a couple of days,"

"There should be one of my grandmother's sticks in Storybook Cottage somewhere," said Gabriel.

He was right. Imogen had a clear mental image of a

walking stick in a dusty alcove by the front door. Odd how the old lady still had a benign presence there in so many ways. Sometimes, fancifully, Imogen half expected to open a door and come across her perhaps reading the newspaper by the French windows in the sitting room or listening to an old-fashioned wireless in the little room Imogen had designated the study.

Her thoughts were interrupted by the rapid tip-tapping of female shoes on the stairs.

"Gabriel!" said a voice brightly, soon revealed as belonging to flippy-haired Louise. The one who was always flirting with Gabriel. Today, in work mode, she appeared with her hair in a smooth, professional-looking chignon and morning fresh makeup despite the late hour.

"And Dr. Simon too, how nice," she added, simpering in Simon's direction.

"And Imogen, I think you've met?" said Gabriel.

Her eyes settled on Imogen, and her face hardened. "I saw you at the village hall," she said. "So, this is the trespasser my clients were referring to."

"I'm afraid it is," said Gabriel. "What do you think we should do with her? Summary execution or just a hundred lashes?" As he spoke, he was pouring and adding milk to a mug of coffee, which she took from him with the barest acknowledgment of someone who was on intimate terms.

"How are the biscuits?" Louise said, with frank accusation, checking out Imogen's bulging cheeks and the scattering of crumbs on her lap.

"Not bad, thanks," she replied cheerily through a large

mouthful. So here was the phantom biscuit maker. With sinking stomach, Imogen began to understand why the once red-hot Imogen and Gabriel connection had lost its heat.

Instinctively disliking the woman, she also remembered the comments of Winifred Hutchinson. This must also be the woman in the red skirt suit who scuppered the holding of the village fête at the Hall by wanting to charge a huge fee for the use of the venue. Come to think of it, Joan and Muriel were banging on about a girl planning to get her claws into the lord of the manor, so . . . what? Did that mean Gabriel was the lord of the manor and this girl Louise was the "brazen hussy"? Surely not . . .

As the penny dropped, Imogen caught such a fearsomely hostile glare from Louise she wondered for a minute if she had spoken aloud.

Hers and Gabriel's was the steamy affair that never was. This woman was clearly the love interest in Gabriel's life. Of course, she was.

"Not too much damage done, then," Louise said tightly, watching Simon strap up the ankle.

"No, except that I saw my life flash before my eyes when your clients jumped out and shot me at point-blank range," said Imogen. "Lucky Gabriel came along when he did."

"You shouldn't have been there," replied Louise testily. "As *Lord* Havenbury will concur, it *is* trespassing—by the way, darling," she added sotto voce to Gabriel, "my guests mentioned you were a little abrupt with them. I am sure you didn't mean to be."

"I didn't," said Gabriel. "I meant to be a lot abrupt."

Louise looked put out for a moment, and then resumed her smooth demeanor with obvious difficulty.

"Actually, Louise, Imogen isn't a trespasser," Gabriel went on, "at least strictly speaking. She's the one who bought Storybook Cottage a few months ago."

"Oh, I see," said Louise grudgingly. Imogen could see Louise reluctantly adjusting her attitude to take into account this new, clearly unwelcome information, and then her face brightened. "Well, if that's the case, Gabriel, it would seem now is the perfect time for us to deal with this issue of—" Louise stopped mid-sentence.

Transferring her gaze to Gabriel, Imogen saw the reason why. He had a terrifying scowl on his face. "This is absolutely *not* the time," he ground out.

"As you will, my lord," she said stiffly, giving a little bow of the head in acknowledgment of the dressing down.

"Anyway," said Simon cheerfully, tying off the bandage with a neat bow, "that's you done. How about a lift home?"

Imogen gratefully accepted, suddenly keen to be alone to lick her wounds, both physical and—she admitted to herself—emotional. Louise clearly didn't regard Imogen as competition, and why would she? Being heavily pregnant and covered in bright yellow goo, she wasn't exactly the catch of the century. Especially to the lord of the manor. Fancy.

Her only regret around leaving was that Louise also looked tetchily relieved at Imogen's departure, settling down with Gabriel to drink the rest of the coffee with the barest of goodbyes to them both.

IMOGEN HAD TO admit Simon's bandaging had done a good job. The following morning, her ankle was only really painful if she tried to walk on it, and the swelling had definitely gone down a bit, she thought, examining it critically. It clearly wasn't broken, anyhow. Just a nuisance.

That was little consolation for an uncomfortable night. She had been relieved to see the blue dawn light soak through the curtains. Given how she was feeling—thick head and gritty eyes from lack of sleep, plus the additional mobility issues—making the late morning train to London for her meeting with Rowena was going to be a challenge.

Two laborious hours later, Imogen had just about managed to wash, dress, and get her suitcase down from the top of the wardrobe. Sitting disconsolately on the bed, she was seriously wondering how she was going to get through the day. Even with the walking stick, which Gabriel had reminded her about, the trip to London was looking extremely daunting. The practicalities of managing the stick, which took up a whole hand, as well as carrying her suitcase and portfolio looked impossible, let alone having to impress in a business meeting.

"Hellooo?" a voice came faintly from downstairs. After a brief series of yells to and fro, the owner of the voice clambered up the narrow attic stairs to Imogen's bedroom.

"Why do you sleep all the way up here?" said Genny, slightly breathlessly as she, at last, arrived.

"I like it," said Imogen simply, tilting her cheek to be kissed.

"Simon told me you might need a hand, poor you!" she exclaimed, cooing over the bandaged foot. "He dropped me off on the way to the surgery so I could help out—if you need me, that is."

"I totally do," said Imogen, relieved. "Didn't I lock the door last night, by the way?"

"Oh yes, you did, don't worry. I just got the key off Gabriel—didn't want you to have to stagger all the way to the door without needing to," replied Genny breezily. She didn't think it the slightest bit odd that Gabriel should apparently have access to the house at any time, Imogen noticed. Maybe she should change the locks.

"No school today, then?" Imogen inquired.

"Nope. Half term, thank goodness. And much needed, I might add, now we've had an entire half term without the head."

"Mrs. Marshall?"

Genny nodded. "She's really unwell. It's cancer, actually—don't tell anyone, most people don't know—it's not going too well, to be honest. It's really starting to look like she won't be working again, but the hope of coming back to the school gives her something to focus on, so no one has the heart to go out and recruit another head teacher."

"So, you're still acting head?" said Imogen.

"Yep. Still, it's good experience if I can survive it. Anyway, talking about careers, how is yours going?"

Imogen told her briefly about the important meeting with the publisher and waved off the confident assertions with a nervous grin.

It seemed no time until the bags had been efficiently packed and put by the front door. Genny even made them both some breakfast and left the washed plates draining by the sink. "It's awful to come back to a mess," she explained when Imogen thanked her yet again.

"How long will you be away, do you reckon?"

"The meeting's tomorrow, but I want to spend some time with Sally and her husband. Sally was a bit out of sorts when I saw her last."

Aren't we all? Imogen told herself, thinking first of her tetchy non-relationship with Gabriel and then of her apparent sham of a marriage with Nigel.

Genny nodded sympathetically. "Anyway, you'll be wanting to get off. I'll give Gabriel a call."

"No! Don't do that," exclaimed Imogen. "Why on earth would you do that?" Her voice rose as she remembered their uncomfortable encounter the previous evening.

Genny looked surprised. "Well, my car's at the garage having its MOT—otherwise I'd drive you myself. When I collected the key, Gabriel said he'd be happy to come over and give you a lift."

"I'd rather get a taxi, honestly," blurted Imogen. He had been pretty irritated with her last night, and she surprised herself with her reluctance to see or hear any more about that Louise woman.

"Don't be silly," said Genny. "He told me he was happy to do it, plus he mentioned he needed to see you about something—I forget what."

"That trust stuff, probably," said Imogen.

Genny looked inquiring.

"It's just something boring to do with the house, I've

no idea what. He mentioned I'd be getting a letter, but I haven't heard anything more. It's probably nothing. Anyway, I don't need to go for ages yet," she added, glancing at her watch.

"Pity, because here he is now," said Genny.

And she was right.

 *Chapter Fifteen*

Imogen looked up at Gabriel searchingly. He appeared cross again—also disheveled, and his eyes were puffy, as if he hadn't slept much. Obviously that snotty Louise had showed him a good time last night.

"How are you?" he asked, neutrally enough.

"Fine," she replied. It was no business of hers who he decided to spend the night with.

"So, you're a lord, then?" she blurted, for something to say.

"I am," he replied. "Actually, to be technical, I'm an earl."

"Not that it makes you a posh twit, or anything."

"God forbid," he said, one side of his mouth twitching up.

"I thought you were the caretaker or manager for the Hall or something."

"I am, in most senses of the word," he agreed wryly.

"So . . ." said Imogen, feeling that the conversation was not really going anywhere, "why are you insisting on giving me a lift? I could easily get a taxi."

"I need to speak to you."

Oh God. He was going to talk about his relationship with Louise, she thought. Apologize for kissing her, leading her on and stuff, probably beg her not to rock the boat.

"No, you don't," she insisted, urgently. After spending weeks longing for him to bring it up, she badly wanted to be excused from the conversation. She needed to play it cool. Play it cool, play it cool, she repeated to herself.

"I'm sorry, but I *do* need to speak to you." He sat down opposite her and leaned forward, his hands clasped loosely between his knees.

He took a deep breath. "How much do you know about the obligations the owner of Storybook Cottage has for repairs at the Hall?" he said.

What? thought Imogen, immediately disappointed now that it wasn't the other thing. "Storybook Cottage?" she repeated slowly, repositioning herself mentally with an effort. "What *should* I know? What obligations?"

"Your late husband carried out his own conveyancing, you mentioned?"

Imogen nodded nervously. "He insisted on it," she said. "He *was* a solicitor," she added, "although not actually a conveyer or conveyancer, whatever you call them."

"Sure," said Gabriel briskly, as if he had made up his mind about something. "Okay, well, I've been speaking to the trustees of the estate, and the deal is this. My grandmother lived in Storybook Cottage for a long time—more than forty years, actually—and even before then, it belonged to our family."

"Okay," said Imogen, trying to look alert, "like in Jane Austen and stuff. The widow moves to the storybook house to let the son take over the big house."

"Yeah, basically," Gabriel said slowly, "the problem is, the owner of Storybook Cottage, in purchasing the house, takes on an obligation to the estate. The onerous part in this case is that the estate can call on the Storybook Cottage owner to contribute to repairs."

"Okay," said Imogen. "But—asking a stupid question—are there repairs?"

"That's the trouble," said Gabriel, rubbing his face. "There are."

"How much?"

"Your share? For the foreseeable scheduled repairs?"

Imogen nodded, pleased her ankle meant that she was sitting down.

"About four hundred and sixty thousand pounds."

"No way!"

"Way, sadly," said Gabriel reluctantly. "Most of it is for the perimeter wall of the land surrounding the manor. There's six miles of it, and it needs repointing. Huge job."

She didn't doubt it.

"But how on earth—and, it has to be said, *why* on earth—should I find nearly half a million pounds to pay for it? I mean, you know I don't have it, right?"

She couldn't decide whether to laugh or cry. Such a huge and completely unobtainable sum was so beyond her reach it was laughable that they should even ask for it.

"How far would they—you—go to get it?" she said at last.

"That's beside the point," said Gabriel briskly, "because I'm doing everything I can to stop it."

"Oh?" she said, daring to hope.

"I was going to suggest we look through your original deeds, to see if there was any loophole we can use to get out of it."

"The other trustees?" interrupted Imogen.

"Yeah, there's six of us," said Gabriel.

"Well, you're actually the earl, or whatever?"

Gabriel nodded.

"Surely it's your choice whether or not you decide to bankrupt a pregnant widow for half a million quid?" She glared at Gabriel, aware that her chest was heaving like a romantic heroine but unable to stop it. Worse, as always in times of fury and stress, she felt tears springing to her eyes.

"Imogen, I—" He looked anguished.

"That's enough," barked Genny, simultaneously throwing Gabriel a fierce look and putting her arm around Imogen's shoulders. "Can't you see she's upset? And I'm not surprised," she added.

"Imogen," he said, desperately, "I don't want to put pressure on you—God forbid—but I can't just make this go away without your help. It's not just about us. If it was . . ." He shook his head helplessly. "I have family obligations. I wish I didn't. Anyhow, I am simply offering to look at the deeds with you to see where everyone stands, that's all—"

"You know what?" said Imogen, brushing the tears from her eyes angrily. "The last thing I want to do is show *you* the deeds. We are on different sides, aren't we? Not to put too fine a point on it, you're the enemy." Her voice broke on the last word.

"I'm sorry you feel like that about it," said Gabriel quietly.

"How else should I feel?" retorted Imogen. "And I have to say, a little less of the 'droit du seigneur' stuff, going around snogging all the women who fleetingly take your fancy, wouldn't do any harm either."

Imogen was vaguely aware of Genny looking aghast, staring at them both in turn. "Oh yes," Imogen continued, nodding at Genny to confirm that her supposition was correct. "I suppose you thought a little charm wouldn't go amiss," she ranted at Gabriel, "softening up the lonely old widow before you kick her in the teeth. I bet you could barely wait for me to arrive after you found out someone had actually been suckered into buying the house. You'll have been cracking open the champagne with your grasping girlfriend once you realized what a pushover I would be, without even a husband to fight it out with you. I bet you were both just laughing your heads off."

"Imogen," Gabriel implored, "that's not how it is." He reached out to her, but she brushed him off and staggered out of the kitchen, dragging her bag to his car, desperate to get away from him, the village, and even the house she had started to think of as home.

THE DRIVE TO the station was carried out in stony silence, with Imogen, in the front passenger seat, doing everything she could to physically distance herself from Gabriel. She was practically hanging out of the window. Genny was crouching in the back seat, doggedly making polite conversation—largely with herself. Imogen had thought about sneaking into the study before they left to see if she could lay her hands on the house purchase papers, but a) sneaking anywhere was difficult to pull off alongside the Long John Silver issues caused by the dodgy ankle, and b) she had suddenly remembered with immense relief that the papers were still lodged in the offices of Nigel's old law firm in London. At least there was no danger of him finding them in her absence. Seeing this new, apparently ruthless side of him, she wouldn't put snooping past him. With keys to the house, there would be nothing to stop him. No, she was going to fight him on this, and it never did any good to let the enemy see all your weapons.

In no time at all, Genny was loading Imogen and her bags into the waiting train and giving her a hasty, warm hug of farewell.

"Take care," she said, looking intensely at Imogen, suddenly serious and older than her years.

"Tango!" screeched Imogen suddenly, making several people turn to stare at her oddly. "I'm such an appalling mother, I completely forgot about the cat," she explained to the puzzled Genny.

"Food and a cuddle twice a day?"

"Please!"

"Done. Now get on the train before it goes without you."

Exhausted by the unexpected emotion of the morning, Imogen amazed herself by falling into a deep slumber before the train even got to Didcot. She was embarrassed to have woken up from a limb-numbingly heavy sleep with her head on the shoulder of a formidable old lady with corrugated blue hair. She heaved herself upright, muttering an apology and checking for signs of dribble on the old lady's shoulder. Fortunately, there was nothing, but she knew there was still an excellent chance that she had both snored and slept with her mouth wide open.

Minutes later, they were pulling into Paddington Station, going from watery autumn sunlight to the gray, echoing spaces of the concourse. Imogen was relieved it was the end of the line. At least she had time to organize her luggage and her painful ankle without being whisked off to somewhere she didn't want to go. Better still, a kindly guard—who had obviously noticed her earlier—turned up specially to put out her bags and lend an arm to help her off the train. Once he had also fetched a luggage trolley for her, she had decided that with both hands now free to lean on the trolley, she could progress quite well. So well, in fact, she nearly cannoned into a skinny, dark-haired man who was standing by the ticket office with his back to her. As she executed a swift veer to the right to avoid him, he turned at the crucial moment.

"Alistair!" Imogen exclaimed, aborting her maneuver in her surprise and hacking painfully at his ankles.

"Imo!" he replied. "I thought you must have missed it—I was just looking to see when the next one was."

Ever the gentleman, Alistair refrained, with an almost invisible effort, from rubbing his ankles and instead leaned forward to give her a kiss on both cheeks.

"Sally sends her apologies. Some crisis at the office, apparently. Plus ça change."

"Thanks."

"'S okay. I wasn't doing anything." He smiled ruefully. "Actually—there's more. There's some do on tonight at work that she can't get out of, so I wondered if I could take you out to supper at Caro's?"

"That would be great," said Imogen, pleased. Caro's

was her favorite Wimbledon bistro, and Alistair was good company—although not in a paint-the-town-red sort of way.

THEY HAD JUST got back to Sally and Alistair's house, where Alistair had settled Imogen in the kitchen and put the kettle on, when there was a crash as the front door was flung open, followed by the thunder of feet along the hallway.

"Hi, Ed," said Imogen as a grubby schoolboy tumbled into the room. "How was school?"

"Rubbish!" he snorted. "We had double chemistry—yuck—and Tristan Parker told Mrs. Simkins I punched him."

"And did you?" asked Alistair.

"Well, yeah," he replied defensively. "He set fire to Mark's chemistry book, so we had to have a fight in the playground."

"Did you?"

"Yeah, course," Ed insisted. "'S okay, though, Dad, I totally thrashed him," he added, reassuringly.

Imogen stifled a giggle and turned away so she wouldn't catch Alistair's eye.

"I'm sure Mrs. Simkins will give me a blow-by-blow account when I come for sports day," said Alistair with resignation.

"Is Mum coming?"

"She'd like to, Ed, but she can't get away from work—you know that."

"She never can!" shouted Ed.

"Ed, come on—"

"No! Shut up! Shut up!" he yelled, crashing his way out of the kitchen and slamming the door.

Alistair and Imogen listened to the receding thunder of steps up the stairs, ended by the distant slamming of a door.

"Sorry," said Alistair.

The joys of being a parent, thought Imogen ruefully, stroking her bump. *And* she would be a single mum. Yikes. The almost impossible question of how to raise a child single-handedly whilst also earning a living, whilst also living in the middle of nowhere was ever-present in her mind these days. And that was before this latest challenge of magicking half a million pounds out of midair was presented to her on top of everything else. The stress of it all was giving her heartburn to go with the heartache whenever she thought of Gabriel.

WITH HER DEAD phone on charge, at least no one—including Gabriel—could contact her with any more bad news. Imogen got Alistair to bring her the landline phone so she could call Nigel's old office.

"Imogen!" said Richard. "How are you, my dear?"

"Very well," lied Imogen, and then she filled Richard in on key events since the funeral, not least the baby, plus the bombshell from Gabriel that morning.

"I'm sure everything is absolutely fine," Richard reassured her. "I'll get the property department to comb through the paperwork today. Let's meet for lunch later in the week—I'll get my secretary to give you a call. I am sure I will be able to put your mind at rest."

Imogen certainly hoped so. Richard was a kindly, avuncular soul, and lunch with him would be no hardship in return for peace of mind.

IMOGEN AND ALISTAIR chose a window seat at Caro's, and the horrors of the morning began to recede. She was ensconced on the curved, padded seat gazing out at the polished early evening theater crowd mingled with work-wilted office staff all scurrying past with umbrellas and collars turned up against the rain. She rejected Alistair's offer of even a small glass of wine and had soda water with lemon and tons of ice. It was so nicely chilled the condensation was already running down the outside of the glass, matching the drops streaming down the window. Her favorite slow-roasted pork belly with mashed potato and apple was on its way, and she had earmarked the chocolate fondant with salted caramel for pudding. She sighed with pleasure.

The chat between Imogen and Alistair was largely inconsequential. Imogen didn't have the heart to bring him down with her looming money disasters. Instead, they stuck with talking about the baby and the possibility of Imogen's lucky break into publishing.

"Children's books are where it's at," he told her encouragingly. "Getting books published for the adult market is too hard nowadays. Books for children are massive in comparison, especially if you get something that the grown-ups like too. Look at the whole *The Boy, the Mole, the Fox and the Horse*, for example."

"I love that stuff!" exclaimed Imogen. God, if she could somehow, miraculously, hit on some success like that, maybe Gabriel's revelations wouldn't be so disastrous after all. But it would never happen.

"I could never . . ." she said, spooning up the last mouthful of her pudding with a sigh.

"Why not?" challenged Alistair.

Maybe he was right, thought Imogen. Certainly, her Instagram followers—who were presumably adult—seemed quite keen on her stuff. She smiled at Alistair. He was such a lovely man.

Later, over coffee, he became nervous, twitching little bits off the wrapper from the amaretto biscuits that had arrived in the saucers and rolling it into little balls.

Imogen waited.

"You know that Sally told me about the other woman, right?" he asked.

Her heart flip-flopped. After stuffing the letter in the pocket of her briefcase, she had successfully managed to push "the other woman" to the recesses of her mind in the box marked "To Be Examined Only When Feeling Strong." Which wasn't now.

"We don't know if that's what it was," she said.

"True," Alistair replied enthusiastically. "We don't, and personally I think it's pretty unlikely given that Nigel . . . er . . ."

"What?"

"Well, he just didn't seem the type. I mean, he was a muppet, but . . . Sorry."

"I sort of know what you mean," said Imogen. "But it does look like he cheated on me, and—" Weighing her words, she added slowly, "I think I want to know why."

He nodded. "Sally thought you would. What do you have to go on?"

"A love letter," said Imogen. "Lots of gushy stuff about feeling like they've known each other all their lives and then a bit about not being able to wait until he can introduce her to friends and family."

She felt a surge of anger at the last, in no doubt that it referred to Nigel removing her from the equation before bringing in the replacement.

"Names? Addresses?" Alistair prompted.

"A first name and half the address, a street name but no house number or postcode."

"Right. Well, there's this woman I met."

Imogen nodded, and Alistair continued, emboldened.

"She's a private investigator."

"Sally said," confirmed Imogen, intrigued.

"Not that I had anything personally for her to investigate, you understand," he explained hurriedly, noting Imogen's expression. "No—it was for a story I was looking at doing, on gangland crime. Turns out the police might sometimes use PIs as an easy way of going undercover to gather intelligence on people they suspect."

"Seriously? Do they really?"

"Don't know, actually," he admitted. "I suspected so but never really managed to nail the evidence, so I had to drop the story in the end. Anyway, this woman was pretty impressive. Mind like a steel trap—and discreet isn't the word," he added with the faintest hint of pique.

"So, you think I should contact her?" said Imogen, nervous at the prospect of discovering more.

"Yes, I do," said Alistair firmly. "I'll give you her number, and you can arrange a meeting with her before you go back to Devon."

 *Chapter Sixteen*

Rowena Plummer-Jones swept into the cramped office like a ship in full sail, an impression created by her formidable size and by a dress sense that relied heavily on the more-is-more school of thought. She wore an Orla Kiely print skirt with a purple—what looked like Monsoon—blouse worn loose and liberally adorned with a collection of heavy chains and pendants. The whole towering confection was accessorized with a velvet devoré scarf. She boomed a welcome to Imogen, who was sitting nervously at the desk, clutching her portfolio on her knee.

After placing orders for coffee and tea with an invisible and silent person in the other room, Rowena sat down with a gusty sigh, crossing her ankles and drawing attention to feet that Imogen noticed were surprisingly small and delicate.

"So, why am I spending my precious time seeing you, then?" she inquired bluntly.

"Er . . ." For a moment Imogen actually had no idea why, and she almost decided that perhaps the best thing would be to just quietly leave now.

"M-my friend Sally spoke to your colleague," she eventually blurted.

"Ah yes, so she did," Rowena recalled, warming slightly. "And very persuasive she was too, by all accounts. You're lucky to have friends like that."

"I am," agreed Imogen humbly.

"Come on, then. I think I saw a couple of bits that looked vaguely promising on your Insta account, didn't I? Let's have a look at what you've got."

Taking the portfolio from Imogen, she laid it on the desk, undoing the tapes and opening it with confident care.

Imogen had planned the order of her work with great thought, deciding to warm up with a few conceptual sketches, including a few of her greeting card designs, and then hitting her with the book illustrations. She had been working well since the summer and had a whole Tango and Ruth story fully illustrated with the text as well, plus sketches and outlines for another two.

Barely breathing at first, and then with deflated gloom, she saw Rowena flick peremptorily through the initial work, laying it all to one side with barely a glance. Eyes alighting on the Tango and Ruth cover illustration, she slowed.

"Now, this is interesting," she muttered to herself, carefully leafing through the pages, scanning the text Imogen had written on acetate and taped carefully over the artwork, the old-fashioned method to avoid writing on the drawings themselves, pausing and chuckling—Imogen was pleased to see—at the little visual jokes and whimsical detail. On one page there was a tiny mouse, spiriting away a chunk of meat from Tango's bowl while he snoozed, oblivious. On a later page there was a hedgehog with leaves skewered on its spines trailing to bed with cocoa and nightcap while Tango and Ruth played in the autumn garden.

Reaching the end of the fully illustrated story, Rowena paid nearly equal attention to the pencil sketches Imogen had done to map out the second story. Finishing her appraisal, she reassembled the papers and folded the portfolio, tying the tapes and settling it squarely on the tabletop before resuming her seat.

"You don't work digitally?" she inquired.

Crestfallen, Imogen admitted she did not. "I can't," she said. "I don't know why . . ." So that was that, then. Everyone worked in digital nowadays. And the software was amazing. Imogen had played with it in wonder when she had the chance. What she had not done was ever successfully use it to produce any artwork that came from her heart. The disconnect was profound. It was pencil or paintbrush to paper, and that was it. What a shame Rowena didn't know that before they met. It would have saved Imogen the trip to London and the exquisite anguish of hope.

Preceded by a timid knock, the door opened. A mousey secretary came gingerly into the office with a loaded tray.

Waiting for the girl to leave and then pouring, adding cream, and offering biscuits to Imogen, it was a tantalizing minute or two until Rowena was comfortably settled once again.

"Well," she said, her disdain over Imogen's working methods apparently forgotten, "I have to say, my dear, your friend was absolutely right about my needing to see you."

Imogen raised her head and started to feel a stirring of optimism.

"Obviously, the only thing of interest to me is the book, which is excellent. The writing is not up to standard, of course."

Imogen's crest plummeted once more.

"But that doesn't matter," Rowena continued. "The publisher I have in mind for you has several good writers on their books, and I even represent someone myself who would also do a superb job. The illustrations, on the other hand, are wonderful. Perfect for seducing the parents." She noted Imogen's puzzled look. "It's the parents who spend the money, my dear. What you have is a marvelous life and vivacity about your drawings that will appeal to the children, but there is a rarely seen wit and nostalgia that the parents will appreciate, and frankly, that is the vital ingredient as far as the publishers are concerned.

"You also have some strong and attractive main characters, offering good spin-off merchandising opportunities, but that's a bridge too far at the moment. Suffice to say that I am prepared to represent you as your agent if that is what you would like."

Rowena finished and met Imogen's eyes, which were squinting slightly as, slack-jawed, she processed the information she had just heard, unable to immediately make the move from the rejection mode she had been preparing for to really-happening-after-all-these-years mode. It was an entirely new and exhilarating experience.

"Would you like me to be your agent?" Rowena inquired, articulating slowly and clearly.

Imogen nodded furiously, still unable to speak.

"Good." Rowena paused, still looking askance at Imogen's

vacant expression. "Right. Well, far be it from me to hurry you, but I understand you don't live in London, so might I suggest you have a look at our standard contract with a view to signing it now so I can get cracking?"

After that, Imogen enjoyed herself hugely. The timid secretary brought in a surprisingly brief contract detailing the rights and responsibilities of both agent and client in, thankfully, straightforward English, and Rowena left her to peruse it over tea and delicious chocolate biscuits. Eventually, Imogen signed with a flourish and shook hands with Rowena, who she had decided was just as intimidating as ever, but—as the Rottweiler working on her behalf—the scary manner was much to be valued.

Not even waiting for Imogen to leave, she was on the telephone.

"Lionel? Rowena," Imogen heard her boom. "Yes, yes, fine, thanks. Now, I have got an absolute treasure for you. I totally guarantee you're going to be thrilled . . ."

"FANTASTIC!" WAS SALLY'S response when Imogen broke the good news over lunch around the corner from Sally's office. "I knew you'd do it. So, it's only a matter of time before my entry ticket to smart parties is telling people I know you," she crowed.

"Dunno about that. I'm not sure children's book illustrators are of much interest to people who throw smart parties," muttered Imogen, absurdly pleased all the same.

"Don't you believe it. Getting anything published is terrifically smart, even children's books—especially children's books, in fact. It's even better if you hardly get any money to start with 'cause that way you can say you're doing it for the artistic satisfaction and then later, when you get hugely rich, you can point to your earlier career and look really unmaterialistic. It's the only way to be nouveau riche nowadays."

"What—sort of accidentally?" said Imogen, fascinated.

"Exactly. It's incredibly uncool to have just won the lottery or even to have been a ruthless businessperson, working twenty-four hours a day and killing every competitor in your path—it's just so passé to actually want to be rich.

"'Course, being privileged from birth is frowned upon too," she added, making Imogen wonder how anyone could be acceptably affluent. Certainly not Gabriel, with all his inherited privilege. But she frankly didn't care how it looked. Thanks to her devastating conversation with Gabriel, she had recently become extremely interested in money.

She decided not to share her worries about whether Storybook Cottage deeds could rob her of everything she owned. The concept of low-income living was great as a theoretical lifestyle choice, but for Imogen it could soon be all too real, unless her meeting with Richard the next day went well.

"YEAH, I REMEMBER 'im," said the raspy, south London voice on the telephone. "Nice bloke. Bit simple, though, bless him—thought I was gonna give 'im a story on a plate as if I didn't 'ave anyfink to lose. Like my life." She chuckled, and Imogen joined in nervously.

Although Alistair had told her his private investigator contact was the link with a London gangland story, Imogen was still taken aback and nervous as she quickly outlined why she needed help.

"You'd better show me this letter, then, love. 'Ow about early next week?"

Imogen admitted apologetically that she was planning to leave London the next day, fully expecting to be told to get lost.

"You'd better come over now, then, 'adn't you?" the voice responded, giving practiced directions and telling her to hurry. "Only I'm meeting my Harry down the boozer at six, and he don't take kindly to bein' kept waiting."

GETTING OFF THE Tube at Shadwell, Imogen made a mental note to be safely back on the train before night descended. Even in daylight, the main street was bleak and gray, graffiti offering the only splash of color in the concrete landscape. A free newspaper, whipped up by the wind, tried to wrap itself around her legs as she walked. Remembering a Substack she had once read on how not to be mugged, she was consciously walking with confidence and purpose, head up and brisk, hoping the directions in her head would prevent her from needing to resort to Google Maps. According to the Substack article, walking alone peering at your phone was a real mug-me-now signal.

Soon, though, she arrived at a peeling, blue-painted door, squeezed between a betting shop and curry house. Its reputation for good cuisine was hardly heightened by what looked suspiciously like a vomit stain on the pavement outside it.

After pressing on a grubby intercom button over a sign

on the doorpost announcing *G. Mitchell PI*, Imogen was admitted with an answering buzzer by a silent inhabitant. She climbed steep stairs covered in a stained and odorous gray carpet, the marks of hundreds of grubby fingers streaking the long-ago-painted-magnolia walls. She arrived at a frosted glass door and rapped timidly.

"Come in," said a distant voice—the voice she recognized from the telephone conversation.

The office was narrow and dark, carved from just part of the original Victorian room. The insensitive partitioning had left a ceiling that was disproportionately high, with coving around just the original perimeter. Two gray filing cabinets flanked an ugly wooden desk. On it the ashtray filled with lipstick-stained butts partly explained the dinginess of the net curtain at the window. The fumes of the incessant traffic below explained the rest.

"Well, sit down, then, love," said the voice, this time attached to a body that bustled through from a dark and gloomy kitchen area. A cerise pink twinset, coupled with brassy blond hair, elaborately coiled and sprayed, completed the impression of faded 1970s glamour.

"I'm Gloria," she said. "Gloria Martin."

She held out a red-taloned hand, knuckles encrusted with rings. Imogen shook it nervously.

Gesturing to an upright chair opposite her desk, Gloria settled herself on the other side and whisked a packet of cigarettes and lighter out of a drawer.

Extracting one, lighting it, and chucking down the pack in a practiced gesture, she took a deep drag and then exhaled, watching Imogen appraisingly all the while.

"So," she said at last, "man trouble, is it?" Her gaze drifted down, lingering on Imogen's swollen belly.

"My husband," said Imogen, handing over the letter from the mystery blonde. Gloria read it, holding the page at arm's length either through long-sightedness or distaste at its contents.

"I take it you want 'im caught on the job, then. Covert surveillance, photo evidence, record of movements, that sort o' fing—give you what you need to divorce him and bury him," she said briskly, looking at Imogen for agreement.

"Um, well, actually, the burying bit's already sorted."

Gloria's eyebrows rose.

"Which means it's a little late for the surveillance bit—although it sounds very good," she added encouragingly.

"This his?" said Gloria, gesturing with her cigarette at Imogen's tummy.

Imogen nodded.

"Killed 'im, did ja?"

"No!"

"Get someone else to do it for you, did ja?"

"Absolutely not," said Imogen firmly. One heard about this sort of thing, she thought, her mind racing, East End gangs and hit men, contract killers propping up the bar in the local pub. This woman was so damned matter-of-fact about it all . . .

"Awright, love, listen," said Gloria, leaning forward on her elbow. "You don't wanna spend the rest of your life all chewed up about this bloke, right? Forget 'im. He's not worf it." She chucked the letter down on the desk between them.

"Take it from me, if there's one fing you can rely on, it's that all men are bastards." She paused reflectively. "And most of 'em are useless tits an' all," she added with some sorrow that spoke of much direct experience.

"So," said Imogen slowly, "you won't help?"

"Can't help love, not won't," Gloria explained. "Catching people on the job is what I do. Can't see meself coming up with much watching a gravestone. It's not as if he's up to any of his old tricks now, is he?"

Imogen nodded reluctantly. The silence stretched between them.

"Look," said Gloria at last, "d'ya want to see 'er? Is that it?"

"I suppose I do," agreed Imogen. "I just want to know who she is. Does she look like me? Sound like me? It's the only way . . . I want to understand . . ."

Gloria sighed, folding the letter and tucking it into her capacious bra. "Awright, darlin'. I'll be in touch."

"Great!" said Imogen, brightening. "How about money? I could pay now," she said, bending to rummage in her bag.

"Nah, 'ave this one on me, darlin'," Gloria replied, taking another world-weary look at Imogen's tummy.

 *Chapter Seventeen*

mogen slept badly, her dreams racked with nightmares of Nigel and a blond woman whose face she couldn't see frolicking in bed together. She covered her eyes, but when she looked again, Nigel and his lover had gone, replaced by Gabriel and Louise. The bed was unfamiliar but the setting, bizarrely, was the main bedroom at Storybook Cottage. In between fondling each other, they were laughing and waving handfuls of money at her in return for what she was holding. Looking down to see what they wanted her to give them, she was horrified to see she had a tiny baby in her arms.

RICHARD HAD CHOSEN his club as the venue for their lunch. When Imogen arrived, exhausted, she was escorted into the dining room, where he was already seated, with a stranger, at a table for four. He was waving a glass of what looked like scotch and was speaking in an overloud voice, apparently telling a joke. Jumping to his feet, he welcomed her solicitously.

Imogen, my dear," he said, kissing her on both cheeks. "Do let me introduce you to Duncan Grant from our property department."

Duncan was a skinny, nervous-looking man in his fifties, and his handshake was unpleasantly damp.

Imogen dared not bring up the reason for their meeting until Richard acknowledged it. This he finally did, once lunch was ordered and wine poured.

He cleared his throat and looked serious. "Imogen, I've asked Duncan to examine the deeds for Storybook Cottage and have obviously told him everything I know about this claim you described on the phone. I'm afraid this is not a subject with a swift and sure resolution."

Imogen's heart sank.

"I suspected as much, Richard," she said. "Perhaps, Duncan, you could tell me where I stand?"

"Gladly," said Duncan, although he looked anything but.

"They have a claim, don't they?" said Imogen, reading his expression.

He nodded, flushing. "I'm afraid they do."

"So, this isn't good, then, basically," said Imogen.

"Er, not brilliant," agreed Duncan. "Then," he continued, "I was looking to see whether such a risk had been insured against."

"You can take out insurance?"

"Oh, yes," he said. "It's quite common."

"Did Nigel take out insurance?" asked Imogen, knowing the answer.

"Nope. I'm afraid not. Although, even if he had, it probably wouldn't have met the requirements for a claim once the company had examined the deeds for themselves."

"Right," she said bitterly. "In other words, Nigel should have known."

"Er, well—yes, basically."

At that moment, Imogen hated her dead husband. The man had obsessed boringly about every other detail of his life, requiring Imogen to match his socks, iron his shirts, and ensure a constant supply of his favorite breakfast cereal, but—when it actually counted, when an error would be utterly catastrophic—he had been criminally careless. It seemed a screaming injustice that he would not even be punished for his ineptitude but that, instead, Imogen had to face this impossible situation on her own.

She squared her shoulders.

"What are my options?" she asked the two men, who were looking at her anxiously. "Can I contest the claim?"

"Legally, this sort of thing is still a bit hazy," admitted Richard.

"Also, any sort of legal action is going to require pretty deep pockets." He gave Imogen an inquiring look, which enraged her.

"If I had deep pockets," she retorted, "being asked to pay for repairs would hardly be such a disaster, would it?"

He nodded, head bowed.

Imogen's rage abated and was replaced quickly with guilt. "I'm so sorry, Richard," she said, thinking she would never have spoken to him so directly when he was Nigel's boss. "You are all being enormously kind. I can't thank you enough for giving me your advice."

"My dear," he replied. "Anything we can do, you know that."

Bunging me half a million quid wouldn't go amiss, she thought.

"Thank you," she said again. "And, talking of advice, what on earth do you suggest I do?"

Richard and Duncan sighed in tandem, neither keen to volunteer, it seemed.

"The only money I have is in the house," mused Imogen aloud. "I suppose I could sell . . ."

Duncan and Richard glanced at one another and then both looked at her miserably.

"Oh, bloody hell, what?" said Imogen.

"Well, the value of any house is always a bit of a 'movable feast,'" ventured Duncan timidly, pausing for Imogen to catch up with his reasoning.

"You mean it's worthless?" she asked bleakly.

Both men lowered their eyes.

"It's worthless," she repeated, and let out a shaky sigh, patting her bump absently, more to comfort herself than a baby who was entirely unaware she was going to be born to a woman with nothing. Literally nothing. Not even a roof over her head.

"Although you could hope a buyer would accidentally overlook the clause?" suggested Duncan.

"Not ethical," said Imogen firmly. And not flipping likely, anyway, she added silently to herself.

"Any other thoughts?" she asked the two men.

"Well," said Richard at last, "I suppose you could always go back to this earl chap and beg."

ON THE WAY back to Alistair and Sally's house, her mind churning over what Richard and Duncan had said, she nearly missed the sound of a text coming in. It was an unknown number and simply said: *Victoria Harris, 23c Ifield Road, Chelsea. Good luck.*

At supper with Sally that evening, she let her old friend wang on about the trials of work and motherhood. It was easier to listen—or, at least, half listen—than it was to try and put into words the turmoil she was feeling. It had been a hell of a day, all right. And she couldn't even have a glass of wine.

THE BIRDS HAD mainly migrated now—there were fewer in London, anyway—and Imogen felt a pang of sadness at a dawn chorus of traffic noise instead. After lying there uncomfortably for half an hour, she got up, tiptoeing to the bathroom for a shower. Pulling on comfortable clothes and deciding not to bother brushing her hair, it was only fifteen minutes later she was sitting at the kitchen table with a cup of tea, gazing out across Sally and Alistair's perfectly manicured London garden. A pair of clipped bay trees stood sentry over the tiny circular lawn. The absence of color— "Actual flowers are sooo last season, darling," Sally's garden designer had said—and the preference for heavy evergreen shrubs over more ephemeral beauties gave the garden a funereal look. The mist of rain and dew graying the outlines made the end of the small garden seem further away, and yet the effect was a cheat, like a stage set.

Imogen found herself wishing fiercely for the orchard at Storybook Cottage, where the grass grew shaggy and wild at the base of the gnarled fruit trees, the meadow studded with wildflowers in the summer adding an impressionist haze of floating color.

Today she would go back home—for as long as she could call it that. But first, there was something she had to do. Taking out her phone, she looked again at the text from her kind private investigator. The mystery of this Victoria who meant so much to Nigel was within her grasp.

JUST HALF AN hour later, Imogen was sitting on a low wall in Chelsea, pretending to wait for a bus midway down Ifield Road. From where she was sitting, she could see number twenty-three, a high, narrow town house converted into flats. The street was lined with expensive-looking cars, but the stucco on a few of the houses was shabby, dreary net curtains at some windows contrasting with elegant shutters at others.

Pretending to have an intense interest in an article in yesterday's *Evening Standard* about rising property prices, she covertly studied the street for activity.

By now it was just after eight o'clock. A businessman in irreproachably tailored pinstripes, rosy cheeked and perfectly shaved, tutted to see that his red Audi had been wedged in overnight by two other cars. She watched with amusement as he edged backward and forward, backward and forward, to ease his car out into the road, having about sixteen goes before accelerating bad-temperedly toward the junction. The lights were red, doubtless not improving his mood.

A bus came, and the short queue that had formed around Imogen got on. She stayed where she was, but no one seemed to notice.

She watched more openly now, newspaper folded on the

wall beside her, as office workers went past, mainly with heads down, intent on getting to the Tube station before the misting rain worsened to a downpour. Imogen considered them all, feeling safe to disregard the men but studying all females. Who was Victoria? Was it this mousey twentysomething with cheap shoes and a too-thin raincoat? Or this fat-bottomed Sloane with her navy tailored trousers and velvet headband? Too old, surely? But then who would Nigel be interested in, anyway? She just didn't know. She wondered if the woman would look like her; from her avid consumption of tabloid newspapers—a habit Nigel had noisily disapproved of—she had often seen the staggering lack of imagination that led serial philanderers to get involved with a string of photofit women. It was as if the near-identical mistress was chosen to be a more accommodating, less jaded version of the original model. On the other hand, why would Imogen flatter herself? After all, he would hardly be looking for a duplicate of a woman he had no interest in being faithful to. And still they all trailed past, with just one woman challenging Imogen with a suspicious look.

A door next to her target house opened, and a harassed mother shepherded two primly dressed little girls down the steps to the street. They were wearing matching wool coats with velvet collars. She quickly gathered from the mother's clucking that they were called Henrietta and Hermione. She was amused to see the mother getting into the station wagon that had been blocking the businessman's Audi. It pulled noisily off toward the junction, and she could see the mother's mouth in constant motion, head half turned to her charges glumly sitting on the back seat. After it passed, she spied a woman on the pavement opposite. She had appeared in the short time the station wagon had blocked Imogen's sight, meaning she must have come from one of the houses nearby. That made her a contender. Imogen studied her closely. Shoulder-length, heavy blond hair, a neat figure in a navy skirt suit, perfect makeup, and—despite the gloom of the day—sunglasses. She checked left and right and then trotted across the road directly toward the bus shelter. Imogen stared at the woman, drinking in every detail. Then her heart crashed as the woman looked directly at her. Imogen did a classic comedy double take.

Victoria?

The utterance seemed to hang in the air between them. The woman's eyes slid past, and Imogen realized she had not spoken out loud. She felt sure this was the mystery blonde. As for that lurch of recognition. It was unmistakable. Visceral. And yet where could she have seen that face before? Frozen with shock and indecision, Imogen watched as the woman walked away, disappearing out of sight around the corner.

THE RAIN WAS falling heavy and monotonous by the time the taxi drew up outside Storybook Cottage. She waited for the driver to unload and carry her bag to the doorstep; obviously he was hoping for a fat tip. Imogen glanced guiltily at her little red Ford Fiesta. Her test was in just a few weeks, and she felt horribly unprepared. She still had a habit of glancing down to the pedals when she braked or changed gear. It was a futile gesture, especially now her belly was too big for her to see her feet anyhow. And she could hardly count on Gabriel to take her out practicing anymore. Not after their last conversation.

The taxi driver departed with his tip, and Imogen let herself in. Glad to be alone at last, she closed the door and leaned on it, tears pricking at her eyes. The house had an expectant air, an electric frisson in the atmosphere as if the telephone had, just that moment, stopped ringing.

She checked her mobile. It was flat and dead in her pocket. God knew how long it had been like that. She remembered Rowena insisted on taking her landline only, professing to hate mobiles. Chiding her superstition and half hoping her sixth sense was telling her the new London agent had been trying to contact her already, she grabbed the hall phone and dialed 1471. A local number had called much earlier in the day. Probably Genny checking if she was back or, more likely, Gabriel calling to complain about something she had done. Or even more probably—on the basis of recent history—to break some more appalling news.

There was a thud on the floor above, making Imogen jump. Then Tango trotted down the stairs toward her, yowling resentfully to distract her from the near certainty that he had been illicitly sleeping on her bed.

Unfortunately for him, bumping down the stairs made his mews come out jerky, and Imogen laughed, to his fury. He stalked ahead of her to the kitchen and stood whinging over his bowl until she filled it. Waiting until he was sure she was watching, he turned up his nose at the food and crashed through the cat flap into the rain.

Lulled by the drumming of the water on the roof, Imogen

stood in the kitchen waiting for the kettle to boil. Beans on toast for supper, followed by an early night—simple comforts seemed like untold luxuries after the highs and lows of the last few days.

Not entirely relaxing, though, were the implications of the curtain of water sluicing down from the roof past the kitchen window and spattering onto the stone path. Clearly a gutter was blocked. She thanked her lucky stars the kitchen was only a ground floor extension, since she knew she would have to clean it out.

NEXT AFTERNOON, WHEN the rain had stopped, Imogen dragged out the heavy old stepladder from the shed and tried it up against the kitchen wall for size. It was only just tall enough, and her big belly meant it had to go a bit further away from the wall than she would have liked, leaving her to lean precariously forward. Armed with a black plastic bucket, she got started and was amazed to discover that the gutter was filled to the brim with the black, rotting remnants of leaves from many autumns with the soggy cornflake remains of this year's crop in a layer on the top. Entertaining herself with a spirited rendition of the soprano line of the final quartet from *The Marriage of Figaro*, filling in the rest of the parts in her head, Imogen scooped and chucked handfuls of gunk with enthusiasm.

"What the hell do you call this?" roared a familiar voice, causing Imogen to sway and clutch the gutter for a moment. "Oh, Christ, don't fall off . . ." he added, grabbing her legs firmly.

"It's Mozart, actually." Imogen deliberately misunderstood

as she gazed down into Gabriel's ever-scowling face. Good God, it was rich that he always seemed furious with her. She had a lot more cause to be cross than him when you thought about it.

"That's not what I meant, as you well know," he replied. "Although I have to say, I've never heard it sung quite like that before." His mouth twitched into his familiar almost-smile. "Anyway, you'd better get down, for God's sake. I don't want you falling on your head and the village gossips saying I pushed you or something."

"They would? Why?" Imogen muttered to herself, picturing Joan and Muriel gassing in the village store.

"Because you're so annoying, obviously," replied Gabriel testily. "Now, get me some coffee, why don't you?"

By the time Imogen returned with the mug, which steamed like dry ice when it encountered the sharp autumn air, Gabriel had finished clearing out the gutter and was chucking the evil-looking sludge at the feet of the rosebushes.

"Good fertilizer," he said, taking the mug and handing back the bucket with a mock bow.

"That looks like a few years' worth of gunge."

"So?" he snapped.

"Well—I—obviously it hasn't been done for a while," she continued, "not surprisingly, given that an elderly lady lived here before."

"Not just any old lady," he said bleakly, "my grandmother."

"Ah, yes. It must have been nice for her having you so close."

"Mmm, well, I wasn't always on the spot."

Ah, guilt, she thought, the little voice that says, *I could have done more.*

"There's a few other jobs to do before winter, you know," he said as if he had heard her thoughts.

"The garden, yes, I know." She nodded guiltily, looking at drooping brown stems in the flower beds and tussocks of grass, still frost-rimed in the shade. There was obviously a velvet lawn there once, now shamefully neglected, to say nothing of the windfall fruit rotting on the ground in the orchard beyond.

"Don't waste your effort on the aesthetics," he said roughly. "I mean the important stuff. Come and look at this," he barked, marching toward the orchard.

Stopping on the little wooden bridge at the entrance to the orchard so suddenly that she almost cannoned into him, he pointed.

The stream was no longer the grass-lined bubbling brook of summer. After the heavy rain, the water rushed, red-brown with soil, in a torrent, the seething surface nearly reaching the underside of the bridge.

"See this?" Gabriel was pointing to the borders of the narrow gully made narrower still—Imogen noticed for the first time—by the copious growth of the hedgerow plants lining the bank.

"All this greenery has to be cleared away, or the stream will choke. It's fed by all the fields around here"—his arm swung comprehensively—"so it gets blocked, and the whole lot's under water in no time."

She nodded, wide-eyed. "It's almost a river, I hadn't noticed . . ."

"You're right. Basically, it's the river that comes out at Portneath," he said. "Or a tributary that feeds into it, anyhow. All this water is coming right off the moors. With the rain we've been having, it's going to come straight down and straight through. It's not interested in what's in its path."

She thought of the broad, serene river that ran alongside the road toward Portneath, just a couple of miles before it reached the sea.

"Wow," she said. "No wonder."

"I'll get a couple of the lads from the estate down to clear it out in the next week or so," he said briskly.

"No, you don't have to do that," she began, fed up with so very obviously being considered unable to look after herself.

"Yeah, I really do," he said shortly, giving her an unreadable look, and with that, the interview was over, it seemed. He handed back the mug with a nod of thanks and marched back across the orchard, lightly vaulting the stone wall, ignoring the recently built stile. She watched him go, loping across the fields to the manor, even his back view broadcasting negativity.

"Of course, you want to clear the stream," she said aloud to his departing back, although he was too far away to hear. "We must protect your assets, mustn't we?" She looked at him disappearing now into the forest, out of sight, with a painful yearning. And then she reminded herself Gabriel must have known about the clause when Storybook Cottage was put up for sale. Had he and the trustees been waiting and hoping someone would fall into their trap? Come to think of it, the house had been on the market for a while when she and Nigel saw it. Maybe they were the only ones stupid enough to buy it?

"Sod him," she said aloud, and went back inside, realizing that not only had neither of them mentioned the elephant in the room of their last conversation, he had not even asked about her trip to London. At the same time, she was relieved he had come. It was a perverse comfort to see they were still—apparently—on talking terms, even though the atmosphere was frosty. It would be worse—her heart whispered—to have to bear the thought of not seeing him at all, even though he was simultaneously the best and the worst thing that had ever happened to her.

 *Chapter Eighteen*

Feeling terrible about having left it so long, Imogen whipped up a batch of walnut-studded brownies and made the most of a brief cessation in the rain to drop in on Winifred with them.

"My dear, what a lovely surprise," said the older woman.

The two women settled in the neat, overcrowded little sitting room with tea and brownies still warm from the oven. Imogen was shocked at how much more gray and frail Winifred looked. It was poignant that there was no snoring, hairy lump of chestnut brown taking up all the space in front of the fire.

"I do miss the old boy," admitted Winifred, seeing Imogen looking. "I'm a silly old fool, but I only managed to steel myself to get rid of his bed, lead, and bowl last week."

"I'm so sorry," said Imogen. "I've been meaning to say—"

But Winifred wasn't interested in hearing Imogen's list of her own failures. "Ah, well, we must buck up," she announced. "It's nearly Christmas, after all, and there's such a lot to do, with cards and baking and—of course—all the volunteering with the school refurbishment. But enough about me, my dear, tell me about you!"

Imogen obediently told the story of her extraordinary breakthrough in Rowena's representation. Sensing Winifred was keen on distraction, she led her through the exciting developments. Imogen plastered on a happy face at the thought that Tango and Ruth were soon to be released on the world, if only Rowena would update her on what potential publishers were saying about her work.

"It all sounds so splendid, and yet . . . What is it that is troubling you, my dear?" said Winifred, fixing her with calm, all-seeing gray eyes. "You are far too miserable for a soon-to-be debut author with the world at her feet. Tell me, what is amiss?"

And so, Imogen did. As soon as she mentioned the obligation in the house deeds, the old woman's intelligent eyes focused sharply on her, and she went still.

"You know about this," said Imogen. It wasn't a question.

Winifred sighed. "Oh, my dear," she said. "It sounds like the Middlemass Hall curse strikes again."

Imogen inclined her head, urging Winifred to disclose what she clearly knew.

"My lovely friend Deirdre, sadly passed now," Winifred began. "She lived in the Old Rectory, you know the one? Old red-brick house with a huge, beautiful garden, just at the bottom of the hill that leads to Paddy's shop?"

Imogen nodded. "A barrister guy lives there with his family now?"

"That's right, well—until a couple of years ago—it was the home of Deirdre and her family. Her husband died eons ago, and her children are all grown-up—she was ninety when she died. The same as for you, there was a letter from the Middlemass estate demanding an unimaginable sum, just a few years ago. I blame that flibbertigibbet child, Louise, who is always demanding this and that, just because her company has some hiring agreement with the place."

Much as Imogen enjoyed hearing Louise being bitched about, she was keen for Winifred to get on with the story.

"So, anyway, Deirdre was terribly shocked, of course," Winifred went on. "She came from a good family—old money—and she wasn't poor, but she led a life of relative genteel poverty. The money she did have was mostly in the house. She certainly didn't have the kind of sum they were demanding just sloshing around in the bank. And—in any case—the expectation was that she was going to leave the house to her grandchildren, to give them a jolly good start in life, to pay for university and suchlike."

"So did she have to move out?"

"No," said Winifred decisively, causing Imogen's heart to give a little leap of hope, but then Winifred continued.

"She was in her late eighties before all this came up, and she had inherited the house from her own grandmother, raised all her children there, lived there for decades with her husband until he died . . . and darling Lord Havenbury made an agreement with her that she could continue to live in the house for the rest of her days," said Winifred, her eyes shining. "Wasn't that kind?"

"Very," said Imogen bitterly. She could think of lots of things to call it, but "kind" was not the first word to spring to mind. And Gabriel had so far made it quite clear the same accommodation was not to be extended to her. Even though Deirdre's family had only enjoyed what she wanted for herself, to be able to raise her child in that house, to make it her home forever. Albeit she was bound to live for longer, only being thirty-two to Deirdre's late eighties.

"So, what happened in the end?" she asked, hoping against hope for something she could take some comfort from.

"When Deirdre died—it was only a couple of years later—the house was sold to pay the debt to the Middlemass estate," explained Winifred gloomily.

"But it can't have been worth anything?" said Imogen, remembering Duncan's and Richard's gloomy faces when she proposed doing the same.

"I suppose not," said Winifred. "I don't know the detail, but I think Lord Havenbury came to an arrangement with them so it could happen."

"And the grandchildren?"

"They got a little something," conceded Winifred. "Not really enough to transform their lives as she had hoped. She would have been very distressed about that aspect of things."

"Do you think it's fair?"

"Would it make a difference if I did?" asked Winifred gently. "I have some sympathy for Lord Havenbury. It's not easy running these huge country estates. Society has changed so dramatically, really it's difficult to say what these enormous, expensively crumbling houses are for anymore. But blood is blood, isn't it?" she said, putting her head on one side and regarding Imogen sadly. "People will do anything for those they love, won't they?"

IN THE END, after days trapped in the house by torrential rain, watching the telephone crouching silently in the hall, and cursing Rowena's insistence on refusing her mobile number—although the signal was rubbish in the house anyway—Imogen nearly missed the call.

Nervous about her approaching driving test and horrified at the thought of being in a car with Gabriel again, she had booked a couple of emergency lessons with a kindly sounding local instructor called Trevor. Waddling out to greet him, because a waddle was required nowadays, she was inserting herself clumsily into the driving seat when a sound, or even just an echo of a sound, told her the telephone was ringing in the house.

Cursing, she apologized, extricated herself with difficulty, and galumphed back to the door at an almost run. Knowing for a fact that if it was just her mother she would be forced to drive to Surrey, driving license or no, and strangle her, Imogen grabbed the telephone.

"Imogen speaking," she said breathlessly.

"Rowena," boomed the voice at the other end.

"Oh, hi!" she squeaked, checking her reflection in the hall mirror and frantically smoothing hopelessly rain-frizzed hair as if the call were about to convert to Zoom.

"Hi," replied Rowena in kind, with faint sarcasm.

Imogen cringed.

"Good news, darling," she continued more warmly, "splendid, actually . . ." She paused for effect.

Imogen waited.

"I spoke to the usual crowd about you, obviously." She

reeled off a few imprints that Imogen had heard of. "But it was Tiger Books I really wanted for you . . ."

Imogen was unable to prevent herself giving a tiny squeal of excitement. Tiger Books was huge. She had submitted to them—un-agented, of course—years before and been rebuffed by an echoing silence.

Tiger Books was synonymous with most of the children's classic books. Her childhood bookshelves had groaned with the weight of them, and when the hugely successful pop star Angel had decided to write a children's story last year, it had been Tiger Books who scooped her up and hyped the truly execrable Curly the Caterpillar series with champagne launches and podcast interviews.

". . . so anyway, they agreed, of course," Rowena was saying.

"Sorry?"

"They agreed! Well, I say they agreed—they did more than that, actually. Far be it from me to blow my own trumpet"—at this Rowena laughed conspiratorially—"but I can't remember the last time I struck a keener deal."

"You are marvelous," responded Imogen fervently.

"Oh, I don't know about that, my dear," she replied with false deprecation. "Anyway, as I was saying, are you sitting down?"

"Yes, yes!" she lied impatiently.

"Well, they instantly took *Autumn in the Park*, but only if they can have one for spring, summer, and winter as well—a set of four just to launch with, my dear—I am sure I don't need to tell you this is quite exceptional for a new author. Of course, they want their own writer . . ."

Imogen's pang at the rejection of her own words was fleeting.

"And in fact, they already have someone looking at *Autumn*, although I did say I reserved the right for you to do your storyboard first, words second, for the others too. They seemed to find that perfectly acceptable. You really are a bit of a hot property, my dear!"

By this time, Imogen had sat down, sinking onto the hall chair and staring blankly ahead. After years of rejection and self-doubt, success was destabilizing. It was a disconcerting sensation of opening a familiar door into a familiar room only to discover that something quite astonishingly wonderful unexpectedly lay beyond. A slow smile crept across her face as she half listened to Rowena boom on about advances, launch marketing strategies, and revenue from overseas rights.

Eventually, noticing the still-open front door, Imogen gasped, "Trevor!"

"I beg your pardon, my dear?" replied Rowena, interrupted in midflow.

"I'm so sorry, Rowena, my poor driving instructor is waiting to give me a lesson, I really must go.

"Absolutely, and I think you had better start thinking about what car you would like to buy when you've passed your test. I have a very good feeling about this. In my estimation, Tango and Ruth are shaping up to be the new *Tiger Who Came to Tea*."

THE DRIVING LESSON was not one of Imogen's best. Trevor was sweet and kindly thrilled at her news. However, even he was impatient when she tried to pull away in reverse for the third time. And when she shocked herself by trying to go round a roundabout anticlockwise, causing a formidable lady driving a Land Rover to swerve onto the central island, Trevor asked Imogen to pull into the lay-by.

"On the whole, my love, you've got some good skills. You did a beautiful three-point turn earlier, and your hill starts are definitely improving, but we can't afford to be making mistakes like that, can we?" He smiled encouragingly.

Imogen hung her head.

"Don't worry. We'll get you through the test all right. I'm just a bit concerned that it's coming up so soon. We only have a few lessons, after all," he said, kindly ignoring the appalling display of attention deficit she had shown that day. "I don't need to tell you how much you'll need to be able to drive, living around here, once the little one arrives."

Imogen nodded dumbly.

"The main thing is to get you into your little Ford in between our lessons," he continued briskly. "I want you to find someone you can drive with for at least an hour every day from now until the test."

"Oh no," she groaned. Only one person had offered, and that was the man she now thought of as the devil incarnate. She couldn't ask Gabriel. She just couldn't.

"I WOULD ABSOLUTELY love to help, sweetheart," said Genny sympathetically later that day, "but I just don't know when we would do it. School is just ridiculous at the moment."

"How's it all going?" asked Imogen, ashamed that she was thinking of herself when this was all going on.

"Well, okayish, although this half of term we have to get through a huge amount of curriculum stuff, just in case we don't have all the facilities back after the Christmas refurbishment. Gabriel's been practicing driving with you, hasn't he?"

"I don't think driving lessons with Gabriel are good for the mental health at the moment. His or mine," said Imogen gloomily.

"Ah yes," said Genny. "The repairs clause. I can tell he's feeling really bad about it."

"That's a great comfort to know," said Imogen with a wry smile.

Genny sighed. "It's *so* tricky, though," she went on. "He is under a huge amount of pressure. I know the conference company who rent the Hall are really demanding. It's probably them who are insisting on the repairs. I mean, there's always stuff to do on an estate that big, but it's a case of waiting until there's the money to do it."

"If he gets what he wants from me, he'll certainly have a useful repair budget," said Imogen, unable to keep the bitterness out of her voice. "Given what you are saying about the conference company putting the pressure on, he's probably doing it to show off to his girlfriend."

"Louise?" Genny grimaced.

Imogen's stomach fell. Even if she hadn't admitted it to herself, referencing Gabriel's "girlfriend" had been fishing. And now Genny had confirmed her suspicions.

"Not anyone's favorite person," Genny was continuing. "It's weird how she seems to have some sort of a hold over him . . . She's got a nerve, being so brazen, don't you think?"

She looked at Imogen for backing. "There she is chucking herself at him, and let's face it, he could pretty much have anyone he wanted, after all."

"I actually thought he was a little bit fond of me," admitted Imogen.

There, she had said it.

"He is," said Genny. "I'm sure of it."

"I mean, obviously he treats me like a bit of an idiot—"

"Yeah, obviously," agreed Genny, a bit too readily in Imogen's view.

"But no, clearly money is what drives him," Imogen went on. "He would rather see me ruined and on the street than have his precious estate wall go another few years without repointing."

"I just can't believe Gabriel would do that," said Genny. "You should talk to him. Although he's in a funny mood at the moment. Now I think we know why."

In the end, Imogen had no choice but to swallow her pride and ask Gabriel to help her practice her driving. Now the worst of the situation was out in the open, he seemed keen to see her and certainly very keen to be helpful. It was probably guilt.

Out with him the following day, with neither of them acknowledging the elephant in the car, she was feeling pretty chipper about her driving, at least. Under his surprisingly calm instruction, she had even gone all the way to Exeter with him and buzzed confidently around mammoth roundabouts with multiple sets of traffic lights and more lanes than an American highway, as well as doing a series of competent hill starts on the fearsomely steep road out of Portneath. Tootling through the narrow, high-sided lanes that led back to Middlemass, she allowed her speed to rise to a carefree forty miles an hour. She swung around the final corner of the switchback into the village. Then she froze, eyes fixed on the sea of sheep filling the road in front of her. A millisecond later, she stamped hard on the brake and wrenched the wheel, sending the car into a sideways slide, taking her the remaining yards toward the nearest animals and stopping inches short of their noses.

Gabriel muttered furiously under his breath.

"Sorry," said Imogen, and then, just to make conversation, "Are they yours?"

"Yes," he said heavily. "Although funnily enough, it's not a good idea to plow a car into a flock of sheep, even if you don't have the owner sitting next to you."

Jumping out, Gabriel waved and shrugged placatingly at the shepherd on the far side of the dusty, milling river of bleating wool still filling the lane. He came around to the driver's side and opened Imogen's door.

"Out you get, then," he said impatiently. Imogen got.

He jumped in and restarted the stalled engine. Making to drive off, he looked with irritated surprise at Imogen standing hunched on the steep bank.

"Staying here?" he asked sarcastically.

Imogen scuttled around the back—the sheep were now filling the lane to the front of the car, jostling against the bonnet, spilling down the sides of the lane—and levered herself into the passenger seat.

Gabriel nodded curtly, put the car into gear, and rested his arm along the back of her seat, reversing confidently along the lane with just one hand on the wheel.

She kept her eyes fixed firmly on the sheep until they were lost to sight as Gabriel reversed skillfully around a bend and continued, aiming for the gateway they had passed some hundred or so yards back. She was acutely aware of his hand, hanging relaxed just an inch from her jaw. In her mind, his thumb ran caressingly down her cheek, his strong, tanned fingers stroking her neck as she ached for more and then, suddenly, they were closing convulsively around her throat, clenching shut, stopping the air, choking her . . . Imogen recoiled, gasping as if it were real, sitting rigidly upright in her seat, staring through the windscreen.

Gabriel appeared not to notice anything unusual. He merely braked when he reached the gate, executed a perfect three-point turn using the extra width provided by the gap in the hedge where the gate was, and then jumped out of the car again to swing open the gate in readiness for the sheep as they appeared around the bend.

Climbing back into the driver's seat and restarting the engine, he said, "I'll take us back now—unless you want to drive again." But it was a statement, not a question.

Pulling up alongside his Land Rover at the front of Storybook Cottage, he killed the engine but then just sat, hands on the wheel, staring through the windscreen.

She waited.

"So, you talked to your solicitors in London?" he said at last.

She nodded mutely.

"And?"

"They said . . . well, basically, they said I'm stuffed," she admitted.

"Our guys say you should claim on your insurance."

"Well, I can't," she retorted. "There isn't any."

"Of all the bloody idiocy!" he fumed. "You should sue them for incompetence."

"Yes, all right," she snapped back. "Not sure where to send the papers, though. Heaven or hell? Do say which . . . To be honest, I have a few issues I'd like to raise with my dead husband at the moment. I'll add this to the list." She threw open the car door and stomped out.

By the time she got to the front door, Gabriel was already there, barring her way.

"You're doing this to me," she said. "It's not Nigel. It's you. And you're doing it because your precious Louise is telling you to."

She glared up at him, furious that he could see her eyes filling with tears.

"You're wrong, that's not it at all," he said, clutching his temples. Then, taking a deep breath, he held out his arms. "Imogen," he said, gently. "Come here. I'm sorry."

"No," she said, pushing past him. Inside the house, she leaned against the front door, legs trembling. She had been mad to think she could cope with seeing him just so she could practice her driving. It was agony. She waited, motionless. After several moments, she heard his car door slam and the engine start. As she heard him go, her knees gave way, and she sank to the floor.

 *Chapter Nineteen*

"So, how's the tall, dark, handsome stranger?" said Sally irrepressibly.

"What, you mean the lord of the manor, stomping about his domain shagging all the servant girls? Arrogant sod."

"Ooh, really?" said Sally. "Droit du seigneur. How exciting. When are you going to succumb?"

"Never," said Imogen, not prepared to confess she had basically succumbed already but that there was no future in it.

"You just don't recognize class male totty when you see it," replied Sally. "It doesn't have to be anything serious, does it? Why not just have a little fling? He's just the type I'd love to find in my Christmas stocking. Talking of Christmas, what are your plans?"

"Hadn't thought," lied Imogen, who had actually told her mother, just the day before, that she couldn't join her and Gerald in Surrey because she had already been invited to go to Sally and Alistair. It was a lie, but it got her off the hook, plus she was half hoping for an invite.

"Well, normally we'd love to have you here, but work's been such a 'mare we've decided to bog off to Austria for skiing."

"Lovely!" said Imogen. her heart sinking. "You've earned a break." That was that, then.

Putting down the phone felt like cutting off a lifeline. Imogen grabbed it back a split second before it hit the rest, suddenly and irrationally panic-stricken, like she had stepped on the cracks in the pavement.

"Sal?" she gasped, but Sally had already disconnected. Imogen could picture her moving confidently on to the next task, chivvying for homework to be done, checking her mobile for urgent work texts, dumping stuff on the worktop for supper . . . In Storybook Cottage, though, Imogen's ears rang with the silence. She replaced the receiver reluctantly and thought about calling her back. But what would she say? *I'm not ready to stop talking* or, simply, *I'm lonely?*

There was nothing to stop her calling her mother. *Actually, Mum, I'm free after all—I'll come up and stay, shall I?* she could say, forcing herself to be jolly, to be fussed over and brought cups of tea in bed in deference to her condition. But then she had lied to get out of it, so surely, she couldn't want to go? She prodded her psyche experimentally. Nonsense, she told herself. I'm a grown-up, sensible woman of resources—and grown-ups don't mind being on their own.

"Not that I am on my own," she said out loud, resting her hand on her now huge bump. The baby squirmed, pressing painfully on her left hip for a moment and then settled, reluctantly it seemed, in her cramped quarters.

"Miaow," came a cross voice.

"Of course," sighed Imogen. "I'm never alone while I have you, Your Serene Majesty."

Taking the key off the dresser to unlock the back door,

she opened it with a sarcastic bow. Tango stalked in, giving her no more attention than an inanimate object such as—for example—the cat flap, which he studiously denied the existence of.

A SHARP FROST silvered the landscape when Imogen pulled back the curtains. She was due at the school later that morning to see Genny about the nativity play props. She hoped Genny wasn't expecting too much.

Anxious about finishing as much work as possible, before Christmas and before the baby came, she decided to set off early, giving herself time to stop at the pond and make a start on one of her winter book pages. It was one she had planned where Tango and Ruth were watching the ducks skating around on the ice. She wasn't expecting the ducks to oblige her by walking on water in the absence of a complete freeze, but she could get the basic composition down at least.

It was so pretty by the pond with the sun low in the sky and the usual bright colors bleached by the frost. Frozen dewdrops hung like crystals on the bare branches of the willow overhanging the water, putting Imogen in mind of fairy lights. It would be Christmas soon. Her first Christmas in Storybook Cottage. And probably her last.

The only strategy she had been able to find to cope with the stress of the issue with the house and Gabriel was to immerse herself in work. When she was engrossed, she was content, and able to forget about her sorrows for ages. She was sketching away happily when a shout sent her pencil skittering across the page.

"Imogen!" came an instantly recognizable voice.

Okay, so *now* she was thinking about losing the house again. She sighed.

"Hello, Gabriel, why are you shouting at me?" she said wearily, turning toward him as he came at her from the direction of the village shop.

"Christ, can you just get away from the edge of the pond, woman?" he said, arriving beside her. "Don't you know that bank is unstable?"

"Actually, I didn't, but what I *do* know is—if anything is going to make me fall in the pond, it's people yelling my name when I'm least expecting it," she reasoned.

"Anyhow, I saw you there as I drove past, and thought you needed warming up." He handed her a paper cup with a lid. "Hot chocolate from Paddy's new drinks machine. It's not the best, but at least it's warm," he explained, prising the lid off his own cup and looking at the foamy contents suspiciously.

"That was actually quite kind," said Imogen grudgingly, taking a sip. It was sweet, smooth, and—if she was honest—very welcome.

"Also," he went on, still peering into his cup, "I was unforgivably rude when I saw you last. It's not your fault you weren't insured against the Hall estate repairs claim. I was just—well—I'm angry at the situation. Not you. And I just wanted to say I didn't mean it. I'm sorry."

"Apology duly noted," said Imogen tightly. If only he would apologize for demanding practically everything she had and tell her he didn't mean *that*.

"I just wonder . . . well, I wonder if you appreciate that I'm just in the most appalling position."

Tell me about it, thought Imogen, very much hoping he wouldn't.

"So," he continued relentlessly, "it's a pressure, you know? Nine generations of Havenburys at Middlemass Hall. All those fortunes lost and won. All those death duties paid for somehow, by hook or by crook. Hanging on to my inheritance like grim death, just so I can shackle my own son to the responsibility one day—poor bastard—but, the truth is, *I* don't want to be the one who bankrupts the estate. I can't be the one, in such a long line, that fails in my duty, that's all."

She could feel him looking at her anxiously, but Imogen was struck dumb. She had nothing.

"Anyhow, it's . . . Well, it's all a bit crap, isn't it?"

She looked up at last, to see him smiling crookedly down at her. "Friends?" he proffered.

"Friends," she replied, doing her best to smile back with trembling lips. She desperately wanted to reassure him—just to see if she could iron out that furrow on his brow.

As if "friends" would ever be enough. As if "friends" was even remotely possible.

Because she loved him.

The realization in that moment was so ironic—and so utterly, utterly hopeless—it was all she could do to stifle a cry of pain.

"I must go," she said, when she could trust herself to speak. She drained her cup and handed it back to him. "Genny's expecting me at the school."

 *Chapter Twenty*

warn you, they do need a little work," said Genny breath-lessly, as she hauled the main backdrop out for Imogen to see. "I'll just get the manger and stuff."

Imogen looked at the scenery propped against the wall. "Hmmm. It is a little surprising."

"It's the pig, isn't it?" came a muffled voice from the storeroom.

"Yeah, mainly," said Imogen in what she felt was a masterly understatement as she looked at the row of animals leaning jovially and anthropomorphically over the top of the stable stall.

"The ox and the ass are okay, but I somehow don't feel that, given the predominantly Jewish population at the time, there would have been a pig in the stable where Jesus was born," Genny explained, appearing at Imogen's side and brushing her hair out of her eyes with a grimy hand. "After all, Christianity hadn't been invented, when you think about it."

"There's that aspect, now you mention it," said Imogen slowly, "but, more than anything, I think it's the hat."

"Ah, yes—the hat," said Genny, mouth twitching into a

grin. They both tilted their heads to better appreciate the pig's headgear.

"It is what is known, I believe, as a porkpie hat— appropriately enough. Did I mention the bloke who did this for us was seriously bonkers?"

"You're not kidding. How long have you been having to use it?"

"Twelve years. He died in the spring."

"Hence, finally, the opportunity for a rethink?"

"Exactly," said Genny with fervor. "I've been waiting a long time for this."

LIKE IMOGEN, BRIAN the carpenter had been desperate to start work on the school refurbishment. Having the nativity play scenery to do in the meantime was a welcome diversion from the delay, and he cheerfully knocked out the designs she sketched for him. Decoration was not his bag, though, he had explained, and crawling around on her knees to paint it all herself had been quite a strain on Imogen's heavily pregnant body.

Now, on the day of the nativity play, she was at least as skittish as the children, who scampered shrieking around the school hall, ignoring teachers trying to fasten on head-dresses and fix angel wings.

"We encouraged the children to choose their own parts," explained Genny as a horde of angels with a pink fairy in its midst trotted past.

"Ahhh," said Imogen, beginning to understand. "Which one's Mary?" she added as two little girls in blue walked past demurely holding hands.

"Both, nearly," chuckled Genny. "In the end we persuaded Katy to be Mary's sister Helen, who's just come to stay to help out with the baby."

"Good thought," replied Imogen seriously.

"Yes, well, we thought Helen could lend a hand getting ready for the three kings to arrive. Only there's five of them—plus a queen—so there's quite a bit to do."

As they spoke, the hall was filling up with parents and grandparents waving proudly to their children, who were now more or less corralled at the front of the hall.

A lot of the mothers looked casually glamorous with artfully lightened hair and gym-toned bodies in the latest gear. These were the sociable ones too, hooting to each other across the hall, catching up on the schoolgate gossip. Some were running cake stalls and a raffle to boost PTA funds, doling out tea and coffee from tables set along the perimeter of the hall. Fathers mainly shuffled uncomfortably, heads down. Every now and then, one would sidle, stiff-legged, toward another that he knew, and they would clap hands on each other's shoulders awkwardly, looking relieved at having someone to talk to.

And then Imogen's heart pounded as she spotted Gabriel, glowering fiercely at the back of the hall, standing apart from everyone and staring in her direction.

Their eyes met, and they stared helplessly at each other. Then, Louise, dressed in a red swirly dress with a fur collar—literally a sexy Santa, registered Imogen—arrived beside him, handing him a paper cup of mulled wine. Instantly, his ferocious expression lifted, and he smiled as he turned to her in a toast, apparently delighted as she ran her fingers down his arm.

Swine.

Imogen turned away from this devastating scene furiously, just as Genny shuffled onto the stage, twiddling the ends of her hair and waiting for everyone to notice she was there.

Simon smiled encouragingly at her from the back of the hall and folded his arms to listen.

"As well as the children, who have all worked so hard," she said eventually, her voice quivering just a little, "we should thank the PTA for organizing the stalls; the mummies, grandparents, and daddies who contributed cakes and prizes for the raffle; and also Imogen and Brian for quite miraculously transforming the stage sets we have this year." She paused, as the audience obediently applauded.

"I think you are all aware," she went on, her nerves returning a little, "how precious our school is to this community and how highly we all value it as a service for our children and our community. I think you all know, also, that our school is in danger. Thanks to the efforts of those who are working on the refurbishments which will bring the building up to standard, we have a real chance to fight against closure. I would like you all to be aware of the great sacrifice those people are making, a team led by Bill"— she stopped for the audience to give a cheer, and for a delighted, red-faced Bill at the back of the hall to duck his head—"and help the fundraisers by all supporting the raffle and tombola before you leave.

"And now, without further ado, I give you—our play!"

Genny edged crablike along the narrow space in the front of the stage and disappeared behind the curtain.

After some frantic whispering and shuffling, plus a couple of heavy thuds, the curtains squeaked jerkily open onto the first tableau. As the children launched, almost tunefully, into "Little Donkey, Little Donkey . . ." Imogen felt the hairs stand up on the back of her neck, and her eyes prick with tears. Seeing the wobbly smiles of the mothers and even the fathers surreptitiously wiping moistened eyes, she stroked her tummy thoughtfully and allowed herself a little daydream about a solemn dark-haired girl playing an angel. The vision was so vivid, she found she could examine every feature on the little girl's face—more Imogen than Nigel, everyone said—and see the white socks, one pulled up and one concertinaed around the ankle below a baggy white smock.

Her mind on her inner eye, it was a second before she clocked that she was staring, unseeing, at Gabriel, who had snuck to the front at the start. He gave her an unreadable look and then turned abruptly, pushing through the crowds to the door. She blushed and was glad she was sitting down, as her heart began to pound. Even after he was gone, the image of his face seemed burnt onto her retina.

CHRISTMAS CAROL SING-ALONG *at the Village Hall,* trumpeted the notice by the post office counter. *Rediscover the True Meaning of Christmas with Rudolph the Reindeer and Frosty the Snowman,* it continued improbably.

Imogen smiled to herself and looked around for something a little more edifying. She failed. Instead, she found Genny scratching her head over a poor choice of Christmas wrapping paper. Spotting Imogen, Genny grinned conspiratorially and whispered so that Muriel couldn't hear, "I'm torn between the fat Father Christmases jammed in the chimney and the one with red and green bells all over it."

"Not sure I'd want to be confronted with either without a dimly lit room or a pair of sunglasses," said Imogen.

"Simon's such a kid, I think he'd probably be a bit disappointed if I presented him with something discreet and tasteful—just as well, given this choice." Genny sighed. "I should go into Exeter, but I just can't face it."

"I'm desperate to go in, actually," admitted Imogen, "but not for Christmas shopping. I've really got to get big bulky stuff like a cot for the baby, so I'm hoping to do it with my little car."

"Have you passed your test?"

"Actually, it's this afternoon." She was so nervous about it the trip to the village store had been a ploy to push it to the back of her mind.

"Ooh! Good luck. I'm sure you'll be fine, though. Getting your wheels will certainly help with the Christmas shopping. Or have you done it all? You'll make me feel hideously disorganized if you have."

"I have."

"I'm impressed."

"Don't be. I sort of cheated quite a bit," admitted Imogen. "I found this brilliant charity online that lets you buy stuff for underdeveloped countries. It's all on the website, you choose something really vital for a village in Africa, pay for it, and the charity sends your recipient a card saying what you've bought."

"What sort of stuff?"

"Well, my mum really likes goats—"

"She does?"

"Oh yes, loves them, so I got a goat for a family in a country in Africa. You get to give it a name and everything, and it changes their fortunes completely. They milk it, obviously, plus they can breed from it, so then they can sell the kids."

"And then they can kill it and eat it," Genny finished, nodding thoughtfully.

"Mm, yes, I suppose so," said Imogen uncertainly, seeing Genny in a new light. Imogen had seriously considered getting Sally a goat too. In the end, though, she decided on some lime and elderflower bath oil from Jo Malone. All mail order, conveniently.

"So, it's true," admitted Imogen, "I've done all my Christmas shopping, apart from local friends. I thought I might make some chocolate truffles. I can pop them around to people on my bike if I don't pass my test. Or even if I do, I suppose."

"Yum! I hope we're getting some," said Genny, "although I'm not sure cycling it to people is a good plan."

"How do you think I got here? I am starting to get a few funny looks, though." She felt she looked a bit like Humpty Dumpty, balanced on her bike with her huge tummy out in front of her. Also, admittedly, it was getting pretty uncomfortable, and she found herself running out of puff at anything more than the most sedate pace.

"I think we had better hope you pass your test today. When's your due date again?"

"Two to three weeks, pretty much, Morag reckons. A couple of days into the new year, although actually it would be nice if she came on New Year's Day, don't you think?"

"Yes and no," said Genny thoughtfully. "On the one hand, she will always have her birthday on a bank holiday, which is nice, but have you thought about having to organize all those noisy children's parties with a post–New Year's Eve hangover?"

"Good point, but Morag and Simon have both told me that first babies tend to be late, so I think I'm pretty safe."

"Gosh, it really is about time you got the baby stuff in, though, isn't it? I'm so excited. Aren't you?"

Imogen smiled, not wanting to rain on Genny's parade by admitting that she was worried sick, not least about what she and the baby were going to do financially, with Gabriel out to ruin her. In truth, leaving shopping for the baby so late was mostly because she worried about spending money.

"When are you and Simon going to hark to the patter of tiny feet?" Imogen asked, summoning up a smile.

"Simon would love to any time, but we've agreed to put the family thing on ice for a couple of years. The school is such a big job—it's like my baby, really," Genny said, looking weary.

"How's it all going?" said Imogen, feeling bad for not having asked sooner.

Genny glanced over to Muriel. Seeing her nattering contentedly to her sister Joan, she leaned in closer. "You remember me saying about Mrs. Marshall being ill?"

Imogen nodded.

"Well, the truth is she's dying." Genny pressed her hand

over her mouth to hide a sudden quiver. Imogen put a hand sympathetically on her shoulder, but Genny waved her away.

"No, don't be nice," she said quickly, dabbing the tears from the corners of her eyes. "She's such an inspiration. She knows she hasn't got much time left, but all she wants to do is help with everything. She's been so incredible getting us ready for the inspection—did I tell you the Ofsted report was 'outstanding,' by the way? Don't tell anyone. It's not official yet—and she said she wants me to apply for the head teacher job permanently. It's a lot. We're just hoping the LEA committee meeting after Christmas will see sense. Of course, we will have the building work pretty much complete, so they can't use the dilapidations as an excuse to close us down. Bill's been amazing, and Gabriel's been there all hours laboring away. I went up at ten last night with a flask of coffee, and he was there on his own, painting the corridor in the new toilet block. He looks exhausted. But whether all this is going to do us any good . . . ?"

Genny's chin quivered again, and she brushed away another fat tear with her finger, sniffing.

"They've got to admire what's been achieved," said Imogen. "And of *course*, you should apply for the head teacher job. You're doing it now anyway and doing really well from what I've seen. I've got this little one signed up already," she said, patting her tummy.

"Let's hope we're still open for her to attend," said Genny bleakly.

"I just wonder if *we* will still even be here in the village at all," Imogen fretted in turn.

 *Chapter Twenty-one*

The driving instructor carrying out the test looked such a nervous man Imogen found herself wondering which had come first, the job or the nerves. If he was inherently twitchy, surely choosing a career as a driving instructor had disaster written all over it? On the other hand, perhaps he had been virtually horizontal with serenity as a young man but had been ground down mentally after years of botched emergency stops and sixteen-point turns. Clutching his clipboard, he eyed Imogen's tummy with frank alarm. She was feeling pretty jumpy herself.

Her lovely last-minute instructor, Trevor, had gently dissuaded her from driving her own car in the test.

"All I'm saying, my love," he had explained tactfully, "is that the examiner doing your test isn't going to be thinking 'dodgy handbrake' when you roll back doing your hill start. He's going to think—quite wrongly, in my view—that you're a tiny bit rubbish."

He had a point.

That said, she was even more nervous at having to drive one of the school cars rather than her lovely, familiar Ford Fiesta, even with its ever so slightly knackered handbrake.

Getting into the car with the instructor alongside her, Imogen discovered that—humiliatingly—the previous occupant had clearly been a teeny, slim person with very short arms. By the time Imogen had wrestled the seat far enough back for her to insert her huge tummy in front of the steering wheel and hauled the ridiculously unaccommodating seat belt across herself far enough to do it up, there was a fine sheen of sweat on her brow. Glancing across to her now goggle-eyed tester, she noticed he too had beads of perspiration on his upper lip, and he seemed to have turned puce. She hoped it was just embarrassment and not an incipient stroke.

Driving out of the car park, she tried furiously to concentrate. All she could think about was the scary stories Sally had told her on the phone the previous evening about other people taking their tests, like the woman who got into the wrong side of the car and then looked in vain for the steering wheel, or the man who ran over the examiner's dog on the way out of the test center car park. Actually, that one was more upsetting than funny, and she preferred to think it wasn't true. As if Sally's tales weren't bad enough, Trevor had told her that morning about a driver who panicked so much about which way to go around the roundabout that she, allegedly, drove right over the top, crushing a track through a carpet of lobelia and dianthus spelling out *Portneath in Bloom*.

Her parallel parking was going fairly well until it occurred to her that she was maneuvering ridiculously slowly. Could he fail her for being too slow? She gunned the engine, shot forward, and promptly stalled. The instructor gave her another pop-eyed look, and she stifled a nervous giggle. Trying to focus, she heard Gabriel's calming voice in her head as she carried out the checks. Handbrake on, gearstick in neutral, turn on ignition, depress clutch. Nothing happened. She tried again. The engine coughed reluctantly into life. Next, they traveled toward the behemoth roundabout that Imogen loathed. She always got flustered about what lane she needed to be in and especially hated turning right.

"Take the third exit from the roundabout," whined the instructor nasally, "and then follow the road ahead."

Imogen cursed her luck. She had never managed this maneuver without panicking, even with Gabriel beside her. Middle lane, left lane, she thought frantically, checking mirrors and whipping her head round right, then left, before tentatively moving. "Damn!" A car was sneaking up the inside. She slammed on the brakes and whipped in behind it. By the time she was back on the road with the hated roundabout behind, her heart was pounding. She must have failed by now, she thought, remembering what Trevor had said about never abandoning a test: "Even if it all goes wrong—which it won't—you will need to get to the end. Unless you are an appalling danger, they won't let you stop."

Blinking back tears of frustration and despair, she stole a glance at the instructor, who was gazing stonily ahead. She could see his Adam's apple in profile; it stuck out so much in his scrawny neck, and it was bobbling up and down as he swallowed. At least he hadn't told her to pull over. That meant she must at least have avoided being "an appalling danger." Either that or he was catatonic with fear and no longer had the communication ability to stop her killing them both.

At last, they pulled into the test center car park. Imogen's body felt so heavy she thought it quite possible she would spend the rest of her life welded to the car seat.

Staring fixedly through the windscreen, she heard a distant voice.

". . . so, I am pleased to tell you—er—Ms. Hewitt . . ." He stressed the *Ms.* slightly as he gazed, still apparently fascinated, at her belly. "That you have passed your driving test."

Imogen took a huge breath and turned. Seeing her move toward him, his eyes widened in terror, clearly afraid she was going to involve him in an unseemly display of joy—possibly involving touching.

She was. Catching his expression, though, and more to the point, catching a whiff of stale perspiration wafting from his polyester shirt, Imogen regained her self-control without difficulty.

BY THE TIME she had—thrillingly—driven herself home from the test center, Imogen was beginning to feel more confident at being alone in a car. Parking neatly outside the house, she stroked the bonnet of her dear little red Ford Fiesta, promising it a proper car wash with wheel wash and wax to celebrate their newfound freedom.

"And the first big adventure needs to be shopping for the baby," she told it excitedly.

The sense of the world opening up was exhilarating, making Imogen realize how trapped she had begun to feel, in her big house with no easy way of getting further than the confines of the village.

"Not long to go now," came a female voice, making Imogen jump. She spun around to see her arch-irritant and love rival. Louise was looking with faint disapproval at Imogen's huge belly and disheveled appearance. As always, she was immaculately groomed and looked, Imogen thought, like a glamorous advertisement for country living, with her far-too-clean waxed jacket and brand-new Hunter wellies.

Imogen attempted to smile. "I'll be glad when the baby comes, to be honest," she admitted. "Being pregnant has now officially become a bore."

"I'm sure," said Louise with a barely suppressed shudder. "It must be really weird losing control of your body like— er—that," the subtext clearly being *like you totally have.*

"Have you decided what you're going to do yet?" Louise added.

"About what?" said Imogen.

"Well, about meeting your share of the repair bills," said Louise, apparently irritated that Imogen was so slow on the uptake and managing to intimate that this must only be because she didn't treat the issue nearly responsibly enough.

"And you're involved how?"

"Well," Louise said smugly, "of course, Gabriel and I— sorry, *Lord* Havenbury," she corrected with a simper, "are very close." She glared at Imogen to ensure she got the point.

Yeah, right, pillow talk—I get you, thought Imogen, planting her finger over her lip to physically prevent it coming out. She confined herself to a nod, distantly astonished at how furious and betrayed she felt that Gabriel was not only frolicking with the ghastly woman but discussing her most private business with her too.

"Yes," said Louise, getting into her stride, "Lord Havenbury has an enormous range of responsibilities—being in his position—and I like to think I ease the burden by offering a sympathetic ear."

Imogen wondered if she called him Lord Havenbury in bed.

"Actually, I am frequently able to offer helpful advice too," Louise added. "Then, of course, I hold a rather responsible position within the company, which is what threw the two of us together in the first place." Her smile invited Imogen to join her in marveling at how fate had conspired to unite them. "Lord Havenbury says it was my professionalism that first impressed him." She smiled into the middle distance.

"How nice," muttered Imogen. Not just your big tits, then, she added to herself. God, the woman really was a monster. Yet again she asked herself why she felt anything at all for a man who not only wanted to ruin her but who also had such unspeakable taste in women. That said, given their own—undisputed, if former—mutual attraction, it probably said nothing flattering about her either.

"So, what are you doing for Christmas, then?" she said, determined to change the subject and seeing that Louise had no intention of leaving.

"Ah, well," Louise simpered again. "Hard to say at the moment, but Lord Havenbury has just asked me to join him for an intimate dinner tomorrow. We have a—how shall I describe it—an important agreement to celebrate together."

"Mm. Christmas Eve, eh?" said Imogen, trying hard.

"Well, quite," said Louise, bridling. "I rather think he might . . ." She left the end of the sentence unsaid but wafted her left hand at Imogen, her ring finger prominently displayed, leaving her meaning in little doubt.

"And then, of course, we will need to break the news. Christmas is such a lovely time to do it, don't you think? With families already together. A double celebration."

Imogen felt utterly bleak and desperately wished Louise would go away. "Great, yeah. Bye, then," she said firmly with the last of her reserve.

"Oh! Goodbye," said Louise, managing to convey with arched eyebrows how puzzling she found Imogen's rudeness, at the same time as intimating that she expected nothing else from such an unsatisfactory specimen.

A COUPLE OF minutes later, Imogen was still muttering to herself furiously as she polished the Fiesta's bonnet with an energy she had no idea she had.

"It'll never love you back, you know," came a shout from the lane.

Imogen whipped around, flushing scarlet to match her little car. Joining in his laughter, shamefaced, she walked toward Simon's car.

"I wasn't talking to the car, you know. Actually, I was talking to myself," she explained, not feeling that she was being particularly successful at reclaiming her dignity.

"Whatever you say," he teased. "I generally find the baby addles the brain at around this stage in the pregnancy."

She was absurdly pleased to see him, though, and told him the good news about passing her test.

"Champagne to celebrate, I think!" he exclaimed about the test. "Not that I happen to have any about my person, but I would happily join in if you've got some."

"SHOULDN'T YOU BE healing the sick or something?" asked Imogen when they had jointly decided—okay, Simon decided—that sparkling elderflower was more suitable than alcohol.

"Probably," he said, propping his feet onto the tea towel bar on the stove and holding his glass to the light to admire the bubbles. "But I've just done my house calls, and it's not my turn to do evening surgery today. Thankfully, I think the inhabitants of Middlemass can survive until tomorrow without my help."

They drank in companionable silence for a minute, Imogen taking tiny sips for fear of setting off the heartburn that plagued her almost continually now.

"So, who's sick and who's well?" she asked at last, just to make conversation.

"Well, obviously it's all strictly confidential," he said.

"Of course," replied Imogen, feeling chastised, but Simon was grinning.

"So, if I tell you, I'll have to kill you," he went on. "You know about Mrs. Marshall, the headmistress, of course?"

Imogen nodded. "Genny told me she hasn't got long," she said, choked to remember Genny's distress, but then she could barely listen to the news on the radio without bursting into tears. It must be her hormones. How wonderful to be Simon and to have such composure when talking about things like that. Imogen was sure that, even if she had been clever enough to be a doctor, she would have been hopeless, probably in permanent floods.

"I've just seen your mate Winifred Hutchinson too, actually," he added. "She asked after you. Mentioned you'd dropped by to commiserate after the dog died?"

"I did, but that was weeks ago," admitted Imogen, feeling a pang of guilt she hadn't been back. She had barely seen Winifred since then, being so wrapped up in the pregnancy and her work.

"Is she all right?" Imogen asked, cringing.

"Fine. It's nothing other than old age, really," he said reassuringly. "And she's lonely. She should get another dog, but she says she won't consider it because she doesn't want to risk a dog outliving her and needing to be rehomed."

Imogen's eyes filled. "That's so selfless, but—yes—it must be lonely. I don't know what I'd do without Tango," she said, looking down at him. Overwhelmed with emotion, she gathered him up for a hug, but he locked his legs rigid to push her away, jumping off her lap with a bad-tempered yowl.

"Yep, he's a peach, all right." Simon grinned as the cat crashed through the flap and stalked down the garden path, twitching his tail. "You might want to find someone a bit more reliable than a grouchy old cat, you know. Like Gabriel, for example," he added mischievously.

"Oh right, yes. I'll swap a grouchy old cat for a grouchy old bloke any day. Good plan."

There was an awkward pause while Imogen decided not to mention the conversation she had just had with Louise. She didn't think Simon would be thrilled to hear that she and Gabriel were getting hitched, and she didn't fancy being the bearer of bad tidings. It was unutterably bleak just knowing about it herself.

"Genny mentioned you bumped into each other in the post office," he said instead. "She was cross with herself because she meant to ask what your plans were for Christmas, but she forgot."

Briefly, Imogen considered making up a visit to her mother. "Nothing, really," she admitted.

"I hoped you'd say that. I can't imagine you'd want to be traveling far with the baby due so soon. Genny and I would really love it if you would come to us on Christmas Day."

"And be a third wheel? No fear," said Imogen. "It's really kind of you, but honestly—"

"You won't be."

"I couldn't imagine anything worse for you than having me crashing your day—"

"I'm trying to persuade Gabriel to join us too."

"Except that," Imogen said, with finality.

"Honestly, you two are the limit!" Simon said, exasperated. "Here we are, me and Genny, trying to pull off a perfectly legitimate bit of matchmaking, and you are both kicking and struggling against it like a pair of Tangos."

Imogen, open-mouthed, felt bound to protest but couldn't think of a thing to defend herself. "How can you think for a minute that we're suited?" she said, eventually. "We can barely be in the same room together. You know about the money. He wants to ruin me."

"He doesn't want to ruin you."

"He doesn't care enough not to."

"I don't believe that. And he's steamed in to the rescue a couple of times," added Simon persuasively.

"He's got Louise," Imogen said, adding provocatively, "She seems to think she's in with the main chance too."

"God, not that Louise woman, surely?" said Simon immediately. "He's been so weird the last few months—"

"Even more than normal?"

"Yes, *even* more," acknowledged Simon with a nod. "Pretty much since you got here," he said. "I thought it was because of you, but maybe she's the real reason why. And she's probably the one pushing him to get the repair money from you too."

"No one seems to think much of her," said Imogen, taking some satisfaction that her view was so widely shared.

"Loony Louise," said Simon with a faint shudder. "We think we've managed to prise him away from her for Christmas Day, thank goodness."

"I wouldn't count on it," Imogen muttered under her breath, remembering Louise's confidence in the outcome of her Christmas Eve dinner à deux.

"Good, that's settled, then," said Simon, jumping to his feet and popping his dirty glass into the dishwasher. "We'll see you for Christmas lunch at about midday." He pulled a teasing face as she remonstrated helplessly.

"Good grief, it's Christmas Eve tomorrow," he said. "God help me. I must get into Portneath and do some shopping." He was shrugging on his jacket, his mind elsewhere already. "Goodbye, little Imogen," he said, gathering her up in a big, warm hug.

Not expecting it and starved of physical contact with

anyone, she found his warmth and strength meltingly comforting. How lovely it would be to find such a kind man, she thought longingly.

"Genny's so lucky," she said when, eventually, he let go.

"Be sure to remind her of that on Christmas Day," he said. "She should appreciate me more. I'm always telling her . . . See you then, but"—he waved a finger admonishingly—"Anything happens with the little one? Anything at all? You call me. Promise?"

 *Chapter Twenty-two*

In the end Imogen couldn't face going to Exeter to buy the last baby things. She had left it so late for fear of spending money, but now, with hardly any time left, the need was unignorable. Instead of going out shopping for new stuff, she made herself a mug of tea and turned to the internet. Using eBay and Facebook Marketplace to source the cheapest and most basic secondhand options she could find, she saved herself a fortune, organizing to go and pick things up in her car in the week between Christmas and New Year. Just in time. Splashing out money when she didn't have any—the book deal advance had been modest—and accumulating stuff when she didn't even know where she would be living soon seemed reckless and idiotic, but thank goodness she could at least do this.

Thinking back to the school nativity, the irony of being pregnant, so near giving birth, *and* so near being homeless quite so close to Christmas did not escape her. Perhaps she and the baby would end up living in her car? Gabriel couldn't take *that* away from her, at least.

It was the early hours of the morning before she slept.

NEXT MORNING, SHE awoke from restless dreams feeling leaden-limbed and deeply weary. This was more than just late-pregnancy fatigue. She placed her hand on her forehead experimentally. It was fiercely hot, and clammy too. Surely she had been too isolated to have picked up a bug, but the evidence was incontrovertible. Someone had shared their germs with her, and just before Christmas too. Delightful. Lightheaded just from heaving herself out of bed, she leaned on the windowsill to catch her breath. Dawn had broken with an evil red glow, backlighting her view of the manor house on the horizon and reminding her of its owner's devilish aura. Storm clouds pressed down from the sky, making day barely lighter than night.

Dragging herself downstairs wrapped in a blanket—her dressing gown gaped so much over her swollen belly she didn't wear it anymore—she thought about calling her mother to report that she was ill but then decided she couldn't be bothered. Worrying her mother pointlessly was even worse than the forlorn thought that no one was expecting to see her all day. The prospect of spending Christmas Eve totally on her own made her feel even more grateful for Simon's last-minute Christmas Day invitation. It would be lovely to see Genny too, although the thought of navigating a day spent with Gabriel—and perhaps Louise too—made her head ache even more. Perhaps she should just stay home and keep her germs to herself.

Listlessly putting aside her latest set of drawings and unable to concentrate on the newspaper, she curled up in front of the television with a cup of hot chocolate. *It's a Wonderful*

Life had just started, and Imogen watched with one eye, her aching head buried in the softest cushion she could find. Barely half an hour in, she was fast asleep.

A THUNDER CRASH shook Imogen violently awake. She sat up, heart pounding, and looked toward the window. Slanting rain was washing in icy sheets down the window-pane. An explosion of light and sound tore through the air, sending Tango scuttling from the room. The lights flickered ominously. The clock on the mantel said four o'clock. What daylight there was would soon be gone.

Whimpering, she staggered, lightheaded and shivering, to the kitchen to find the matches and candles. Matches were easy, but her search for candles produced two blackened stubs and a broken kitchen candle mixed up with the tea towels. Gathering them up, she grabbed an old saucer and arranged her little hoard on the table. No sooner had she turned to put the kettle on when a giant tearing crash she could feel in the soles of her feet shook the house and plunged it into darkness. Fumbling in the gloom and trembling with fever, she snapped the first match striking it against the box. The second time she created a fragile flame, and the candle guttered into life, casting a mean light that seemed to create more shadows than it penetrated.

The amount of rain falling was colossal, Imogen thought, worried now about the culvert that Gabriel had warned her about. It needed to be cleared. As far as Imogen was aware, no one had done it.

"Thank goodness it's not colder," she remarked to Tango,

who had just slunk back in, having failed to find sanctuary elsewhere. "If this were snow, it would be up to the window-sills by now."

Saying it out loud made her feel braver, but her voice was a surprise to them both, raspy and thin as an old lady's. Her throat felt dry and red-raw.

"I'm off to bed," she announced, "and I suggest you come too." She tried to sound like she didn't care either way, but feeling sorry for herself and a tiny bit lonely, she hoped Tango would join her. In an unusual shared agenda, he tried to look like he didn't care either, but the storm had made him edgy, and he was happy to lead the way. She crawled into bed, with him on her thighs, and slept.

PARALYZED WITH FRIGHT, Imogen watched the motor-bike ahead of her on the long, straight road. It was barely a smudge on the horizon, but she knew it was Nigel. The engine snarled and roared as the black BMW raced toward her. She sweated and moaned as she tried to dive out of its way, but nothing would make her legs move. The bike was screaming now, yards away, spraying gravel from its wheels. Daring to look into the darkened visor as it filled her vision, the last thing she saw was a ghastly, grinning skull, shreds of flesh still clinging to the cheekbones as the bike plowed into her, doubling her up in agony as it hit her middle . . .

A breathless, sleep-paralyzed scream escaped from her as she woke. She struggled to get up, pushing away the bedclothes that pinned her down. A tearing pain ripped through her body, crushing her bones as she pressed her face into the pillow, groaning.

At last, it lifted. She lay bathed in a cold sweat, listening and letting the last images of the nightmare dissipate. The rain still lashed the window in violent flurries like gravel flung against the glass by a giant hand. The wind wailed down the chimney. She clicked the switch on the lamp. Damn. Still no power. Trying to breathe calmly, she did a mental check. Her head was pounding as hard as her heart and the bedclothes were soaked in sweat. More than just the effect of the nightmare and the pregnancy, this was definitely a vicious dose of flu. Obviously, the pain in the tummy didn't fit the diagnosis. Imogen had just persuaded herself it was one of those Braxton-Hicks contractions— practice contractions—that Morag had told her about, when it crept up again, crushing her in a vise of unbearable pain. She found herself gripping the bed rail, rocking and moaning until she thought she couldn't bear it anymore. Long seconds later, it started to ease.

"Okay, not Braxton-Hicks," she commented to Tango, who merely registered his disgust at her inability to stay still so he could sit on her.

She picked up her mobile, scrabbling at the smooth cover. The action of bringing it to life expended its last gasp of battery life, and it shut down in her hand as she wailed in disbelief. With no electricity, there was no point in even feeling around for the charging cord in the dark.

She staggered down the attic stairs, leaning on the walls with her hands. As she picked up the old-fashioned landline telephone in the main bedroom, her stomach lurched with dread. Instead of a dial tone, the line buzzed dully. Could she even remember anybody's number? No one memorized numbers anymore . . . And then—her heart leaping in hope—her eyes fell on the note Gabriel had sent her after their lunch all those months ago. His offer of driving lessons was written on a stiff, white postcard with the address and phone number of Middlemass Hall printed at the top. With shaking fingers, she dialed but there was no ringing, just the infernal faint buzzing of a damaged line.

Going to the window, she looked across the valley to the manor. Hallelujah. The lights winked reassuringly in the near distance. No power cut there, apparently. There was nothing for it—the Hall was her nearest sanctuary—she would have to walk across. Following the path through the wood, and with a torch, she could get help within half an hour. Vaguely she remembered Morag saying that babies took ages to come, and first babies longest of all—that she should stay at home for as long as possible in labor. She'd also said to make sure Imogen had someone with her.

Imogen put on the first pair of shoes she could find, never mind about socks. Her coat was in the hallway downstairs, and so was the torch. Feeling her way, she went down the last flight, but she stopped short of the bottom, puzzled. Her eyes were playing tricks on her—it had to be the effect of the flu—but the moonlight breaking through the clouds was eerily reflected on the hall floor. The normally gray flagstone floor was like a pool of oil, glossy and smooth, and three feet too high. Straining her eyes to make sense of this nonsense, she carried on and gasped as her foot disappeared into the glassy lake. Water. It gleamed evilly, returning to stillness in seconds, unlike the tumult that continued outside.

Imogen sank onto the step, sobbing. A yomp through the woods, in the dark, ill and in labor, during a storm had seemed briefly reasonable. The terror of wading through floodwater, its calm surface hiding currents and obstacles, made the journey impossible.

Carefully, shivering, she waded to the coat stand and found her coat, holding it above her head as she waded back to the stairs. At least the torch was there, in the pocket. Time passed. Contractions came and—thankfully—went. She tried to time them by shining the torch on her wristwatch, but it was impossible to concentrate. She vaguely remembered there was something significant about two minutes but couldn't remember whether it was the length of the contractions or the time between them. She checked her watch—nearly two o'clock in the morning. There would be no one dropping in, no fortuitous visit from the postman or Morag the midwife on Christmas Day. Her only hope was that Simon and Genny might eventually wonder where she was, but she wasn't even due at their house until midday. How long would they wait before they seriously queried her absence? She was alone. Worse still, her torch was fading, so she switched it off and sat in darkness. Drawing her coat around her, she closed her eyes. Time passed, and she stopped counting the contractions as they ripped through her.

THE PHANTOM MOTORBIKE with its terrifying rider had returned, its headlight burning across her retinas as it careered toward her, swerving right and left. Twitching with terror in her dream, she longed to run away as the ghastly figure on the bike loomed over her.

A shattering crash woke her, and nightmare met reality as she opened her eyes to find there really was a bright light veering from side to side, illuminating the hallway. She watched in horror at the smashed stained-glass window next to the door as a hand reached around to lift the latch. Finding her voice at last, she launched herself screaming up the stairs, clambering on her hands and knees as the door slowly opened against the weight of the floodwater.

"Imogen! You're there. Are you all right? For Christ's sake, stop making that noise."

She was vaguely aware of Gabriel next to her, holding her face in his hands, then putting his arms around her. Never mind that this was the man who wanted to ruin her life and who had spent that very evening proposing to another woman. At that moment he was the only person in the world that Imogen wanted to see.

"You weren't there!" she wailed, finding words at last.

"I'm sorry."

"I was all on my own," she sobbed helplessly.

"I'm here now. I'm here now," he said softly, stroking her hair.

She clung to him. Despite—or perhaps because of—the relief, she couldn't stop sobbing and gasping convulsively, her tears and snot soaking his shoulder. She gradually noticed it was the one bit of him that seemed to have stayed dry until that point. He was sodden from his feet to his waist.

"Imo?" came another reassuringly familiar voice.

Simon loomed into the circle of torchlight around them, throwing ten-foot shadows onto the wall.

"Hullo, darling. Did you leave the bath running?" he joked.

"What are you both doing here?" asked Imogen.

"We've been at the Hall, thinking we should probably check on you in the morning with this storm, and then the phone rang, but there was no one there. Why aren't you tucked up in bed asleep?"

"Not feeling too good," Imogen muttered. He held a hand to Imogen's forehead and then to the pulse in her neck.

"Christ, she's as pyretic as hell, and tachycardic," he muttered to himself. "Darling, what have you been up to?" he said, louder.

Imogen started to explain about falling ill, but another contraction caught her by surprise. Blimey, they were getting overwhelming now. She was oblivious to both men for a while and then found herself clutching Gabriel's hand.

"Okay, I think we can assume the baby's planning to make an appearance," Simon said lightly, but his face was stern. "When did the contractions start?"

"Don't know. It was dark—I think. What time is it?"

"Nearly dawn," said Gabriel. "We tried to call you, but you didn't answer."

"It wouldn't have been ringing at this end," explained Imogen. "There's something the matter with the line, I think, and my mobile's dead."

Simon waded to the telephone table and lifted the receiver. "It must be the flood," he said. "And"—he fumbled in his jacket pocket—"yes, damn it, my mobile's got no signal here either."

He smiled reassuringly. "Imogen, I'm going to have to examine you to see how far on you are. Gabriel, could you hold the torch?"

"Nooo!" shrieked Imogen like an outraged maiden aunt, drawing her pajamas around her in an attempt at dignity.

This time Simon was a little more firm. "Come on now, darling. I *am* a doctor, and I really do need to check."

"Can't it wait?" interrupted Gabriel. "She can hardly have her baby on the stairs in the middle of a flood anyhow. Let's get her back to the Hall. At least there's light and heat there. I can take the Land Rover and fetch Morag from the village."

Suddenly Imogen wanted the uncompromising and taciturn Morag with her very much indeed. She nodded at Simon eagerly, looking from him to Gabriel, who hugged her to his side reassuringly.

"Okay, well, I don't think we've got many other options. Given the water levels here, there's no chance an ambulance is going to get through the valley."

Gabriel gathered her up into his arms, not for the first time.

"Sorry," said Imogen. "This seems to be becoming a habit."

"I don't mind," he said, puffing exaggeratedly to make her laugh, "but I can't say I don't wish you'd lose a little weight."

Simon grinned. "She will. Soon."

 *Chapter Twenty-three*

nfinitely reassured that she was no longer alone, Imogen remembered little about the short trip back to the Hall. Taking the back drive to avoid the worst of the floodwater meant
a diversion of over a mile. At one point, the water breached
even the high body of the Land Rover to pour in over their
feet, and Gabriel swore repeatedly under his breath as he
gunned the engine to keep the water from getting into the
exhaust.

Carrying her again up the narrow stairs to his apartment, he laid her tenderly on the sofa where he had placed
her weeks before with her twisted ankle.

The contractions had miraculously receded on the
short journey, but after she sank with huge relief into a
deep bubble bath drawn by Gabriel while Simon fetched
Morag, they returned. No longer panicking, Imogen
found them less painful but increasingly powerful and
purposeful. By the time Gabriel had helped her out, dried
her, and dressed her in one of his shirts, she could hear
herself moaning loudly with each one, as she rocked to
and fro on the bed.

"Well, well, this one looks like it's ready to make its

mummy's acquaintance," announced Morag, bustling into the room and pushing Gabriel out of the way with casual disdain.

Imogen started to cry again with relief at the sight of the formidable old woman.

"There, there," soothed Morag, "I'm here now, and all's going well, by the look of it. Let's just see what's going on with the little one," she crooned. "You. Out," she barked over her shoulder at the two men. Simon, who was hovering in the doorway, looking like a whipped dog, gave a mock salute and winked at Imogen behind Morag's back.

In the end, though, while Simon paced the sitting room like the anxious father, Gabriel stayed in the bedroom, barely tolerated by Morag and clung to by Imogen as he gave sips of iced water, mopped her brow, and let her crush his hand when she needed to. Here was the man who seemed to wish her more harm than anyone else on the earth, but the comfort of having him there was overwhelming.

"She's so beautiful," Genny gasped reverently, stroking the tiny baby's mouse-soft hair. Just three hours old, she gazed solemnly into Genny's face, content in the crook of Imogen's arm. Genny, panicked at waking up and discovering Simon had not returned home, had called him and insisted he come and collect her immediately.

"What are you going to call her?"

"Should be Holly, really, being born on Christmas Day," said Simon.

"Ruth," said Imogen quietly. "She's called Ruth." Closing her eyes, she drifted off to sleep.

AFTER THAT, THE days flowed one into another without form. There was a memory of Christmas dinner, brought over by Genny but abandoned untouched by the bed. Morag came in twice a day to fuss over Imogen and to bathe the baby. Simon checked in on her frequently as the flu kept her in its grip. More than once, while he was examining her chest with a stethoscope, Imogen nearly deafened him with a sudden coughing fit, and he continued to mutter about secondary infections and pneumonia.

Gabriel was a continuous and calming presence, popping up regularly with food and cups of tea, changing nappies, and bringing the baby to be fed when she cried, which she hardly ever did. Sometimes they just sat together on the bed, quietly companionable, each wrapped in their own thoughts.

Finding Imogen tearful and lonely one afternoon, Gabriel took them both down to his workshop and installed her on an oak settle padded with cushions and blankets. He put Ruth in a cradle alongside her—the cradle he had used as a baby himself, he told her. Mother and baby spent hours mesmerized by the flames of the forge, watching his sweat-slicked forearms as he combined strength and delicacy, teasing elegance out of the glowing iron rods. Imogen would doze and then wake again to see him still working, utterly absorbed.

One afternoon, Genny came over to babysit them both so Gabriel could go out, which he did, having shaved and showered. He returned late, looking tired. A couple of days later, he disappeared again, and Imogen heard Louise's name mentioned in a muttered conversation between him and Genny on his return.

Imogen was grateful he was visiting his fiancée away from the house. She said nothing about it, nor did Gabriel. Instead, by mutual unspoken consent, neither of them mentioned either Louise or the repair bill but existed instead in a strangely timeless and intimate world where Gabriel seemed happy to protect her from the intrusion of real life.

She knew quietly and absolutely that she loved him. She couldn't say, of course.

It was hopeless. She knew that. She could only savor her time with him while it lasted. And then? Well, she had Ruth now. The tiny girl was the center of a universe that would soon no longer have Gabriel in it. Imogen thought she might have given up without her baby to live for. So much loss in a single year . . . her husband, her house, and now the love of her life?

But she had Ruth. And that was everything.

"What about Storybook Cottage?" she finally asked, one morning. It was a red-letter day because Simon had finally let her get up and get dressed. She sat at Gabriel's dining table eating delicious flaky croissants and—joy of joy—drinking freshly filtered coffee.

"I've been down to take a look," Gabriel said slowly, watching to see how much to tell. Tears were still infuriatingly close to the surface, and she was aware of being handled with care.

"The floodwater's gone," he said. "It was gone by the end of Christmas Day, actually, but I'm afraid it's all a bit of a mess. A major insurance job."

"I'd better see for myself," said Imogen briskly. "I don't

suppose you could take us down today?" Gabriel hesitated. "I mean, I appreciate you're really busy, but it would be brilliant. Maybe Simon—"

"No, no—it's fine. I'll take you. But you need to seriously wrap up warm, and we're not taking Ruth with us. No way."

"Okay." She could see his point. "Well, Genny mentioned dropping in this morning, and I don't delude myself that she's interested in me. She only wants to see Ruth, so I'm sure she'll babysit for a bit."

Genny was delighted at being in sole charge of Ruth. She came by daily to gaze in wonder at her and was dreading the beginning of term because she would have less time.

"We'll get on just fine, won't we, my darling?" she cooed. "Take as long as you like," she added, dismissing them with an airy wave.

Imogen's heart thumped as they approached the house. The flower beds and gravel at the front of the house were merged into one revolting mud slick but—other than that— the house looked normal. The broken glass by the front door reminded her of Christmas Eve with a jolt.

"Sorry about that," said Gabriel following her gaze. "I was in such a rush to get to you, I forgot to bring my key. I know a guy who does stained glass. I'll get him to restore it. It'll be good as new, I promise."

"I'm not sure I want it invisibly repaired. It sort of reminds me of you being a hero and steaming in to rescue me," she said, smiling shyly at him.

"Mm. Not for the first time, either," he said forbiddingly, but grinned. "Mind you, I feel pretty guilty, actually."

"Why on earth would you?"

"Well, if the culvert had been cleared properly in the autumn, it might have been able to carry away the floodwater a little better. I knew it needed doing, just one of the many jobs on the list."

"You don't have to look after me, you know."

"Ah, but clearly I do, don't I?" said Gabriel. "Now, look, you don't have to do this. I can just kick the insurance company up the arse and get it sorted."

"No. You've done so much already. Let me see."

He pushed open the front door slowly. It caught and dragged a piece of debris with it as it swept across the floor, clearing a fan-shaped sweep through the thick reddish-gray silt that covered the floor. Imogen stepped inside gingerly. The smell was the next thing that hit her. It was the musty, damp odor of the tomb, a clammy cold that touched her face with icy fingers. She shuddered. Inside, the house was gloomy and silent. A tidemark nearly three feet up the wall showed the worst extent of the flood. It was already turning green with algae at the margins, and the wallpaper was peeling in big, flabby blisters.

Gabriel held her elbow, steadying her as she took the few steps to the main drawing room, a room she had hardly gone into before the flood. Nigel's precious Eames chair was on its side against the fireplace, its black calf leather cracked and dull. The green algae had begun to stake its claim here too, and the parquet floor was silted thickly. In places, she could see the oak blocks had lifted with the damp. She reached down to prise one up.

"Don't!" barked Gabriel.

Imogen froze.

"You really don't want to touch anything. As it is, we need to change our clothes and shower when we get back to the Hall. It's not just rainwater. It's tainted with sewage where the drains backed up. The whole place needs decontaminating."

Imogen swallowed. "It's quite a job, then?"

"Afraid so. The electrics need redoing. All the plaster below the line of the floodwater needs to be chipped off and replaced and then the whole place will need redecorating. You've got no central heating at the moment either. The kitchen is completely out of action, and all the base units need ripping out . . ." He tailed off. "You can't live here, Imogen. Not with Ruth, and not anyway, frankly. Not for months, anyhow."

"Oh my God, what happened to Tango?" gasped Imogen, going pale. "He loathes water. And what has he been eating? I feel so terrible . . . I kept forgetting to ask you," she said, stricken.

"You've had your mind on a couple of other things," commented Gabriel dryly. "Still—lucky I didn't forget him too. I came down on Christmas Day to fetch him. It was nice to have him pleased to see me for a change. He's been bunked up with the stable cats at the Hall for the past week having a wonderful time. We'll turn him into a decent ratter yet."

"Tango doesn't do hunting. He doesn't agree with it," she said repressively.

"He does now. I had to stop him bringing you a dead mole as a present just this morning."

"Really?" She was astonished.

"Really," said Gabriel. "He's gone full-on country life at last. I always had him down as a bit of a wussy town cat, but he's coming on really well. We'll have him chewing straw and entering welly wanging competitions in no time."

THE REST OF Imogen's exploration was no more uplifting than the start. The little study where she had spent so much time was littered with ruined books, and the furniture was all past redemption. She riffled through the low drawer in the bureau where she had kept the old photographs of Nigel's family. It was a shame the original house deeds were not still there in the drawer. If they had been ruined in the flood, she might have been able to wangle a way out of her predicament. As it was, she had heard nothing from the law firm since the week before Christmas and she still hadn't taken Richard's advice—which was simply to beg Gabriel for mercy.

She found a dry cardboard folder and stored the few photographs that had escaped ruin. She needed something to help her tell Ruth about her father, she rationalized, and it just seemed too heartless to have them chucked on the skip with all the other rubbish. Thank goodness she had been using one of the attic rooms as her art studio. Losing her latest drawings would have been a disaster. She would need to collect them too, not knowing when she would be back.

Looking around upstairs was a bit more cheerful, although she had to agree with Gabriel about the impossibility of living there for now. Even in the rooms where the floodwaters hadn't reached, the damp and the smell had pervaded. Gabriel helped her gather some clothes and bits and pieces in a suitcase. She packed the pile of baby clothes her mother had sent in preparation. "White, not yellow, darling. Yellow just looks grim on newborns," she had said. "Matches their little faces too well if they're a bit jaundiced, which they often are." She had, of course, offered to come down; Imogen had wearily put her off, at least for now. The poor woman was dying to see her first grandchild and had been wondering loudly and repeatedly when she would get the chance.

The memory reminded Imogen, cocooned in her little world since Ruth was born, she had a lot of news to break to people who would be miffed at not being tipped off earlier.

"Tired?" said Gabriel, looking anxiously at Imogen's face. "Of course, you are. We should go back. I can always come and do this later," he added, shutting the case and plonking it on the floor. "Simon'll go nuts if I let you overdo it on your first day up."

It was true, she was suddenly exhausted—she admitted—and a tiny bit tearful. Gratefully, she let him lead her back to the car.

 *Chapter Twenty-four*

"You must come and stay with us, of course," said Sally firmly when she had stopped shrieking over the birth and gasping over tales of the biblical flood. "Al and I would love to have you. Also, frankly, what else can you do?"

She was right. Her agent, Rowena, called daily now that Imogen had reluctantly given her Gabriel's number. Being child-free herself—Rowena's own words—she regarded baby Ruth as an inconvenience in the same category as a sprained ankle or a failed car MOT, briefly acknowledging Imogen's split agenda and then making no concessions for it as she called for her to attend this meeting and that, just as soon as circumstances would allow.

Imogen had made the initial call to her insurers the day before. They promised a loss adjuster's visit but apologized for the delay in the same breath. They were stretched to breaking with new claims "flooding in," if Imogen would excuse the expression.

She had examined her car at the same time. The carpets were saturated and stinking, but the little treasure started after only a few seconds' reluctance and now it was in a garage at the Hall with carpets washed and a heater on the back seat to dry it out.

BREAKING THE NEWS of her inevitable departure to her friends was harder.

"You can't!" said Genny and Simon in unison, distracted from bickering amiably over the last custard cream.

"You belong here now," said Genny. "And anyway, imagine how unsettled Ruth will be being carted from pillar to post at such a young age," she added. Ruth dozed, impervious, in Genny's arms, a trickle of spat-up milk running from the corner of her mouth and her head blissfully lolling to one side.

"I—I just need a bit of distance," explained Imogen, "to sort things out. Sally's au pair's just left, and she needs a bit of help. I've got to be in London for the whole book publishing thing, and then there's the solicitors dealing with the repair bills thing . . ." She trailed off, overwhelmed at the enormity of the task ahead. "There is something else I wanted to ask you all before I go, though," she said. "Even if I don't come back to live here . . ." Seeing Genny's stricken face, she added hastily, "Which I will—probably—I don't want to lose touch with you all. And I especially don't want you to lose touch with Ruth. In fact, I was wondering"—she took a deep breath—"if you would agree to be godparents? Both of you, that is." She smiled.

"Wow!" said Simon, giving her a hug. "I've always wanted to be one of those. I can be an appalling influence and take her to gambling dens for her birthday."

"You can see why no one's asked you before," Genny joked. "Don't worry, Imogen, I'll be the grown-up."

"What about Gabriel?" asked Simon.

"What about him?" said Imogen, hoping he would drop it. She was trying to be upbeat but having to dredge through the leaving-Gabriel thing would shatter her composure completely.

"Well, you can't just cut off contact with him," said Simon. He and Genny met each other's eyes with an exasperated look.

"There is—as you say—the whole repair bill thing for a start," said Genny reasonably, taking up the baton, seeing Simon was struggling to think how to raise it. "How are you going to pay?"

"No idea. My only asset was the house, and that's worthless now."

"Because of the flood damage?" said Simon.

"That, and the impossibility of selling it to anyone with half a brain while the estate repair liabilities are there," said Imogen hopelessly. "Let's face it, only my idiot husband would have bought it in the first place."

"We don't want you to leave," said Genny, cuddling Ruth even tighter.

"Nor do I," admitted Imogen quietly.

SADLY, IMOGEN PACKED up her scant belongings. Gabriel had brought her art materials from Storybook Cottage, and she packed them carefully into the boot of the car. They represented her future now, her success as a book illustrator being the only reasonable way she could ever see herself and Ruth financially secure.

She waited until Gabriel was sweating and swearing over the installation of the baby car seat before raising it again.

"I don't really want to go, you know," she said gently.

He didn't reply.

"I need to pursue my career."

"Who will look after Ruth?" he said, glaring at her reproachfully.

"I'm not the first single mother who needs to work," she snapped back. "You forget, somehow I have to find half a million pounds. Plus, of course, we have to have somewhere to live."

"Live here," said Gabriel.

"I can't," said Imogen quietly. "I need to get my head straight."

"What if you could somehow sell Storybook Cottage without the repair responsibility clause? Pay off the current estate repairs with the proceeds?"

Imogen froze. If he could get the clause removed for her to sell, why couldn't he get it removed altogether and release her from this appalling situation?

"You want me to sell?" she said, trying to keep her voice level.

Gabriel put his hands up to his head, massaging his temples hard.

"It might solve a few problems," he said at last.

There was a silence while Imogen bit back all the responses she could give. There was no point. She hadn't been able to raise the issue of Louise with him. Nor had she seen her, and she was grateful Gabriel had kept her away. She couldn't cope with congratulating him or seeing her nemesis any more than she could cope with talking to Gabriel about how he had—for whatever reason—chosen to be with another woman over her. What was it with her and men? First, she married a man who was unfaithful, then she was encouraged to fall in love with a man who bankrupted her and got engaged to someone else. Actions were what counted. And he had made his position very clear.

"I would be grateful if you would keep Tango here for the time being, just until I find somewhere suitable for us all in London," she said, stiffly.

"Of course," replied Gabriel, equally stiffly. He opened his mouth to say something else, but Imogen begged him with her eyes to stay silent. She just couldn't go there.

They stared into each other's eyes for a long moment. It was Imogen who looked away first, not wanting him to see her tears.

Soon there was no further reason to delay. The car seat was in, her bags packed, and Ruth, freshly changed and fed, was dozing in the car. She couldn't even find Tango to give him a last cuddle. The lure of his exciting new country-cat life clearly outweighed such petty loyalties.

Gabriel stared after her with an inscrutable expression as she drove away.

The pressure on Imogen's chest and the ache in her throat worsened as she turned the corner and lost sight of him. She barely managed to get clear of the village before the tears began to fall.

IMOGEN RUMMAGED THROUGH her luggage, chucking knickers and socks into empty drawers while Alistair cuddled Ruth. Her country wardrobe had appeared sad even in Devon, but it looked particularly inadequate in Alistair and Sally's posh London spare room, recently vacated by the posh London au pair. Imogen's knickers were a post-pregnancy disgrace, showing much less ability to spring back to their previous shape than Imogen, whose dose of flu had had the sort of dramatic effect on her figure that postpartum film stars paid a fortune for.

"It's really nice to have you here," said Alistair shyly.

"That is so sweet," said Imogen. "It's not everyone who wants their wife's BFF moving in with them. Actually, never mind 'not everyone,' it's 'not anyone,' now I come to think of it. And that's the friends without a screeching baby in tow."

"She's not a screeching baby, are you, gorgeous?" he cooed at Ruth, who gurgled encouragingly. "And it's genuinely great having you here. We're all fond of you, and—well—Sally's sort of nicer when you're around."

AT LEAST SALLY and Alistair still have each other, Imogen reflected. Nigel and I had a failing marriage, and I didn't even know it. If he'd stayed alive for longer, I could have found out about the blonde, slapped him in the face, and chucked him out in time-honored fashion. More likely, she thought, I would have become one of those stoic embittered old women who turn a blind eye in the spirit of duty. No, it was too late to challenge Nigel, but she could sure as hell give the mystery blonde a piece of her mind.

THE NEXT MORNING, she placed herself by the bus stop in Ifield Road again, watching the morning commuter tableau unfold and keeping an eye on the door of number twenty-three. This time Ruth was bundled up complete with hat in the baby carrier, strapped to her chest with legs dangling. She loved to look down on Ruth's little crumpled face as she slept and had to keep reminding herself to watch the street. Her memory of Victoria was vivid, and her heart quickened at the thought. At that moment, a lorry rumbled past, blocking the opposite side of the street from view. Damn! When it had gone, a slim blond woman had already appeared from one of the houses, walking briskly away. She wasn't sure if it was the right house, but even from behind, it was her, Imogen was certain.

"Victoria!" she called.

The woman glanced behind and kept walking.

"Victoria!" she called again. This time, the woman turned around, searching the street for a familiar face. By this time, Imogen was dashing across the road toward her, holding Ruth's head to her chest to stop it being jolted as she ran.

"Are you Victoria?" she asked breathlessly, struck again, as she saw the woman's face, by the strong sense of recognition she had had before. This was obviously not reciprocated by the other woman, who just looked perplexed and slightly nervous.

"I'm so sorry, do I . . . ? Have we met?" she asked politely, guarded.

"Are you Victoria?"

"Er, yes," she replied uncertainly.

"The Victoria who knew Nigel Hewitt."

"What do you mean, 'knew'?" Victoria replied. "I know him, yes." And then, higher, she repeated, "What do you mean, 'knew'? Where is he?" Her voice shook, and she pressed her hand to her mouth. "Something's happened to him, hasn't it?" Her eyes met Imogen's. "Tell me, quickly."

Here was the woman she had decided to hate. The woman her husband had an affair with. And yet she felt a rush of pity for her.

"He died," Imogen said gently.

The disintegration was dramatic. Imogen grabbed Victoria's elbow as she swayed. Her face crumpled, and she covered it with her hands, letting out a couple of gasping sobs. Imogen thought about giving her a hug, but . . . They had only just met, after all, and the woman *was* her husband's mistress.

After further reflection, Imogen gave her a hug anyway, briefly squeezing Ruth between the two of them.

She remembered reading a piece in the newspaper about mistresses. There had been a woman who had a lover for thirty years, talking about how she couldn't be at his deathbed because of his wife. She couldn't attend the funeral either. Despite herself, Imogen felt her eyes filling with tears in sympathy for Victoria, who was trying desperately to compose herself as people, staring curiously, flowed around the three of them as they huddled in the middle of the pavement.

"Come on," said Imogen at last. "We'd better have a talk." She steered the slightly less hysterical Victoria to the Costa

Coffee by the station. Bunging her in a chair facing the corner, she got a couple of lattes from the intrigued barista and grabbed an extra handful of napkins for Victoria to mop herself up. Ruth, all the while, was snoozing contentedly in her harness, thank goodness.

Victoria nodded her thanks and cradled the coffee cup in both hands as if she craved its warmth.

"His mobile stopped working," she said. "First it was on answerphone all the time, and then it just went dead." She gulped, trembling. "I thought he had decided to cut off contact with me. There was no other way of getting hold of him, you see."

"I take it you always met at your flat, then, did you?" said Imogen, trying and failing to eradicate an image of Victoria and Nigel having sex in her marital bed.

"Well, yes, mainly—after the first time. We met here, then, actually," she said, looking around the café with a wan smile.

"We sat over there. In the window. I couldn't believe we had finally got together after all those years."

Blimey, thought Imogen. It's a bit rich expecting me to listen to a bunch of we-were-just-meant-for-each-other stories, even though I feel a bit sorry for her.

Victoria's eyes widened suddenly. "You're his sister, aren't you? Anne, the barrister?"

"Er, no," said Imogen. No wonder she thought the romantic reminiscences appropriate. "Actually, I'm his widow." Imogen enjoyed the soap opera drama of saying it. That'll floor her, she thought uncharitably.

She was disappointed.

"You're Imogen!" Victoria gushed, apparently delighted. "Of course, you are. He told me so much about you, about your art and everything. He was really proud."

"He did? He was?" she managed to mutter incredulously.

"And this little one is his, I take it?" she said, cooing at Ruth, who had started to stir.

"She certainly is," said Imogen, having another stab at the wronged wife getting vengeance. "I suppose he told you we didn't have sex anymore?"

Victoria looked startled. "I don't remember him mentioning it, actually," she said, blushing slightly.

Imogen decided to press home her advantage.

"Yes, well, I suppose he told you I didn't understand him and all that rubbish."

"No. No . . ." Victoria looked anguished and puzzled. "He only said nice things about you, honestly."

"Well," said Imogen, unable to hide a note of sarcasm, "didn't you think it a bit odd he was looking for a bit on the side when he and I were—apparently—so deliriously happy?"

"A bit on the side?" Victoria echoed blankly. And then her face cleared.

"Oh, my goodness! You think Nigel and I were having an affair!"

"Well, weren't you?" Imogen challenged. "Worse than that, it sounded like you were planning to come out in the open too, all that stuff in your letter about hating to keep your relationship secret, wanting to meet his family and friends but understanding there were 'obstacles' to be cleared out of the way . . . Well, here's the obstacle," she said, pointing to herself.

"No, no, no, no . . . How could you think. Oh, my goodness, no . . ." Victoria trailed off weakly. Then, grabbing Imogen's arm, she looked into her eyes intently.

"Nigel wasn't my lover," she said. "He was my brother."

 *Chapter Twenty-five*

Finishing their coffee, they decamped to Victoria's flat so Ruth could have a clean nappy and a feed—Imogen was still shy about whipping her tits out in public. As Ruth snoozed on a blanket, they exchanged stories.

"I only found out I had a brother and sister eighteen months ago," said Victoria sadly. "My mum never wanted to tell me about my father. I only knew that he sent her money to support me—quite a lot, actually—but it stopped when he died. That was about ten years ago. It was hard on both of us, because I had to be taken out of private school just before A levels."

"So, you're about my age, then," said Imogen, doing the maths quickly.

"Thirty-two," confirmed Victoria, smiling.

"I was jealous when I first saw you," Imogen confessed. "You were like me only prettier, blonder and everything, you know . . . I even thought you looked familiar, but I couldn't work out why."

"We look a bit like each other, Nigel and me, don't we?" she asked. "We decided we did—same nose and mouth but different coloring."

Imogen nodded, smiling sadly.

"It's so hard to lose him before we've had a chance to get to know each other better," Victoria said. " I was always desperate to have a big brother when I was growing up. It was just mum and me, of course. She was great, but it was a bit lonely a lot of the time."

"Was?"

"She died two years ago. It was only when she knew she was dying she let me have my father's name. She hoped I would be able to trace some family for myself. She didn't want me to be completely on my own when she'd gone."

Victoria was impressively lacking in self-pity, Imogen noted. And what a story . . . It even made her want to call her own mother to arrange a visit, spend some time with her. Well, almost. Chances were, when Sally and Alistair got fed up, she and Ruth were going to have to move back home. Her mother would love it, of course, but the idea filled Imogen with dread. Guiltily, she dragged herself back to what Victoria was saying.

"Anyway," Victoria continued, "his details took me to the national records office, so I found out he had a son and daughter, Nigel and Anne. Trouble is, since they had grown up and moved away, it took me a while to track them down. I only found Nigel, and that was a bit of a long shot. Hewitt's a pretty common name."

"With the address you were given, you could have just contacted your father's wife," suggested Imogen, thinking, with a wince, of her ghastly mother-in-law, who would certainly be needing a visit soon.

"I promised Mum I wouldn't," she explained. "Apparently his wife never knew about the affair, although my own thoughts are that she probably did know or at least must have found out after he died. Presumably the money we got from him over all those years will have showed up when they went through his estate."

"I suppose it might have come up," said Imogen slowly. Not having met Nigel's mother until after his father's death, she began to wonder if the corrosive bitterness that consumed her had developed after finding out about the affair, either before or after her husband's death. She's a miserable, self-obsessed old rat bag, Imogen opined to herself, not for the first time. But she may have had her reasons.

"Anyway," Victoria continued, "you saw my letter to Nigel, so you know he was sort of preparing the way for me to meet Anne, my sister." Tears threatened again. "She's the only family I have left." Victoria dabbed at her eyes with a corner of the sodden tissue. "God, sorry, all the time, I just can't stop—"

"I'll get you two together," promised Imogen. "She's not, though."

"Not what?"

"Not your only family. There's me for a start, if in-laws count. More importantly, how about Ruth? Tragic to lose a brother, but you've gained a niece today."

"Oh, my goodness! Yes, of course. Little Ruth." This time the tears really did start again, and Imogen had to give her another hug.

"What I don't understand," said Imogen, trying to disguise the hurt in her voice, "is why Nigel didn't tell *me* about you. I can see the difficulty with his mum, sure, but there's no obvious reason—"

"I'm sorry about that. You must be angry that he didn't confide," empathized Victoria, squeezing Imogen's hand. "I can't speak for him, obviously, but—if it makes any sense at all—we were kind of enjoying this golden 'thing' together, and that was partly because it was a secret. I got the impression Nigel was quite grown-up and commanding in the rest of his life, but the two of us together? We were like giggly kids. It was nice." She looked out of the window, misty-eyed. "I'm so glad we had that."

Victoria looked back at Imogen, imploringly. "Does that make any sense at all? If it's any consolation, I think he was gearing himself up for the big reveal. He was dreading telling his mum and paranoid that she would find out. I suppose he thought telling as few people as possible made us safer."

In other words, thought Imogen, he didn't tell her because he was worried she couldn't keep a secret. Okay, fair enough. She did have a reputation for putting her foot in it—for blurting things out—especially when it came to his mother, because the old baggage made Imogen feel so nervous.

With relief, she noted that the pain from the thorn in her side that was Nigel's perceived infidelity had gone. She could start to make her peace with his death at last.

"Now, JUST LET me do the talking," said Rowena firmly. Imogen nodded, only too happy to comply. She knew nothing about marketing, and the publishing house's invitation for her and Rowena to attend their planning meeting felt more like a trip to the dentist than the privilege her agent assured her it was.

"Are you up to this?" she barked, looking doubtfully at Imogen's slight frame. "You certainly don't look like you've just had a baby," she said, "although I can see the sleep deprivation is having an effect."

It was true. Her face was gray and her eyes heavily ringed, although not much of it was down to Ruth, who slept angelically and was only waking once a night for a feed, despite being just two months old.

In the end, the meeting was amazing. Imogen was introduced to the marketing team, whose names she immediately forgot.

There was a little, pretty blond girl with pearl earrings who had made the coffee, said hi shyly, and spent the rest of the meeting assiduously taking notes in silence.

The marketing director was a tall, dark Hooray Henry in a pink shirt with cuff links. He kept talking enthusiastically about "parent power"—which Imogen thought she understood—and "vertical audiences"—which she absolutely knew she didn't. As he talked, he was scribbling notes on a whiteboard, and soon it had *Tango and Ruth* in the middle of a big circle with lines flying out from it to point at random words, which were apparently meaningful to everyone else. It looked a bit like a giant spider with massive shoes on, thought Imogen vaguely, beginning to enjoy herself.

She was given to understand that the launch of the first four books was being heavily supported by marketing spend, including a significant linkup with a supermarket chain, and that they were hopeful of some media coverage if they could wangle it.

A sharp-faced press officer had asked her if there was any personal reason for the choice of the character names.

"Well, I do have a cat called Tango," said Imogen tentatively, with a pang of regret that she had not seen him for so long.

The press officer was guardedly pleased.

"So, is the character like your cat?"

"Oh no. The Tango in the book is much nicer. The real Tango's a bit of a sociopath," she added, missing him terribly.

The press officer looked disappointed.

"They're the same color, though," added Imogen, trying to be encouraging. "And of course, my daughter is called Ruth."

"No way! That's fantastic, you called the character after your daughter. It'll be like Christopher Robin and Winnie-the-Pooh. How old is she?"

"Eight weeks."

"Ah, the books aren't inspired by her, then," he said, disappointed.

"Absolutely they are. Or she's inspired by them. I'm not sure which . . ." said Imogen, wondering if it was appropriate to drag Ruth into it at all. Perhaps she should change the character's name.

"Mind you," said the press officer, brightening, "I love that you're a widow." The pretty blond girl caught her eye and smiled apologetically. "That's just sooo great!" he continued. "It's the whole single mother fighting against adversity thing—we can definitely use that. I'm thinking *Sunday Times Magazine* Best of Times, Worst of Times column or Loose Women maybe—yeah—definitely Loose Women."

Imogen trembled at the thought of having to talk to the press. She couldn't imagine what she could possibly say that would be of interest to anyone.

Still fretting about this, she hardly noticed as the talk moved on, incomprehensibly again, to residuals and overseas distribution and merchandise licensing deals. Rowena got quite strident over some percentages, which seemed important, although Imogen couldn't see why. She was impressed at her agent, though, as the whole publishing team looked scared and seemed to be capitulating over these incomprehensible battles.

SPRING BARELY REGISTERED in a London that still seemed unrelentingly gray, or perhaps that was just Imogen's mood. She wondered if the crocuses were out at Storybook Cottage. They must be by now. Wanting to check up on Tango but too shy and upset to call Gabriel, Imogen phoned Genny instead. Touchingly, she seemed pleased to hear from her.

"So, how is he?" she said eagerly once they got through the preliminaries.

"To be honest, Simon and I think he's very unhappy at the moment," Genny said.

"Oh no!" Imogen felt appallingly guilty. "Is he off his food? Because if he is, I find warming it up before you give it to him really helps."

"Right. Well, he is looking a bit thin, now you mention

it, although I took him round a shepherd's pie a couple of days ago, and he's brought back the empty dish, so I assume he ate it. I would imagine he heated it up first. I probably should have told him to—I just didn't think . . ."

Imogen was flummoxed. Tango hated shepherd's pie. "Oh, you mean Gabriel!" she said eventually. "Hmm. Well, it's not up to me to make sure he's happy."

It's that woman Louise's job, she thought bitterly. God, I must be a bitch. If I'm honest, I *like* the idea Louise isn't making him happy.

"Is he really unhappy?" she queried.

"Oh yes," said Genny. "He's not been this miserable since—well—since Annabel was killed. Plus, he's just so busy with the conferences—that Louise girl is useless as well as horrible—and all the other hours of the day, he's in the forge working away. Then, of course, everyone is cracking the whip to get Storybook Cottage repaired."

"That's so sweet of you all," said Imogen. "I should be there, not just leaving it to you."

"It's fine, sorry, I didn't mean to sound like it was a problem. As for the practical site management stuff, Gabriel does most of it, of course, because he has the keys. I know he's been checking their work and so on. He said something about dragging the plasterer back because he wasn't too impressed with the job they did in the hall or something."

"I could come back," said Imogen longingly, despite her mixed feelings about seeing Gabriel again.

"Ye-e-s. I mean—no. I don't think you should," said Genny slowly. "For one thing, you wouldn't have anywhere to stay."

Imogen was a tiny bit hurt. It was true Storybook Cottage was uninhabitable, and staying with Gabriel probably wasn't an option with Louise around, but she was a little bit surprised Genny wasn't offering a room.

"The insurance company has offered to pay for me to rent somewhere. I could easily find something in the village, couldn't I?" said Imogen, trying to sound brisk and businesslike. "It's wintertime, so there must be a holiday let available."

"I can't think of anywhere," said Genny dismissively. "Anyway, I just don't think it's a good idea. You've got all that work to do in London with your books, and well"—she paused—"it would just be difficult for you to be here now."

"I see," said Imogen in a small voice. She'd thought Genny was a friend. Obviously, her loyalty to Gabriel came first, and naturally Genny understood how awkward it would be for everyone with Gabriel and Louise being together. Imogen could hardly expect anything else.

"Actually," she added experimentally, "I was thinking I'll just sell it when it's fixed. I think it's what Gabriel wants too. He was talking about getting the repairs liability clause removed in return for payment of the current bill." He had mentioned this before she left but, rather than being grateful, she had bitten his head off that he could remove the clause but wouldn't until he had his pound of flesh.

"Oh, really?" said Genny. "That's not a bad idea. You'll get a reasonable price when it's all done up, I'm sure."

Imogen felt like she had been thumped in the chest. They had moved on without her, all of them. Even Genny, she thought sadly.

". . . AND BRUSH YOUR teeth!" yelled Alistair after his son, who was dragging himself up the stairs.

"Why?" came the reply.

"Because they'll fall out if you don't," shouted Sally wearily, in support.

"Good. I want them to fall out," Ed shouted back. "Sam got five quid for one of his last week."

They all laughed, but only once they were sure Ed was out of earshot.

"Kids, eh?" said Alistair, sighing. "Can't live with 'em, can't kill 'em. Anyway, tell us about your high-powered publisher meeting," he added as he poured Imogen another glass of wine.

"Well, I am just blown away," said Alistair once she had told them all the bits she could remember and understand. "Getting a four-book deal and talking about merchandise and animation deals before they are even launched is exceptional. You do realize that, don't you?"

"Only because Rowena keeps telling me," she admitted. Apparently, it's something to do with them losing the whole Terence the Tractor series to a rival publisher six months ago. Not only are they furious and feeling deeply competitive, they also have a whole load of budget allocated to this business year and nothing to spend it on until Rowena dropped my stuff into their laps. It's just a timing thing, really."

"Nothing to do with your genius, then," said Sally. "Honestly, honey, I am just so bloody proud of you. You've had the crappiest year ever. During which I've been a rubbish friend—no, let me finish," she said as Imogen demurred.

"And, after all that slog getting nowhere for years, you've pulled this amazing triumph out of the hat less than twelve months after losing your husband. Respect. They don't come more impressive than that."

"Talking about amazing triumphs," said Imogen, "my other, far more impressive achievement this year seems to be making her presence felt."

They listened. Ruth had woken up and was making polite but strident noises to let them know she was ready to join the party again.

"I'll go," said Alistair, leaping up. "I expect she'll be needing a nappy too . . ."

"It's about time I found a place for me and Ruth to stay," announced Imogen when Alistair had reappeared with Ruth in his arms.

"You've got a place here," protested Alistair.

"Yes, plus you don't want to waste money on rent," added Sally sensibly. "You're not a multimillionaire author yet, after all."

"We need to have our own space," explained Imogen. "And so do you. You've been really kind, but I outstayed my welcome with Gabriel, and I don't want to do the same with you both."

They were a little mollified when she told them about the insurance company money and the little two-bed flat she had found just a couple of streets away. Alistair even offered to help settle her in at the weekend.

 *Chapter Twenty-six*

The garden flat had languished on the rental market for a while, the agent had admitted. Mainly this was because sharers looking for a two bedder weren't keen on the narrow, north-facing second bedroom at the front. For Imogen, though, it was perfect. Her drawing board would fit nicely in the space under the window, the north light in there was ideal, and all the other space she needed was a few shelves for her art materials. It was hardly as if Ruth needed her own room. She was in with Imogen anyway. That would change, but Imogen couldn't bear to think of the longer term.

Alistair was as good as his word, spending most of Saturday moving Imogen's stuff the half mile from the house. He then spent hours fixing up the shelves and a few blinds at the windows where the curtains were too awful to stay. Of course, what little furniture she owned was still in Devon, much of it in a skip by now, she thought.

The flat was basically furnished including a double bed in the main bedroom, which left plenty of room for Ruth's cot. A bleak, cramped little place with limited natural daylight, the flat was a million miles away from Storybook Cottage, but she wanted no reminder of what she had lost. It was home for now. It would do.

THE TWO OF them settled into a routine of sorts. Ruth was happy with an endless round of cuddles, milk, trips out in the pram, and naps. Imogen accommodated her completely, happy to work at her drawing board during the daytime naps and the dead hours of the night. She would rather be at work than enduring the restless dreams that accompanied her sleep. The most common and upsetting was about Storybook Cottage, where Gabriel would stand in the doorway, holding out his arms toward her. Running to him, she would find Louise in his place, slamming the door as she arrived.

As Ruth grew, the work intensified. The publisher's response to Imogen's prolific output was to pack more and more into the schedule, their ambitions growing by the month as the launch date for the first book approached.

"BIN . . . BIN . . . BIN," chanted Sally, as she decimated Imogen's wardrobe, chucking most of it into a black plastic bag. As summer arrived, Imogen found her clothes selection was more inadequate than ever, and Sally—sick of seeing her in the same pair of jeans—had decided on direct action.

"Good grief, woman, you haven't still got these," said Sally, holding up a favorite pair of tracksuit bottoms with spotty patches on the knees. "These were hideous when you were wearing them fifteen years ago."

"They were very cool, I'll have you know," she said defensively. "Ellie Goulding had a pair just like them."

"I rest my case," said Sally, snatching them back from Imogen and consigning them to the pile. "Shopping trip, I think."

"Nope," said Imogen sulkily. "Mum's coming to stay this afternoon. Anyway, shouldn't you be working?"

"Excellent. I love your mum, plus I finished a big proposal last night," said Sally, "so we've got time for lunch at Harvey Nicks too."

"We-ell," said Imogen consideringly, "I do have to find something to wear for my launch party, although I was actually wondering if I could borrow your little black dress again?"

"The one you wore to Nigel's funeral?"

Imogen nodded.

"No, you may not. You looked like Little Orphan Annie in it then, for heaven's sake, and I reckon you've lost another dress size since. Anyway, what's this launch party all about? Sounds like an excuse for both of us to have a new outfit . . ."

Luckily Imogen's mother, June, was all for a trip to the shops and was delighted to have Sally's company, despite Imogen protesting that she must be tired, having just got back from a week in Bali with Gerald.

"Nonsense, dear. I've been doing nothing but sleeping, eating, and having sex all week. Fantastic for one's pelvic floor. Incidentally, darling, that's what you should be doing if you don't want to end up in nappies when you're my age," she added. "I shall be thrilled to stretch my legs, and I'm keen to see what I can find for this little darling to wear." She gave butterfly kisses to Ruth, who chortled rewardingly.

THEY STARTED, AS promised, with a late lunch at a restaurant where huge white linen napkins and even bigger wineglasses were the norm. It was full of ladies who lunch grazing on smoked salmon and rocket. Sally and her mother urged Imogen to go for something more substantial.

"You're feeding Ruth, remember," said her mother. "I nearly disappeared when I was feeding you, until I discovered sticky toffee pudding, that is."

Imogen was pressured into ordering double-chocolate cheesecake for dessert. The thick, dry texture stuck in her throat, and her knotted stomach rebelled against its richness.

After an age of shopping, they eventually decided on a luscious Missoni silk dress for Imogen to wear at the launch. Her mother and Sally refused to let her see the price. It was striped in all the colors she could imagine, cupping her rather magnificent breastfeeding bosom. Better still, the high waist lengthened her legs so that—when she wasn't standing next to Sally, who was genuinely tall—you could almost be fooled that she too was one of the leggy, insouciant young women who strolled the length of Kensington High Street. The jeweled sandals they found for her to wear with it added to her height too. Imogen was terrified about falling off them after years of wearing trainers, flip-flops, or nothing at all on her feet.

Imogen's mother found some shockingly expensive but utterly gorgeous clothes for Ruth. Imogen at least succeeded in stopping her from buying the onesies, which, as she pointed out, at one hundred percent cashmere, would need dry-cleaning or at least hand washing, which was insane, especially as they wouldn't even show under the adorable little pinafore dress and cardigan she had bought to go with them.

"Nonsense, darling," she had said. "Nothing is too good for my granddaughter. And after all, she has inspired a whole new canon of children's literature. The least she deserves is a new frock."

SETTLING HER GUESTS in the flat's little courtyard garden where the flagstones were radiating the warmth of the day back into the evening air, Imogen pottered around the kitchen, gathering nibbles to go with the wine they were drinking. Only then did she notice the little notification tag on her phone. Just a handful of people had her number, so she was guessing it was either Rowena or Genny. Instead, though, a male voice boomed out. It was Richard.

"The most extraordinary development on Storybook Cottage situation," he began. "We've had an offer from the trustees to take the house in lieu of the repair fees. What's more, they are offering a tidy sum to you on top. Not a fortune, but enough for a deposit on somewhere modest, perhaps? I gather they've even had wind of a private buyer for the house, once the repairs clause is off the deeds." He went on to mention a sum, which really was—as he said— "modest," but it was an amount that would help her and Ruth to make a home somewhere. Somewhere far away from Middlemass.

"WHAT'S UP?" SAID Sally immediately, as she joined them on the terrace.

Imogen shared the news.

"Well, darling, it does seem like a good way out of a sticky situation, doesn't it?" said her mother.

Imogen nodded. She might hate it, but it was the *only* way out of a sticky situation. Far from feeling relief, though, she couldn't remember a time she had ever felt bleaker.

"It would make sense, though, wouldn't it, honey?" said Sally, her expression mirroring Imogen's. "Obviously we would love having you close by, but—our own selfish reasons apart—wouldn't you want to be in London now that the whole book thing is going on?"

"I suppose," she said, feeling hollow. Could her dream life in Middlemass really be totally over? It had been such a short time, but she had never felt more at home than in the little community. She thought sorrowfully of her friendships—Winifred, Simon, Genny, and Gabriel, of course. But she couldn't have him anyhow, so she might as well be anywhere else in the world.

"So, darling, tell us about this exciting launch party," said her mother, tactfully changing the subject. "I couldn't be more proud of you. Brenda—you know, Brenda with the husband who went off with his secretary—has a niece who once got to the final of some ghastly TV talent show. I'll tell you, darling, I got sick of hearing about the child and her amazing singing voice. I can't wait to tell her how clever *you've* been."

"I'd have thought my life was complete if I'd sung a song on the telly," said Imogen dreamily. "Actually, I'd still think it was pretty amazing—"

"So anyway," pressed Sally, returning to the matter in

hand, "what, when, where, how, and—most importantly—*who* does your launch party involve?"

"I think friends are allowed to come," said Imogen tentatively. Rowena had just said to let her have a vague idea of numbers. "I don't think it'll be so smart there will be Rottweilers at the door asking for details. They probably wouldn't let *me* in, knowing my luck."

"Seeing as the pressure is on, darling, why don't I stay here for a few days? I can look after Ruth for you while you work," said her mother. "Plus, I wouldn't miss this party next week for the world."

"That would be great, Mum," said Imogen, smiling weakly.

"Fab, so that's you, me, your mum, and anyone else we can think of," said Sally, grabbing a pen and paper to write a list. "This is going to be the event of the century."

IMOGEN WAS EMBARRASSED to call Genny again. It wouldn't have mattered so much if she had had the occasional call from her Devon friends, but it was like they couldn't get rid of her fast enough and now she was chasing Genny for information like some deranged stalker.

She called anyway.

"I don't know much about it," said Genny, sounding uninterested. "But—yes—there's already a buyer lined up. I vaguely heard it's a couple. And they've got a baby. That's right, yes, it's a young family. Apparently, he's a bit of a grump, but she's all right. That's what Gabriel says, anyhow. He's the one who's been dealing with it. Anyhow, I've really got to dash. We've got the Local Education Authority sending their funding gestapo over again today."

"Okay, well, good luck and everything," said Imogen. But Genny had already gone.

"Are you there, darling?" came the voice from a distance. "Cooee." A hand was being waved across her face.

"Sorry, Mum," said Imogen. She had been making a cup of tea for them both. Somehow the kettle had boiled dry and Imogen was staring into space with a pint of milk in her hand. She went to pour it into cups that weren't there.

She really had to pull herself together, but she had forgotten how to do it. Her mother made sure Ruth was fed, changed, and put down for naps, watching Imogen with silent concern. Night after night, Imogen stared into the darkness, her eyes stretched wide, and then dragged herself through the days that followed in an exhausted stupor.

The success she had dreamed of for years was in her sights, and she had her precious baby too.

She had never been so miserable in her life.

PUTTING ON HER new dress, Imogen noticed her skin stretched thin across her collarbone, the shadows it created matching the hollows under her eyes. The dress hung even looser on her frame than it had just the week before when she bought it. Without her still full bosom, thanks to feeding Ruth, it would have dropped straight to the floor.

Despite the heat of the June day, she was cold. The chill had settled over her days before and wouldn't lift. Her hands had been dripping with icy sweat as she had opened her post the previous morning, upset that the paperwork for signing over Storybook Cottage had arrived so soon. She had riffled through the pages to the end, where Duncan had marked the places for her to sign. Scribbling her signature without looking, she stuffed the papers into the return envelope and walked straight down to the postbox at the end of the road, shoving them in before she changed her mind. What was the point in delaying?

Sally, who had come over to the flat to help her get ready, tutted impatiently when she saw her.

"You can't afford to let that dress wear you. It's got more life in it than you have at the moment." She sighed. "Thank goodness for makeup."

Imogen didn't generally bother with a lot more than mascara and a bit of much-needed blusher, but resistance was futile. Sally refused Imogen a mirror while she carried out her work. Once satisfied, she led Imogen into the bathroom.

"There," she said. "What do you think?"

Her eyes were huge and dark. The two streaks of blusher with highlighter above emphasized her newly hollowed cheeks with their razor-sharp cheekbones and made her complexion look dramatically pale rather than just wan.

She might just pull off the neurotic author look, Imogen thought, even if she couldn't look as glossy as all the pretty publishing PR girls who would also be there.

Sally and her mother had declined to come with her for the beginning.

"You need to go early, it's your party," they both said. "We'll follow on behind with Ruth when it's started to swing a bit."

 *Chapter Twenty-seven*

The first person she saw when she got to Waterstones on Kensington High Street was, to her relief, the quiet, sympathetic blond girl who had been taking the notes during the publishing meeting. She was looking fresh and pretty in a flippy skirt and a tomato red T-shirt, simple mules on the end of her long brown legs. Next to her, Imogen looked like a corpse.

She smiled a shy greeting. "You're early," she said. "I'm just putting out the press packs."

"Can I help?" begged Imogen, desperate to have something to do. "I was too nervous to stay at home any longer, thinking about all those press interviews."

"If you're sure," said the girl. "Thanks. Most of our authors seem to love being the center of attention."

"Probably because most of them have something to say," muttered Imogen, shuffling papers together and stapling them like the girl was showing her.

As they worked, the caterers arrived and started to set up. Damn it, thought Imogen, even the waitresses, with their smart dark blue shirts and perfect, deadpan faces, were more glamorous than she was. The band, showing up shortly after, were engagingly shambolic, though, scraping their chairs around so they could get eye contact and then cocking their eyebrows at each other as they tuned up.

At last, they launched into a jaunty, jazzed-up version of "Teddy Bear's Picnic," timing it perfectly to be a fanfare for Rowena, who sailed in with the most extraordinarily eye-catching headgear that Imogen had ever seen. She tried not to stare too obviously but was transfixed. A purple velvet turban with a huge jewel in the front was coordinated with the swathes of purple eyeshadow that very nearly swept up to meet it.

Almost without Imogen noticing, the room filled, the waiters and waitresses gliding smoothly among the guests, trays loaded with glasses of wine and delicious-looking canapés that she couldn't face eating.

She found herself making inane remarks to a succession of strangers who passed before her, gushing and smiling. Crowds of people surrounded her, ebbing and flowing, smiling at her stuttering anecdotes of writing with the real Tango on her knee, of the beautiful countryside around Middlemass that had inspired her paintings. The way she had painted her illustrations for each of the seasons in the four books, and how the real-life Ruth had arrived, looking exactly like her mother's depictions of her. Moved by her own rhetoric, talking so evocatively about a life that was no longer hers, was agony.

Later, she saw her mother surrounded by women all cooing over Ruth, who was, as Imogen noted, looking completely gorgeous in her new outfit.

Imogen made her way over to grab a quick cuddle with

Ruth, who—thoroughly excited at all the attention—tweaked Imogen's nose, making her eyes water. Blinking the tears away, her vision blurred, she did a double take. Those broad shoulders were unmistakable. He was across the room with his back to her, talking to a pretty brunette who was fiddling flirtatiously with her hair. It couldn't be . . . As if he sensed her gaze, he turned, meeting her eye.

Gabriel! What on earth was he doing here? He was supposed to be more than a hundred miles away, overseeing the refurbishment of her house and planning his wedding to the ghastly Louise, amongst other things.

Appropriately enough, the band swung into "I've Got You Under My Skin" as, brushing off the brunette, he weaved his way across the room, never once breaking eye contact.

He arrived in front of her, still saying nothing. She reached out and touched his chest, checking he was real. Her hand was shaking, she noticed with detachment. She raised her eyes again to meet his, gasping at the intensity of his gaze.

"You're here," she observed inadequately.

"I am," he replied, catching her sweating hand in both of his own. "You're freezing," he said. His own hands were warm and dry, and she could feel his strength and solidity like energy pouring into her body.

"Now let's get the hell out of here," he said. Grabbing her around the shoulders, he pulled her toward the door. The crowds were pressing in around them, but he pushed his way through, with his other arm, making space.

"Leaving your own party, my dear, we can't allow that," said Rowena, grabbing her as they passed. "I was just telling the *Bookseller* that yours is the most significant launch for the children's sector since *I Will Never Not Ever Eat a Tomato.*"

"She would say that, wouldn't she?" simpered the journalist. "But it's nice to have some good news for the industry for a change."

"Indeed, it is," said Gabriel pleasantly. "I'm Gabriel," he added to Rowena, giving a sort of salute.

"Well, hello," she cooed, fluttering her purple eyelashes.

"Goodbye," said Gabriel firmly, whisking Imogen out of the door as Rowena's jaw dropped in shock.

"Mum's got Ruth," protested Imogen, turning to go back in.

"Yep," he agreed, grabbing her shoulders and propelling her firmly away. "And what better babysitter for your child than her own grandmother? All part of the cunning plan."

"What cunning plan?"

"First rule of the cunning plan? Don't talk about the cunning plan."

"Right. So, you've got it all worked out, the two of you," said Imogen.

"Yep. And there's a few more than two of us," he admitted. "It is a complex and wide-ranging cunning plan, requiring considerable cooperation from a number of parties. I'll share with you, but not yet."

He was hanging on to her upper arm and walking so fast Imogen had to trot in her high heels to keep up with him.

"Where are we going?"

"You'll see," he said, hailing a cab.

"The Royal Opera House, please," he said to the driver as they clambered in. He then ignored Imogen for the whole journey, staring out of the window, his arm resting casually across the back of the seat, his fingertips lightly grazing her bare shoulder.

All around them, workers had spilled out of offices and into bars, the men with jackets slung over shoulders and the women in summer dresses, tilting their faces up to catch the evening breeze and the last of the sun.

When they stepped out of the cab into the cooling air, goose pimples sprung up on Imogen's arms.

"Don't you have a wrap or anything?" said Gabriel impatiently, dropping his jacket onto Imogen's shoulders. It was still warm from his body, and she wrapped it around her gratefully.

"I've not seen you wearing a suit before," she said teasingly.

"I doubt you will again anytime soon. Do you want a drink or anything?"

"I'm fine," said Imogen. "What are we seeing?"

"*Marriage of Figaro*," said Gabriel.

"My favorite!" gasped Imogen, nearly swooning with delight. "How did you know?"

"I heard you massacring it when you were cleaning out your gutters. I just thought you should hear it sung well, for once," he said, still looking stern, but the corner of his mouth twitched upward after he said it.

"So, the cunning plan so far involves abducting me from my party and surprise tickets to my favorite opera," said Imogen, beginning to enjoy herself. "Whatever next?"

"Don't fish," he told her. "All will become clear. Just enjoy the moment. It's what I've been busy doing for bloody ages, while we've been apart. And why the hell haven't you been in touch?"

It seemed to be a rhetorical question, so Imogen didn't reply. A bubble of joy started to rise up from her core. She felt light, as if—at any moment—her feet might leave the floor and she would float to the ceiling of this beautiful, velvet-lined theater, with its gilding and scrolls and opulent splendor. She could hear the orchestra tuning up below and smell Gabriel's aftershave as he sat beside her; she couldn't remember the last time she had ever dared to be that happy.

They had a box to themselves, and Imogen was transported from the minute the conductor struck up the familiar jaunty overture. The world receded as the actors played out the tale told through the most sublime music Imogen had ever heard. The trouble was, the effect of the music, Gabriel's sudden arrival, and the pent-up misery of the last few months finally beginning to lift made her cry. And once she started, she couldn't stop.

By the time the lights went up, she was sobbing in earnest, with a runny nose and swollen eyes.

Unperturbed, Gabriel put his arm around her shoulders and helped her up.

"Hungry?" he said.

She shook her head.

"Yes, I think you are," he told her, "and I know just the place."

WITHIN MINUTES, THEY were in a cozy, dimly lit booth, private enough for Imogen not to feel self-conscious about other diners seeing her tearstained face. She found she couldn't meet Gabriel's eye at all. He ordered for her, and a plate of pad Thai noodles arrived with some cold lager. Sure she wouldn't be able to eat a thing, she amazed herself by emptying the plate and draining the glass. The gnawing stomach pain she had not consciously acknowledged dissipated.

Imogen took a deep breath. It was now or never. "You didn't bring Louise," she said at last, making it a statement not a question.

"Why the hell would I bring Louise on a date with you?"

"Is this a date?"

Gabriel looked away uncomfortably. "If you like," he said reluctantly.

"Okay, whose idea was this?"

"Mine." He paused. "All right, fine, Genny and Simon and that lot had this ridiculous suggestion I should take you out or something," he admitted. "You know, a show, dinner, all that stuff. I thought it was a stupid idea myself."

"I think it's a strange thing for them to suggest when they know you're engaged to Louise," she reasoned, her heart sinking as she remembered this herself. For God's sake, she knew Gabriel's friends weren't Louise's greatest fans, but using her, Imogen, to mess up his relationship with the woman he wanted to marry was a bit much. She, personally, could do without it, for a start.

"News to me!" he said, sounding even more amazed. "Where the bloody hell do you get these ideas from, woman?"

"You proposed to her on Christmas Eve," said Imogen, bolder now. "She told me." Gabriel's brow lowered ominously. "At least," Imogen added as the truth slowly dawned, "she told me you were going to."

"Did she?" he said, eyebrows raised so high they nearly disappeared under his hairline. "Well, I didn't."

"But you invited her to supper, it was the night of the flood," insisted Imogen.

"And you didn't think it odd that it was Simon and me together when we came to rescue you?"

"Oh, yeah," said Imogen, who hadn't given it any thought at all until now.

"I suppose now you think it's me and Simon that are engaged."

"Well, if it's true, I do think someone should tell Genny," she joked feebly.

"I did see Louise that night. I asked her over for supper so I could make it absolutely clear to her there could be nothing between us."

"Ah," said Imogen.

"Yes, 'ah,'" replied Gabriel.

"How did she seem?"

"Thwarted," said Gabriel, remembering.

"Poor Louise."

"Save your sympathy. She was never quite as keen after she found out the whole lord of the manor thing didn't come with a ton of cash. I gather she's already snaffled herself some city boy who had the misfortune to come on one of her conferences. He's got a helicopter and a villa in Mustique apparently, so I shouldn't think she'll be letting him out of her clutches in a hurry."

They sat in silence while Gabriel finished his food. Imogen was unable to process any more information. The idea that she had been wrong about such a fundamental thing, plus the pressure of the last six months leading up to the launch, had left her poleaxed with fatigue. The only way she could support the weight of her head was by propping it on her hand. Twice her elbow slipped and she nearly smashed her nose on the table.

"Bit tired," she muttered to Gabriel, who had finished eating and was watching her silently.

"I'll take you home," he said.

At this, huge tears started to plop onto the table. The thought of waking up tomorrow in her little rented flat without him made her want to howl all over again. Unable to explain, she stumbled to her feet and let Gabriel lead her out of the restaurant. Even though it was well past midnight, the streets were still teeming with people wearily traveling home or those for whom the evening had barely begun, queuing outside the nightclubs.

His car was in an underground car park around the corner. He opened the passenger door for her and even reached across to put on her seat belt. Like an exhausted toddler, she let him, slumping limply in the seat. Feeling the chill of her bare arms with his warm, rough hand, he took his jacket off again and laid it over her. Before he had even negotiated his way to the exit, she was sound asleep, her head resting uncomfortably on the doorjamb. Later, she was vaguely aware of someone lifting her head and resting it back on something lovely and soft. A blanket covered her, and she sighed, settling down into an even deeper sleep, deeper than she had slept for months.

 *Chapter Twenty-eight*

When she next woke, the car was cruising smoothly on the open road. It was dark. Much darker than anywhere in London, where the city never slept.

"Where are we?" she said sharply, sitting up in a panic. "Where are you taking me?"

"We're going home."

"What home?"

"Middlemass, of course."

"I can't!" said Imogen, her voice rising in panic. "What about Ruth?"

"Look behind you."

Turning, she saw Ruth strapped into a car seat in her pajamas. She was sound asleep, her long dark eyelashes fanned across her cheeks.

"Your mother took her back to your flat and got her ready for you. All her stuff's in a bag in the boot, plus some bits and pieces for you."

She turned to face the front. "How far is it now?"

"Not long to go."

Peace stole over Imogen for the first time in weeks. Of course, Gabriel knew that Storybook Cottage had been sold by now, to that couple with the baby. She wondered where he was taking her and then found that she didn't care. She felt safe. She and Ruth were with Gabriel. Louise was gone. Nothing else mattered. Imogen dozed off again.

SHE WOKE AS the car drew to a halt. They were in Middlemass, but not at the Hall as she had expected. Instead, they were outside Simon and Genny's house. Despite it being the middle of the night—the lights in the kitchen were on, and Genny came bouncing out to meet them. Seeing Ruth was still asleep, she stopped bouncing and put her finger to her lips.

"Hi," she whispered, giving Imogen a hug as she clambered stiffly out of the car.

Imogen caught Genny and Gabriel sharing a look. Genny gave a little nod.

"Look at the gorgeous little thing. She's got so huge since I saw her last!" she breathed, looking at Ruth in the car.

"Gabriel, can you get the car seat out, do you think?" she asked. "You could just bring her in asleep. I'll take her bag." Genny bustled efficiently.

"Now, I've got some hot chocolate ready to go. Why don't we have that, and then you can grab a few hours kip while Ruth is asleep—you don't want to be carting her around all over the place. You can go and see the cottage in daylight. That'll be better, won't it? You won't believe how it looks now, all beautiful again. The boys have done a grand job renovating it."

At the talk of the cottage, Imogen almost cried again. She just wanted to get it all over with. She didn't understand why she had to go and see a home that was no longer hers. The place where she had dreamed of raising Ruth. It seemed cruel to dangle what she wanted so much but could no longer have. As they all sat drinking hot chocolate around the kitchen table, she was aware there was an atmosphere, a secret current of communication going on between Genny and Gabriel, which—in her exhausted state—she just couldn't interpret.

Ruth slept on beatifically in the car seat beside Imogen on the terra-cotta floor of the kitchen. She looked around. It was all so familiar and so perfect. Storybook Cottage could have been perfect too but instead it was being painted magnolia and flogged to some couple with their baby, a little family that Genny was already speaking so excitedly about. The idea that life in the Middlemass community would continue without her and Ruth was almost too much to bear.

"Shall we go?" she said, interrupting Simon's easy chat about difficult patients he had seen recently and Genny bringing her up to date on the latest in the school saga, which was, basically, all good, thanks to her brilliant leadership, as Simon claimed proudly.

They all turned to look at her. Genny seemed suffused with excitement, her eyes dancing in anticipation. "It's dawn," she said, pointing out of the kitchen window. "You go, Gabriel. You can leave Ruth here if you like?"

Imogen looked at her daughter doubtfully. She probably wouldn't wake up. Not if she and Gabriel were quick, and why wouldn't they be? It was going to be the most perfunctory check, she was sure.

"I've got breakfast waiting for you when you come back—

fresh croissants and real coffee—but there's no rush. You take as long as you like." She looked at Gabriel for instructions.

"I'm sure it's all fine," Imogen said in a small voice, once they were in the car. "Genny said you kept an eye on the work. I'm really grateful."

Gabriel said nothing.

SWEEPING UP THE drive in front of the house, she noticed fresh gravel had been laid from the light of the headlights. She could see the first light of dawn in the east too, over past the orchard. The garden had recovered well, transforming from a mud slick to a riot of lavender and roses, with a particularly gorgeous honeysuckle over the door, swags of it drooping with the abundance of its flowers.

In the hall, the flagstones had been scrubbed clean, and a Persian rug she didn't recognize laid in the center. In a dream, she wandered into the biggest sitting room off the hallway. The first glimmers of low morning light crept softly into the room, its rays slanting through the French windows across the oak floor, which was now gleaming with beeswax and effort. Overlaying the polish smell was the scent of a jug of billowing roses sitting on a grand piano. A few petals had already dropped onto the glossy wood. In front of the fireplace, a pair of sofas faced each other across a low table. They were simply covered in white linen with a selection of cushions and throws that invited a visitor to sit and relax.

"It's beautiful," said Imogen. "Just like I always imagined it would be one day," she added, remembering how she had kept the door closed on the room with its odd collection of Nigel's furniture—his Eames chair and that heavy mahogany tallboy. She had been unable to make it feel like a home.

"Most of the furniture that was in here went in a skip, I'm afraid," said Gabriel as if reading her thoughts. "I made sure the insurance people valued it all, of course. You'll have a big cheque coming to you. Come and see the rest."

A brief tour of the other downstairs rooms showed fresh new paintwork, mainly in soft, creamy whites and grays that flattered the elegant detailing and made the most of the light. The kitchen was clean and cozy-looking with new cupboards and oak worktops. The stone sink looked just the same but had a new draining board. Strangely, someone had washed and arranged her Denby jugs and put them back on the newly painted dresser.

What was he doing? she wondered. Showing me what I gave up? It was his idea to sell, for goodness' sake. Surely, he knows?

"Gabriel," she said.

"Shush," he replied. "Come upstairs."

He led her up the stairs, not to the attic floor, where her studio and bedroom had been, but to the main bedroom at the front, with its high ceiling and its pair of huge windows.

She gasped.

"It's beautiful," she said at last. And it was. The peeling wallpaper had been removed, the walls painted the most delicate duck egg blue, and the shutters at the window freed from the layers of paint that had glued them closed and obscured their detailing. Painted in a chalk white eggshell and partly open, they filtered the morning light. There was a cheval mirror in the corner, a chest of drawers, and a large iron bedstead.

"How did you do all this?" marveled Imogen. "The colors, the finishes, it's all perfect."

"Oh," said Gabriel rushing to explain, "that wasn't me. Or Genny. My mate's wife did it. Fenella. She's this amazing interior designer when she's not looking after their baby. You'll meet her soon enough."

But will I? thought Imogen. They were all being so insensitive. Clearly Gabriel couldn't know . . . He was examining the bed with interest. It was heaped with inviting plump pillows and eiderdown, all encased in crisp white cotton with ladder-stitched borders.

"That's good," he said. "I asked Genny to make up the bed."

"Gabriel," tried Imogen again.

"Yes," he said at last, turning to face her.

"There's this other family. The house is gone."

"I know."

"It's not mine."

"I know," he said, cupping her face in his hands with such gentleness, it took her breath away.

"The owners could be moving in at any time."

"They just did," he said, stroking her cheek with his thumb and letting his eyes rest on her mouth.

"They're here?" said Imogen, panicking.

"Yep, right here in this room," he breathed, leaning in and brushing her lips with his own.

"I—I don't understand," she stuttered when, thrillingly, his lips moved to her neck.

"It was mine," he said. "You knew that?"

Imogen nodded, understanding at last. That had been the deal, in return for the repairs liability being written off.

"I bought it. And now I'm giving it back to you," he whispered in her ear. "For us, so I hope you like it."

"I do."

"Now, that," he said, "is the response I was hoping for to a number of questions, not least of which is *do you like this new bed?*"

At that, he pushed Imogen gently backward onto it, his arms either side of her, his eyes ranging over her body.

"I've wanted to do this since we met," he said, slipping the straps off her shoulders and stroking her breasts. "Have you any idea how difficult it's been to keep my hands off you?"

"But," protested Imogen, "I thought I annoyed you." She shivered deliciously as he ran his hands down her body to cup her buttocks, pulling her toward him so their hips ground together.

"You do—intensely," agreed Gabriel, "and never more so than when you keep telling me how I feel about things and then running away from me. Now, stop talking."

"But me being here just reminds you how perfect it was when Annabel was alive."

"There you go again," he said, covering her mouth with his own.

And then neither of them said anything much for quite a while.

 *Chapter Twenty-nine*

So, you haven't answered my question," said Gabriel eventually, as Imogen lay in his arms, exhausted.

"You told me not to talk," she said mischievously.

"You have my express permission to tell me what you think about the bed."

"Mmm, it's heavenly," said Imogen, stretching her arms and then letting them flump back onto the pillow, narrowly missing his nose.

"I could stay here for weeks—as long as it was with you," she added, rolling over to face him and resting her head on his chest.

"I was hoping you'd say that," he replied, stroking her hair. "Tempting though it is, we have more to see."

With that, he disentangled himself and slid out of bed, grabbing his clothes from the floor. In just a minute, he was dressed.

She allowed herself the luxury of watching him do his reverse striptease. He had a remarkably well-formed upper body—all that anvil-work—and the rest of him wasn't bad either. Altogether, she was sorry to see it disappear, at least for now.

"Hey, you," he said, grinning. "A little less leering and a little more action, or Genny and Simon are going to be leaping to conclusions."

"Oh, I see. Although I'm feeling they probably have already. They were in on it, of course."

"Very good," teased Gabriel. "What made you suddenly realize?"

"Genny told me the bloke you were going to sell the house to was a grumpy old git. I should have twigged it was you then."

"Cheeky woman," said Gabriel, not making it clear whether he meant her or Genny.

"Anyway, how did you buy the house?" said Imogen suddenly. "If you were so hard up you couldn't afford to repair Middlemass Hall, how did you suddenly summon up the money to buy this?"

"Good question," said Gabriel. For a moment she thought he wasn't going to answer. "I re-leased the Hall," he said at last.

"You didn't!" said Imogen. "It's been in your family forever."

"Yeah, I know," admitted Gabriel. "But we still own it. The relief is that running it, maintaining it, making it useful is now somebody else's problem for the next twenty years. The company want to run it as a wedding venue, so—obviously that's where you and I should . . . Anyway—at the end of the day—I thought, where do I want to bring up my family? Here in the house where I was largely raised myself or surrounded by that crusty old ruin on the hill?"

"I don't think that's a very flattering way to describe Louise," she said mischievously.

Gabriel narrowed his eyes. "Don't mock. That woman saved us both, although she drove a bloody hard bargain."

"You mean you leased to the conference company?" said Imogen.

"Certainly did. Lock, stock, and barrel. I've been working on it for months," he admitted.

"And we all thought you were spending all that time with Louise because you fancied her," said Imogen wonderingly. "That's the most romantic thing you've ever done," she joked.

"Give me time," replied Gabriel, and kissed her again.

WHEN IMOGEN FINALLY had a quick bath and got dressed—still in the striped Missoni dress, now with Gabriel's huge jumper over the top—they wandered out into the garden and strolled hand in hand through the dew-soaked grass, over the bridge to the orchard. There, in the early morning sunshine, Imogen saw the forked apple tree where she had sat with her coffee on the first morning almost exactly a year ago. She squeezed Gabriel's hand. In response he gathered her in for another long kiss.

"Shall we?" he said eventually, leading her to the stile.

"You built this, didn't you?" asked Imogen. "After you saw me climbing over the wall here."

"Clever you," said Gabriel. "I wondered if you realized I was keeping an eye on you."

"Sort of," admitted Imogen, thinking back.

"It wasn't creepy, was it?" asked Gabriel.

"No," Imogen reassured him, "nice. But I'm confused. If you really did care about me all this time, why didn't you say?"

"Why do you think?" said Gabriel, amazed that she had to ask. "Okay, I couldn't resist kissing you that time, but—honestly—not being able to keep my eyes off you was one thing, expecting you to let me get close to you so soon after being widowed and then finding out you were pregnant . . ."

"And you pretend you're so oblivious to people's feelings," she teased.

"And then there was the whole repair bill thing, when I couldn't keep that from you any longer; of course you hated me."

"I didn't!"

"Yeah, you did."

"Whatever gave you that idea?"

"You told me."

"Yes, well, I was a bit stressed," admitted Imogen. "But mostly because I thought you were in love with Louise. Sorry," she added, slipping her arm around his waist to give him a squeeze.

ARM IN ARM, they followed the path through the woods that led to the Hall without talking, Imogen remembering all her walks there the previous year, feeling secure and knowing—as she did now—that Gabriel or, presumably, one of his staff, was there in the background, keeping watch and keeping her safe. No wonder he appeared so quickly on the scene when the paintballers ambushed her that time.

"You used to keep an eye on me here as well, didn't you?" she asked idly.

"It's something I plan to carry on doing," Gabriel agreed. "But yes, I worried about you here on your own."

When they arrived at the Hall, Gabriel led her into his forge, which all looked as Imogen remembered it earlier that year when she had cuddled up on the settle with the newborn Ruth to watch him work. She gave him a questioning look.

"I didn't lease this. It's all ours still."

He led her up the stairs to his apartment, the space she had so admired as the ultimate bachelor pad when she first saw it a year before. Instead of the view she expected, Imogen walked into a light-filled space, which was now nearly empty. Under the central roof light was a drawing board set up in front of an adjustable artist's stool. She went over to it. Within easy reach was a plan chest. Opening its narrow drawers, she found row after row of pristine artist's equipment. Brushes, paints, pastels, assiduously sharpened pencils all lay perfectly arranged, waiting for her to pick them up and start to draw. It all looked as if it was from the art shop on Portneath High Street—a place she could imagine spending a lot more time. She looked up. The light was perfect, the atmosphere was calm. When she looked out of the window, she could see the manor house and the meadows with sheep grazing in the sun; off to the side, she could see the orchard and, beyond it, the roof of Storybook Cottage. Best of all, she was going to be just feet away from her future husband, working in the space below.

"Is it really ours?" she asked wonderingly.

"It really is," said Gabriel. He looked at her, anxious for approval. "Do you think you could work here?"

"I do," said Imogen, looking around her with awe.

"Even with me working in the forge downstairs?"

"I do," she said again.

Gabriel cleared his throat and took her in his arms. "Imogen," he said, "you are the most infuriating, bewitching, artistically talented, musically destitute, lousy driver of a woman I have ever met. My life is meaningless if I can't spend it with you. Do you agree to become my wife?"

"I do," said Imogen, at which loud cheers erupted, making them both jump.

"Thank goodness for that," said Genny, coming up the stairs. "Honestly, the trouble we've all had to go to. Never mind plan B, we were practically on plan Z by the time you ran away to London," she said, arriving at the top with Simon carrying Ruth behind her. Ruth was now fully awake and clinging to Simon like a little monkey, bright-eyed and interested in all the commotion.

"Oh right, so this was all a setup," said Imogen, trying to sound disapproving. "I suppose Sally and Alistair were involved," she said, almost to herself.

"How else did Gabriel know to come to your party?" replied Genny.

"I see. And my mother . . . ?"

"Oh, yes," said Genny, "in every way."

"So really—"

"Absolutely," interrupted Simon briskly. "I must say, all this romantic stuff is making me feel awfully hungry," he said, giving Genny a squeeze.

"Sorry, Gabriel," said Genny. "We just couldn't bear not knowing any longer. So we thought we'd come and find you."

It was lucky they didn't drop in to Storybook Cottage half an hour ago, thought Imogen, catching Gabriel's eye.

"Anyway," continued Simon, "I don't suppose you feel like coming back to our house and having some breakfast?"

Imogen looked at Gabriel again.

"I do," she replied, and reached for his hand.

Acknowledgments

If it takes a village to raise a child, it takes a small town to produce a novel, and this one is no exception. It is such a huge privilege to be allowed to write books for a living. Who wouldn't want to live inside their own head, when they get to create a world for themselves that is as pleasant as Middlemass and Portneath? However, finishing the solitary writing and having to share with the team would be a rude awakening if they weren't all as lovely as the characters in my books. From my wonderful agent, Kevan Lyon, to my inspiring editor, Tessa Woodward, and all the team at Avon, Harper Collins, including Madelyn Blaney, Kelly Dasta, Amanda Hong, Diahann Sturge-Campbell, Ana Deboo, Brittani DiMare, Robin Barletta, and Cari Elliott, it is a positive pleasure to work alongside this talented crew.

Of course, I would have no fantasy life at all if the people who populate my IRL were not as supportive as they are. From the regular coffee (other drinks may also have been consumed) with the gin dog bitches; to the mutual cheerleading from my precious author friends; to my family, who are stoically understanding about all the late suppers and forgotten "to-do list" items; and even to my merry little dog

Saffy, who is so much nicer than Tango and to whom this book is dedicated; to Alex, Nyx, Jonathan, Helen, Clare, Caroline, Carolyn, Lisa, Richard, Chris, other Alex, Sharon, other Lisa, Sally, et al. . . .

This one is for you all, with my love. x

Poppy Alexander wrote her first book when she was five. There was a long gap in her writing career while she was at school, and after studying classical music at university, she decided the world of music was better off without her and took up public relations, campaigning, political lobbying, and a bit of journalism instead. She takes an anthropological interest in family, friends, and life in her West Sussex village (think *The Archers* crossed with *Twin Peaks*), where she lives with her husband, children, and various other pets.

Read more from
POPPY ALEXANDER

25 DAYS 'TIL CHRISTMAS

In this feel-good holiday novel, one woman needs to find a little inspiration in the 25 days leading up to Christmas to help her remember the magic of the season and the magic of falling in love—perfect for fans of Jenny Colgan and Josie Silver.

THE LITTLEST LIBRARY

A literary-themed novel about a woman who turns an ordinary red phone box into the littlest library in England and brings together a struggling town.